BOOKS BY

Carrie Carr

====================

Destiny's Bridge

Faith's Crossing

Hope's Path

Love's Journey

Strength of the Heart

The Way Things Should Be

To Hold Forever

Something to Be Thankful For

Diving Into the Turn

Piperton

Carrie Carr

Yellow Rose Books

Port Arthur, Texas

ISBN 978-1-935053-20-0
1-935053-20-5

First Printing 2009

9 8 7 6 5 4 3 2 1

Cover design by Donna Pawlowski

Published by:

Regal Crest Enterprises, LLC
4700 Highway 365, Suite A, PMB 210
Port Arthur, Texas 77642

Find us on the World Wide Web at
http://www.regalcrest.biz

Printed in the United States of America

Acknowledgements:

They say it takes a village to raise a child. I'd like to think it takes almost as many to bring a book to fruition. I really have to thank the folks on my chat list, Carrie's Crossing—your continued support and interest helped me more than you'll ever know. To my friend and brilliant beta, Cait—you helped round out a rough draft and gave new life to my work. Kudos to the artistic talent of Donna Pawlowski, who was able to take a photo I took and turn it into a fantastic cover. To my wonderful wife, Jan, thank you for going over the manuscript with a magnifying glass and cleaning it up so beautifully. To Patty, my editor, who caught several big boo-boos— thank you! And, as always, my utmost gratitude to Cathy, who gave me a chance so many years ago and continues to be not only a great publisher, but a very good friend.

To my mom, who has a strength that continues to inspire me. To Mrs. H., the English teacher whose classes got me started writing, giving me an outlet for my imagination. And, most of all, my best friend, the woman who shares my life and makes it worth living — my wife, Jan. Thank you for always being there for me. Forever and always, my love.

Chapter
One

THE HOT AUGUST sun beat down on the ancient car as it cruised along the two-lane blacktop. Old turquoise paint had given way to rust on the 1956 two-door Chevy. Samantha Hendrickson yawned widely. Miles upon miles of fields, bursting with cotton, lulled her into a daze. She hadn't seen another car for hours and was beginning to think the flat plains of West Texas were deserted. Sam twisted the knob on the old AM radio until the static cleared and she could make out the words of Tom T. Hall singing of watermelon wine. She remembered the song from her childhood and hummed along. The vague reference to food caused her stomach to growl, which made her realize she hadn't eaten for several hours.

Sam had been on the road, one way or another, for most of her adult life. She'd left home when she was nineteen and hadn't looked back for ten years. Her grandmother had raised her, and after she passed away, Sam saw no need to stay in the small Oklahoma town. She traveled around the southwest, never staying in one place very long.

Five miles later, the welcome sight of the Kamann city limits sign greeted Sam. She took the next exit and checked her fuel gage when she saw the run-down convenience store on the side of the access road ahead. Sam parked beside one of the decades-old pumps and pushed the car's creaky door open. She got out of the Chevy and automatically clipped the keys onto her belt loop, stretching her arms over her head as she walked into the store. Ice cold air hit her in the face, and goose bumps rose on her arms. Her white tank top was a good defense against the summer heat. Even so, she appreciated the blowing fans that helped cool her back, which was damp with perspiration.

The old man working behind the counter barely acknowledged her, intent on the black and white television that collected dust in the corner. The grainy picture jumped as an eighteen wheeler roared down the highway. He adjusted the antennae before coughing several times, spitting in a trash can, and blowing his nose on a wadded tissue.

Sam tamped down her disgust and continued to the back of the store, where glass door refrigerators lined the wall. She picked out a bottled Coke and grabbed a bag of chips on her way to the register. After placing the items on the counter, she took her wallet from her back pocket and took out a twenty. "I need to put whatever's left in gas, please."

"All right." He looked up and noticed her for the first time. The disdain on his face was evident as he slid the bill off the counter and into the register. "You'll have to stop it yourself." With his gray hair sticking up in every direction, he was a comical sight. "Want a bag?"

"No, this is okay." Sam tried to ignore his stare. She'd encountered his attitude everywhere she'd stopped. With her dark hair cut close to the sides of her head but longer on top, and the old tank top and jeans, most people identified her easily as a lesbian. The wallet on a chain didn't dispel the stereotype, nor did the heavy black work boots she wore. "How much gas?"

"Sixteen-o-nine." He hacked again and spit, dismissing her.

Sam took her purchases and left. "Have a nice day," she grumbled as she went through the door.

After filling her car, Sam weighed her options. It was barely past noon. She didn't see anything that interested her so she climbed into the Chevy and decided to stay on the road a while longer.

By late afternoon, the highway led her into the town of Piperton, whose sign boasted a population of thirty-eight thousand. It didn't matter to Sam, who was only interested in getting a hot meal. She exited and followed a smaller road toward the heart of town.

The street wound through an old, dilapidated residential area before finally opening up to a lonely town square. Most of the buildings on the square were in disrepair and many had boarded up windows. Sam was pleasantly surprised to see the statuesque red granite courthouse that dominated the square. The structure was over three stories high, and with its imposing clock tower, the courthouse was quite a sight to behold.

Sam was considering the surrounding buildings when she heard a loud grinding noise coming from under the hood of her car. Not wanting to park on the street, she drove into the nearest alley and stopped her car close to a beat up dumpster. Smoke billowed from the front of the Chevy before the engine died. Sam had a sick feeling her car was doomed.

Sam ignored the urge to check under the hood since her mechanical knowledge was sadly lacking. Instead, she walked through the alley to the sidewalk, wondering what her options would be in this desolate-looking west Texas town.

She stopped under an awning which bore the name, "Danny's". She could hear music coming from behind the faded oak door and cautiously went inside.

Tinny music from a corner jukebox mingled with the quiet murmurings of a handful of customers who were scattered around the dark room. A heavy wooden bar stretched across the left side of the room, and a lone bartender stood behind it. Tall and gangly, the man's dark blue tee shirt hung loosely on his frame. He was cutting up slices of lime and raised his head as Sam approached. "What can I get you?"

"Whatever you have on draft is fine." Sam sat on a stool and placed a five-dollar bill in front of her. "Is there a garage close by? I need to get my car checked out."

He poured her a mug and took the cash, leaving three-fifty in change. "Dell's is a block west. They do just about anything."

"Thanks." Sam took a sip and looked around. There were over a dozen tables scattered about, and she spied a worn upright, console piano in the far corner nearest the bathrooms. It would likely take most of her money to get the car fixed, but she was already coming up with a solution to her lack of funds. "You do much business?"

"Enough to get by." He wiped the counter with a towel. "You're not from around here, are you?"

Sam shook her head. "I was on my way to Dallas when my car died." She tipped her head toward the back of the room. "Do you have live entertainment come in?"

"Not for a while. Can't afford it."

"Are you the owner?"

"Nope. Just the manager." He stopped what he was doing and stared at her. "Why?"

"I'm trying to get a little extra cash together for car repairs. Do you mind if I use the piano? I'll split any tips I get with you."

He shrugged his shoulders. "Doesn't matter to me. You can keep the tips, especially if it brings in any new business." He offered his hand. "I'm Ray."

Sam shook his hand firmly. "Sam." She finished her beer. "I'll be back around six, if that's all right with you."

"Sure." Ray went back to slicing limes after she left.

THE GLASS DOOR slammed so hard behind her that Sam thought it might break. As the only auto mechanic in town, Dell had told her it would be at least two weeks before he had the time to even look at her car. "Goddamn jackass!" Sam rested her hands on her hips and fought the tears that threatened to fall. The clearing of a throat caused her to turn around.

The mechanic she'd previously spoken to stood behind her. He brought out a pocket knife and cleaned his nails with it, then folded the knife and dropped it into the front pocket of his greasy overalls. "You got a number I can reach you when I got an openin'?"

Sam closed her eyes and counted to ten. It didn't help. She still wanted to knock the smirk off his ugly face. "No. Can't I check back with you every now and then?"

"I guess. But it'd be easier if I called you."

"I'm going to be playing the piano at Danny's. You can catch me there. Is there a motel or something close by? I need a place to stay."

Dell sucked at his front teeth and picked at them with his thumbnail. "Nope. The Ramada closed down couple years back. You can probably get a cot down at the Y, though." He gestured with his thumb over his left shoulder. "It's back that away on Birch. Right past the library."

"Thanks." Sam turned and headed back the way she came. She didn't feel like expending any more energy on the man.

A hot breeze ruffled the top of Sam's hair. Still steaming over the mechanic's indifference, she seriously considered looking for the nearest bus stop and getting out of the aggravating town. She turned into the alley and stared at the rusted heap she'd been driving. It seemed safe enough where it was parked. Since it was a small town, and the weather was halfway decent, she decided to forego the Y and sleep in her car. Her innate distrust of the world around her made Sam roll up the windows and lock the doors. She'd air it out before bedding down for the night.

Once inside the bar, she noticed more people had arrived. Sam stepped up to the counter and tapped the scarred wood.

The bartender turned around. It wasn't Ray, but a younger man. "What do you want?"

"My name's Sam. I was in here earlier and Ray said I could sing in the evenings for tips. Is it okay if I leave my car out back?"

He shrugged his shoulders. "Don't bother me none. You going to start singing now?"

"I guess." She took the wallet out of her back pocket. "How much for water?"

He waved her off before sliding a full glass in front of her. "Nuthin'. Ray said he'd furnish your drinks as long as you bring the people in." He frowned when he noticed her slipping the wallet back in her pocket. "You one of those queers?"

Sam's head snapped up. "What?"

"You are, aren't you?" His lip curled in distaste. "Ray didn't say nothing about you bein' a faggot."

The glass that Sam had started to drink from hit the bar heavily when she slammed it down. "What the hell is your problem, Bubba?"

"Name's Fred, not Bubba. And I ain't got no problem." He turned away, but not before tossing one last quip over his shoulder. "Don't be getting no ideas. We got nice ladies around here, not for the likes of you."

Chapter
Two

JANIE CLARKE KNELT beside the four-drawer file cabinet, her face obscured by her hair that fanned over her shoulder. She flipped through the files until she came upon the one she'd been searching for. She removed the folder and stood, straightening her navy blue pleated skirt with her free hand. At the doorway, she accidentally bumped into a well-developed redhead. "Sorry, Andrea. I didn't see you."

"Obviously." Andrea held out her hand. "Is that Mr. Garrett's file? Dr. Reynolds has been waiting forever for it." She tugged it out of Janie's grasp. "Thanks, June." Andrea offered Janie an insincere smile before trotting away.

"It's Janie," she quietly corrected. It was an everyday occurrence. Andrea would call Janie by whatever name she felt like, and Janie would always let it go. Janie had worked as a clerk for the clinic for three years since the last discount store in Piperton closed down, leaving her in need of a change of employment. Even in such a small town, after three years at the clinic, many of her co-workers knew little about her. She could count the number of friends she had on one hand.

Back at her desk, Janie began to enter information into her computer. A loud buzzing from her desk drawer made her look around anxiously. She made sure no one was watching before she removed her cell phone. When Janie noticed the caller ID, she considered not answering. But she knew it would only be a momentary reprieve. "Doug? Why are you calling me while I'm at work?"

"Hey, babe. I'll be over around seven. What are you fixin' for supper?" Doug Howard was Janie's long-time boyfriend. They'd been introduced four years ago by her father, and she had somehow found herself attached to him. Doug often hinted about marriage and frequently asked when she was going to let him move in. She managed to brush off both ideas. At almost thirty-five, Doug still lived at home with his parents, and he was more than ready for someone else to cook and clean for him.

"I'm not going to be home. I told you yesterday I have a dinner date with Sandra tonight."

"You spend more time with her than you do me. I miss you, Janie." Doug lowered his voice. "I was hoping we'd have an early dinner, so we could have a long dessert."

She had begun to hate his kind of dessert. The sex had never been spectacular, and she rarely got any pleasure from it. She often wondered why she was still with Doug. It wasn't as if she loved him. But her father expected it of her, and it was ingrained in Janie to never go against her father's wishes, even if they were the opposite of her own. "I'll call you later to set a day, all right? But I've got to go. Bye, Doug." Janie clicked her phone closed and quietly slipped it back in the drawer.

THE FAINT TINKLING of a piano drew Janie into the smoky bar. She was on her way to meet her friend Sandra for dinner, but the melancholy sound lured her in. Janie passed this same bar every day on her way to work but had rarely gone inside. She stood at the entrance for several moments, waiting until her eyes adjusted to the cramped, dingy room.

A woman was bent over the piano keys, her eyes obscured by the lock of dark hair that fell into her face. The sides and back of her hair were cut close to her head in a style Janie had never seen on a woman before. Her low voice drifted across the room, as she sang of lost love.

Janie stepped slowly toward the bar, and slid onto the stool nearest the piano, which had been turned at an angle to allow the singer to see her audience. She ordered a light beer from the bartender and set a five dollar bill down. He brought back a sweating bottle and handed it to her. "Thanks." She turned on the stool enough so that she could watch the singer, mesmerized by the smooth vocals.

The song ended, and the musician took a deep drink from the glass of water that sat next to a full tip jar on the scarred piano. As the smattering of applause subsided, she said, "Thank you. I'm going to take five, and then I'll play some requests." She stepped away from the keyboard, and headed for the ladies room.

Janie waved the bartender back over. "Who is that?"

"Who? The dyke? That's Sam. She showed up and started playing a few nights ago."

His description of the singer didn't surprise Janie. The small Texas town wasn't known for being progressive, and his attitude was more the norm than not. But the thought of someone so radically different brought an excited chill to Janie's spine. "She's got a very distinctive voice."

"That's one way to put it. First time she started to speak, I thought she was a guy. With that hair, it was hard to tell." He shrugged his shoulders and ambled back to the other end of the bar.

Janie spared a quick glance at her watch and realized she was going to be late meeting her friend. She was torn between wanting to hear more from the mysterious singer and keeping a dinner date she didn't want to go to in the first place. She took a few sips from her bottle and placed it back on the bar, half full. She picked up the change from the five dollar bill she'd used to pay for her beer and added it to the musician's collection before making her way out of the bar.

"WHERE ON EARTH have you been? I thought you skipped out on me." Sandra Wooten squished out her cigarette, and promptly lit another one. "For god's sake, Janie, you need to get out more. I think you've forgotten how to be social."

Janie waved her hand in front of her face, fighting a losing battle with the heavy cigarette smoke. "I'm as social as the next person, Sandra. It's not my fault that I have to work late more often than you do." Janie's job was full of long days, and little appreciation. She went unnoticed by almost everyone. Her light brown eyes were hidden by her glasses, and her brown hair was parted in the middle and hung straight to her shoulders.

Sandra pointed a nicotine stained finger in her friend's direction. It was almost the color of her poorly bleached hair. "You know, if you'd listen to me, you'd have to beat guys off with a stick. Contacts and a decent haircut would go a long way, girl."

"I've got Doug. He's more than enough for me." Janie stared at the water ring her tea glass was leaving. She'd had the same conversation with Sandra more times than she could remember, and she never won.

"Yeah, right. You and he are *so* in love. Not." Sandra took a sip of her vodka and soda. She waved the glass around as she tried to make her point. "When are you going to realize that you can do better than that lout?"

Janie coughed and pointed away from the table. "Here comes our dinner. You're not going to smoke through the meal, are you?"

"Of course not." Sandra mashed out her cigarette. "I've got better manners than that. You should know me well enough by now."

"I didn't mean to hurt your feelings." Janie rolled her eyes and in a sing-song voice said the same thing she'd said for years. "We've known each other since grade school, and I shouldn't have questioned your manners." She quieted when the server placed her salad in front of her. She looked across the table at the chicken-fried steak her friend had. "How can you eat like that and stay so slim?"

Sandra cut a gravy-laden chunk from the steak. "Good genes. My mother is the same way." She peered at her friend's meal. "How can you live on that rabbit food? You're nothing but skin and bones as it is."

With a quick look down at her food, Janie shrugged. "It's easier this way."

"Is your old man still giving you grief?"

"A little." Janie speared her dry lettuce, and put it in her mouth.

"You're nearly forty years old. When are you going to stop letting that bastard dictate your life?" Sandra took a greasy French fry and dipped it in the gravy. "You haven't lived at home for almost twenty years. Don't you think it's time to do what you want?"

Janie continued to eat her salad. She knew her friend had a point. They had the same argument since they were in high school. Sandra kept trying to get her to loosen up, and Janie did her best to appease both Sandra and her father. "I do fine. He has his opinions. I don't always listen to them." She'd learned at an early age to go along with what Harvey Clarke wanted, even if it were contrary to her own wants or needs, or suffer the consequences. He'd bullied her into always wearing dresses or skirts, because slacks or jeans weren't his idea of how a "lady" should dress.

"Right. So that's why you look like a skeleton? Honey, you need to take better care of yourself. And maybe find some decent clothes."

With a shake of her head, Janie tried to ignore her friend. She knew Sandra meant well, but she tended to think that the world revolved around men, and how to look desirable to them. Janie thought about the relationship she'd been in for four years. Doug didn't seem to mind how she looked, and that's what mattered, wasn't it?

THAT VOICE CONTINUED to haunt Janie the rest of the week. She heard the singer's raspy tones at the oddest times. Every morning in the shower, she found herself humming to the last song she had heard. If she closed her eyes, she could almost hear the notes from the piano.

On her way to work Friday, Janie made it a point to walk by Danny's. She wondered where the enigmatic musician went during the off hours, and then privately scolded herself. The woman was obviously not the type she should befriend, or even speak to. Janie scurried to the office before she was too late.

She was greeted by Andrea, who had no qualms about voicing her disapproval. She flicked one hand in the air, showing off her long nails. "It's about time you got here. I was going to have to make the coffee myself."

Janie tossed her purse on her desk. "I'm sorry. I lost track of time." Inside she was fuming. Janie went into the kitchen and started the coffee maker. It was going to be a long morning.

Chapter
Three

SAM ENDED THE song with a flourish and raised her head to acknowledge the sparse crowd. Some she knew were regulars. Even in the dim light of the bar, she noticed a familiar face. On the barstool nearest the piano sat a thin woman, her eyes hidden by a pair of dark framed glasses. Sam had seen her in the same seat every night for the past week. Wanting to get a closer look, she pushed away from the piano and stood.

The woman appeared nervous as she approached the bar. To put her at ease, Sam stood a few feet away and motioned to Fred. "Can I get another glass of ice water?"

"Yeah." Fred set the glass on the bar in front of her and scurried away.

After a few deep swallows, Sam turned to look at the woman sitting close by. "Enjoying the show?"

Janie jumped as if she'd been hit. "What?"

"I figure you must like the music, since you've been here so often." Sam took another sip of her water. "I'm Sam."

"I know." Janie fumbled with her purse. "I mean, I heard the bartender call you by name the other night." She worked the strap furiously, trying to turn it the right direction.

Sam nodded and leaned with her back against the bar. "So, are you into bar music?"

"No." Janie's shaking hand grasped her beer bottle. She turned it around until the label faced her. "It's on the way home from work, that's all."

"Uh-huh." Although she knew it was mean, Sam couldn't help but tease the jittery woman. "You must be awful thirsty, seeing as how you spend a couple of hours a night in here. Work that bad?"

Janie finally looked her in the face. "No. It's fine." She started to peel the label from the bottle. "Is it a crime to have a drink every now and then?"

"Nope."

"Then why all the questions?"

Sam drained her glass and wiggled it at Fred. It gave her a perverse pleasure to make him wait on her. "I'm sorry. I was only trying to get to know you."

"Why?" Janie determinately finished off her warm beer. She grimaced at the taste. "You're new around here, aren't you?"

"What was your first clue?"

Janie suddenly became interested in the paper napkin that sat beneath her empty bottle. "I've never seen you around before." The sudden laugh from Sam startled her.

"Yeah, I guess I'm not like everyone else, am I? What is it? The haircut?" She'd had about enough from the locals about her appearance. She waved her wrist in front of Janie. The plastic men's Timex was bulky and unattractive. "Or maybe it's my big ol' butch watch. How about the wallet on a chain? No? Not used to seeing dykes, huh?" Sam realized how she sounded when Janie appeared ready to bolt. "I'm sorry. You didn't deserve that."

"It's okay." Janie scooted off the stool and hooked her purse strap over her shoulder. "I've got to go." She smiled shyly at Sam. "You have a beautiful voice."

Sam watched Janie hurry out of the bar. She went back to the piano, hoping she'd see the quiet woman again.

JANIE MANAGED TO avoid the bar for a week. She finally lost the battle with her inner self and returned on a Friday night after work. She found a place at the back of the room, not wanting another confrontation with the singer. She was on her second bottle of beer when someone sat at her table. Her heart thudded double time when she was faced with her boyfriend. "Doug? What are you doing here?"

"You weren't home, and Harvey ain't seen you. You don't got that many friends, so I checked all the places on your way home from work. Never seen you in here before, or I would have tried this spot sooner." He took her beer out of her hand and drank from the bottle. "How can you drink this shit?" He set the beer on the table with a slam.

A new song started and Janie tried her best to peek around his head. "If you don't like my beer, you shouldn't try stealing it."

Doug turned to see where she was staring. "Is *that* the reason you're here?"

Janie ignored him, instead focusing on the music that floated across the room. A firm grip on her hand brought Janie's attention back to her boyfriend.

"Let's go. You've been here long enough." Doug got to his feet and tried to bring Janie with him. She continued to sit, angering him. "I said, come on." He pulled harder on her hand.

"Doug, you're hurting me."

Two men at another table turned at Janie's words. One of them made eye contact with her to see if she needed help.

She shook her head and jerked her hand away from Doug's. "Would you please stop? You're making a scene." But she stood and gathered her purse; even though it was the last thing she wanted to do.

Doug forcefully took her arm and led her outside. The night air was cooler than the interior of the bar. "It wouldn't have been a problem if you'd done what I said."

An unusual anger emboldened Janie. She pried his hand away and raised her purse strap higher on her shoulder. "For your information, Doug, you don't own me. So stop trying to act as if you do." She began to walk faster. "I'm going home. Alone."

"Hey!" Doug had to jog to catch up with her. "You're not going anywhere I don't say."

Janie ignored him until she got to her building. The old two-story home had been split into four apartments. She spun around when his hand went to open the door. "Go home. I really don't have the energy to put up with you tonight."

He started to say something, but instead closed his mouth and walked away.

Once Doug was out of sight, Janie's bravado faltered and she leaned against the oak door. She brought her shaking hand to her forehead and tried to catch her breath. Doug's behavior was becoming more and more erratic lately, and had it not been for her father's continued pressure, she would have ended things long ago.

SAM WATCHED EVERY night for the woman she had flirted with, but had begun to lose hope when more than a week had gone by without a sighting. Saturday arrived and it was her busiest night so far. She had to empty her tip jar three times and was almost glad when Ray finally locked the front door. Her voice was hoarse. Not even the cool glass of water soothed her aching throat, and she dreaded having to learn more songs for the patrons. And, if she had to sing one more Faith Hill song, she'd scream.

Ray handed Sam a damp rag. "If you'll wipe down the tables, I'll take care of the glasses tonight." Their deal had come to include her helping with the cleanup in exchange for her drinks and meals and Sam keeping all her tips. It worked out well for them both. The bar was doing more business and he didn't have to hire anyone else, other than the cook and the part-time waitress that both worked the evening shift on Friday and Saturday nights.

"Thanks," Sam croaked. She quickly took care of the tables and chairs, and swept the floor.

Ray patted her on the back after he returned from doing the dishes. "That's good enough, Sam. Thanks for all your help." He followed her to the front door. "You sound horrible. Why don't you skip tomorrow? It's not like there will be much of a crowd."

Sam stood on the sidewalk while he locked up. "I just might do that." She cleared her throat and winced at the pain. "I'll probably nap in my car. If you need any help, come out back and let me know."

He pocketed the keys. "You really should find a place to stay. That can't be too comfortable. Or safe."

"I've been sleeping in my car for years and never had a problem." She walked with him until they reached the mouth of the alley. "This is my stop. 'Night, Ray."

"All right. Take care."

As Sam stepped into the darkening alley, she could hear Ray whistling the last song she had sung. The sound slowly faded away into the night, leaving her all alone. Sam was almost to her car when she noticed it sat unevenly. "What the—" She walked to the opposite side and cursed. The front right tire was flat. In the glow of the security light, she could make out a large gash in the rubber. A careful once-over of the vehicle didn't reveal any other damage. She kicked the tire angrily. "Goddamned assholes! I can't believe this!"

SPRING GARDENS NURSING Home had been built in the early nineteen-fifties. Originally constructed on the outskirts of Piperton, the town's growth during the oil boom years led to it being only eight blocks from downtown. Small shrubbery that once surrounded the single story brick structure had long-ago been choked out with weeds. It was the final stop for the citizens who were considered disposable – seniors who had no families at all, or those who were considered to be too much trouble to care for.

Janie wrinkled her nose at the antiseptic hospital smell she detected the moment she stepped through the door. No matter how long she'd been coming to Spring Gardens, she would never become accustomed to the stale air. She smiled and nodded to the staff as she made her way down the hall. She'd made this same trek since she was seventeen. It hadn't become any easier but she never regretted it for a moment.

Room eighteen came into view and Janie peeked around the open door. Her grandmother sat in the electric wheelchair she'd given her last Christmas, snoring with her chin touching her chest. Before Janie could back away to leave her in peace, her grandmother snorted loudly and opened her eyes.

Lucille Clarke had been a resident of the home for twenty-one years. Following an auto accident in which her son Harvey had been driving, she lost the use of both legs. With no remorse, he shuttled her away to Spring Gardens as soon as a room was available. She'd been there ever since. Her only outside company was the bi-weekly visits from her granddaughter. "Janie, my girl, I didn't see you there." Lucille adjusted the afghan draped across her knees and held out her thin arms. "Come give your Nana a hug."

Janie happily complied. Once in Lucille's arms, it saddened her to feel the weakening muscles that had comforted her all her life. She kissed her forehead. "You're looking good today."

"Pshaw. I'm looking like a dusty old prune." Lucille touched her granddaughter's cheek. "But you look sad, sweetie."

"No, I'm fine." Janie sat on the edge of the bed and glanced around the small, but well-kept room. "When are you going to come home with me? I have more than enough room."

"And leave all of this?" Lucille wheeled closer and patted Janie's leg. "I know it's hard for you to believe, but I'm happy here. I have my friends, and the staff takes very good care of me. Besides, our monthly social is coming up. I may let Mr. Michaels in room four get to second base."

"Nana!"

Lucille cackled. "You're so easy to embarrass, child. But honestly, I wouldn't know what to do with myself if I wasn't here. This is my home."

It was always the same answer. Janie never expected it to change, but she'd never stop asking. "Remember you have another home should you ever want or need it."

"I do. And I truly appreciate it. But you don't need an old lady around. I'm sure you and that young man of yours will need a place to stay once you're married."

Tears pricked the back of Janie's eyes. She didn't want to upset her Nana by crying, but knew better than to lie to her. "I don't think that's ever going to happen."

"Sure it will. You've been dating long enough. It's time to take the next step."

"How did you know you loved Granddad?"

If the sudden change in subject surprised Lucille, it didn't show on her face. "It certainly wasn't love at first sight."

Not the answer she thought she'd receive, Janie was intrigued. "Really?"

"Heavens, no. Bud was quite full of himself in those days. I didn't want to have anything to do with him." Lucille's eyes softened as she thought of long ago. "Even so, I couldn't take my eyes off him. Being in the same room would cause my heart to beat a little faster. He was so handsome, in that rakish, devil-may-care sort of way."

"Are we talking about the same man? Granddad was the kindest, gentlest soul I'd ever known." Janie propped her elbows on her knees and rested her chin on her palms. "Go on, please."

Lucille smiled dreamily. "Back then, he was quite the hell-raiser. My father forbade me to be anywhere near him." She winked. "Which, or course, was all the encouragement I needed to sneak off with Bud on Friday nights. Poppa caught us down by the lake counting the stars."

"How romantic."

"You'd think so, wouldn't you? But when Poppa brought out his shotgun, Bud high-tailed it out of town."

Janie sat up straight. "No! But you obviously got together."

"True." With a shake of her head, Lucille continued her story. "He couldn't stay away. A few months later, Bud returned. But this time, he had a ring. He even got up the nerve to ask Poppa for my hand."

"Aww, how sweet."

Lucille looked at her hand, where the plain gold band still shone. Years of wear and tear had thinned it, but it had never left her finger. "Poppa told him he wasn't good enough for me and sent him packing."

"But—"

"I didn't care. When your granddad came to my window that same night, Poppa or no Poppa, I climbed out and never looked back." She ducked her head enough so she could peer over the rim of her spectacles. "Don't ever let anyone keep you from your true love. I didn't, and not once did I regret a single moment of my life."

"I won't, Nana." Janie couldn't look her in the eyes. She didn't think Doug was that love, and she wondered if she was destined to grow old alone.

Chapter
Four

JANIE DECIDED IT would be best if she stayed away from Danny's. She had spent her entire life avoiding confrontation, yet all she and Doug had done for the past week was argue. The following Saturday she walked to the library, hoping a new book would help her pass the time.

Upon entering the library, Janie waved to a gray-haired woman behind the counter. "Good morning, Mrs. Lowry."

The librarian raised her head and gave Janie a sweet smile. "Good morning to you, dear. I'm so glad you're here. I held back a book I thought you might enjoy." Mrs. Lowry lifted the book from beneath the counter. "It's the new mystery by that woman writer you like." She slid it toward Janie and leaned closer. "I could never get into her work, myself. She's a bit too," her voice lowered to keep others from hearing, "explicit for my tastes. But, to each their own." Mrs. Lowry straightened and her smile returned. "We've also got a lovely new romance novel." She gave Janie a wink. "My nephew's divorce was final last week. Would you like to come over for dinner soon?"

The book Janie had been leafing through hit the counter with a heavy thump. "Ah, well." She paused, trying to think of a way to gently discourage the librarian's eagerness to match Janie with her nephew. "That's very sweet of you to offer, but I'm still with Doug."

The older woman sniffed in disdain. "I don't see a ring on your finger. Perhaps you'd be better off with someone else."

"No, really. I'm fine." The last thing she wanted was to be courted by Mrs. Lowry's nephew. The man reeked of garlic, at least he did the few times she'd been around him. Janie tipped her head toward the back of the building, where a cozy reading space was located. "I think I'm going to read for a while." She waved the book. "Thank you for thinking of me. I'll stop by on my way out."

The reading area consisted of several padded chairs and two sofas, surrounded on three sides by tall cherry bookcases. Only two of the chairs were occupied, and one of them held the owner of a familiar face.

Partially hidden in the corner, Sam appeared engrossed in the local newspaper. Only the top portion of her face was visible. She hadn't noticed Janie's arrival.

Janie didn't want to go back to her apartment, although she considered sneaking out the way she came. When Sam raised the paper higher, Janie took the opportunity to hide on the far side of the room. It barely took a page before Janie was lost in her book. When she felt someone watching her, she looked up from her reading.

Sam stood in front of Janie, the folded newspaper held loosely in her right hand. "Hey there."

"Um, hi." Janie looked around and was relieved to see that the other person had left. "What are you doing here?"

Sam frowned at her harsh tone. "I come in every morning to read the paper. Imagine my surprise when I saw you sitting here."

"I like to read." Janie lowered her voice. "I really shouldn't be talking to you."

"Why not? Afraid I'm contagious or something?"

"No, of course not. I just don't want anyone to get the wrong idea." Janie closed her book since it appeared Sam wasn't going to leave her alone. "I didn't mean that the way it sounded."

The newspaper was slapped against Sam's leg. "Yeah, right. Heaven forbid you're seen actually being civil to me."

"You don't understand."

"I understand perfectly." Sam tossed the paper in Janie's lap. "You might as well take this. It's about as entertaining as the rest of this town. And almost as progressive." Her boot steps echoed through the quiet library as she left.

Janie felt bad about how she had treated Sam, but was too concerned about how it would seem if she followed her. She didn't feel like reading anymore, and folded the paper neatly before making her own exit.

SUNDAY EVENING, SAM had finished a song when a muscular man dropped a quarter into her tip jar. "Do you have a request?"

He rubbed his hand across the top of his head, not disturbing the flat top in the least. Tiny bits of grass and dust floated away, some landing on his dark green tee shirt that bore the name "Doug's Lawn Care" across the left breast. "Yeah. Don't you know anything snappier? You've been singing some depressing shit."

"I sing how I feel." She looked into his dark eyes and became uncomfortable. They reminded her of a shark's. Cold and menacing. "But I'll try to come up with something."

"Good." He clapped her hard on the shoulder. "Know any Faith Hill?"

Sam exhaled heavily. She was beginning to despise country music. "I'll see what I can do." She waited until he returned to his table before she started another song.

Sam finished the song and closed her eyes. Her heart wasn't in performing tonight. She took a sip from the sweating water glass perched on the piano and cleared her throat. "I think that's it for me, folks." She got up and headed toward the back room.

"Hey, where are you going? We're still waiting for our song," Doug yelled. The other three men laughed and made rude comments.

"Come back tomorrow." Sam waved over her shoulder and disappeared through the door.

The heavy humidity hit her in the face when she stepped into the night. She was exhausted, physically and mentally. The scene in the library the day prior made her realize how out of place she was in the small town. Her overture of friendship was thrown back in her face and she'd be glad to be rid of them all. As soon as her car was repaired she would leave Piperton. She would try to avoid small towns and small minds in her future travels.

When Sam reached the back of the alley, the sight of her car listing to one side was more than she could bear. "Goddamnit!" The left rear tire was completely flat. Even from where she stood, the jagged slice was easy to spot. "Not fucking again!" She'd already had to buy one used tire from Dell's. Sam had found out the hard way that her spare was rotted and useless. The last thing she wanted to do was return to the garage for another.

With a heavy heart Sam crawled into the back seat of the Chevy. She punched the foam pillow and covered herself with the ratty blanket she had bought second-hand years ago. She nodded off, wondering when the nightmare would end.

Chapter
Five

JANIE WAS SOUND asleep when heavy knocking on her front door awakened her. She wrapped her yellow chenille robe tightly around her body and peeked through the peep hole. The distorted figure of her boyfriend stood unsteadily in the hall. She considered ignoring him, but feared he would disturb the other occupant of the second floor. She slung the door open with more force than she realized. "Doug, what are you doing here? It's late, and I have to work in the morning."

He blinked a couple of times and swayed slightly. "You're m'glirfend, uh, grillfried, I mean," he swallowed and tried again. "You know what I mean."

"It's after two in the morning and you're stinking drunk. Go home." She began to close the door, but he stumbled forward and fell into her. The stale stench of beer made Janie's stomach turn.

"Gimme kiss." Doug slobbered noisily on her neck. "I wanna fuck ya, Jane. Lemme come in."

Janie tried to push him away but he was much bigger than her. "No. Not like this." She faltered backward as he leaned heavily on her shoulders. "Stop it, Doug. I mean it."

"C'mon. We haven't fucked for months. You owe me." He pawed at her robe until it fell open. The light green satin gown was so thin he could see her rosy nipples through it. "Nice."

She cringed when his rough beard scratched against her throat. The harder Janie struggled, the more intent Doug became on his task. "Doug, no!"

Doug grasped the lacy neckline of her gown and pulled on it harshly. The triumphant look on his face changed quickly to surprise and then to pain, when Janie's knee connected with his groin. "Ah, fuck!" He fell back into the hall and curled into a fetal position, both hands cradling his damaged manhood.

Janie wrapped her robe tightly around her body and slammed the door. She fell back against it while tears fell silently from her eyes.

IT WAS A few minutes after seven when Sam came into Dell's. The office was vacant, which wasn't unusual. He worked alone and spent most of his time in the adjacent garage. She stood at the counter and tapped the bell. Several minutes went by and she tapped it again, much harder.

The interior door opened and Dell stepped inside, wiping his hands on a rag. "Oh. It's you." He went behind the counter and tossed the rag beneath it. "I still ain't got time to look at your car."

"I figured. But that's not why I'm here. I'm going to need another tire."

"Wasn't nothing wrong with the one I got you before." Dell raised the cracked coffee mug by the register and sipped the cold, bitter brew.

Sam crossed her arms over her chest. "I know. But now someone cut a different one."

"Yeah? Who you been pissing off, besides me?"

"No one that I know of."

He scratched his cheek, smearing a stripe of grease along his jaw. "Maybe you aught to wait to get another tire when you're ready to leave town. Could be cheaper."

She moved closer. "You know something I don't?"

Dell's laughter filled the small room. "Hell, gal. I figure you've probably pissed off plenty of folks." He gestured toward her. "You could always try to fit in. Dress like a lady."

Sam's hands drifted to her hips. Her white tee shirt was tucked into her faded jeans, tight enough to show off her small breasts. The wide black leather belt matched her boots, and a chain could be seen going toward her back pocket. "Do I look like a lady to you?"

"Nope. I don't think even a lacy dress with ruffles would help you."

She exhaled heavily. "Tell me about it." Sam rubbed the back of her neck. "Guess I'll wait for you to call, then. Thanks, anyway."

"Sure. I'll let you know." He went through the side door at the same time Sam walked out the front.

In a matter of minutes, Sam stalked down the sidewalk to return to Danny's. Her nose led her to a small café. She rarely wasted money on breakfast but she hoped a good meal and a cup of coffee would sooth her battered nerves better than the greasy fare at the bar. The restaurant looked busy enough to prove its food wouldn't kill her, so she went inside and searched for a table.

The room was full of people readying for the work day. Few seats were available and those were at occupied tables. Sam had decided to get her order to go when she spied a lone person near the window. She stepped quietly up to the table. "Hey."

Janie looked up from her bowl of fruit. Her face reddened at the visitor. "Hello."

"I don't mean to bother you, but is that seat taken?" Sam pointed to the chair across from Janie.

After an apprehensive look around, Janie shrugged. "I was almost finished, anyway."

Sam sat and touched Janie's hand but pulled it away at her quick intake of breath. "Please, don't leave. I'm not going to attack you, I promise."

Once the waitress stopped by and took her order, Sam tried to start a conversation with the shy woman across the table. She wasn't unattractive, although a haircut and smaller glasses would drastically change her appearance for the better. "We were never formally introduced. My name's Sam Hendrickson. I'm here waiting to get my car repaired."

Janie smiled briefly before she studied her bowl again. "I'm Janie." She raised her head and looked around the restaurant. "Are you traveling on vacation?"

"Not hardly." Sam took a sip of coffee and hummed in approval. It tasted a lot better than what she usually got in convenience stores. "I guess you could say I'm on a permanent vacation. I go from place to place, doing odd jobs."

"Oh. Well, that's kind of strange, isn't it? Not having a regular job? How long have you done that?"

Sam shrugged. "Since I was nineteen." She squinted in concentration while she did the math in her head. "Wow. It's been ten years since I left home."

"Don't you miss your family?"

"My family's all dead. No one to miss." Sam's eyes widened when the waitress placed her meal in front of her. "Thanks." She stared at the plate, not sure where to start. Two eggs, four strips of bacon, a pile of hash browns and four slices of toast covered the platter. "Good grief! Am I expected to eat all of this?"

"You're lucky you didn't order the Rancher's special. It has a stack of pancakes and a steak, too."

"You're kidding me."

"No." Janie watched as Sam began to make a sizeable dent in the food. "Hungry?"

Sam winked and continued to eat. She finished most of the eggs and bacon before speaking again. "What do you do for fun around here? Besides frequenting dingy bars and listening to hack singers, I mean."

"I usually don't make a habit of going in there." Janie speared a chunk of melon and nibbled on it daintily. "As a matter of fact, I'd only been in a time or two before."

"Really?"

"Uh-huh."

After swallowing a mouthful of hash browns, Sam chased it down with a gulp of coffee. "What made you come inside the night we met?"

The blush on Janie's face spoke more loudly than any words. "I heard you playing."

"Oh?"

"Yes."

Sam grinned. "Cool."

THE AFTERNOON WORE on for Janie. It had been frequently interrupted by the cell phone which lay on her desk. Every so often it would buzz and dance around. She had tired of the constant calls and changed the ringer to vibrate soon after she arrived at work. The more it buzzed, the more she castigated herself for not turning it off hours ago. Doug had repeatedly tried to reach her all morning, but she refused to answer. She had nothing to say to him and needed time to reassess their relationship. He was usually a decent man, but had recently started drinking more heavily. And when Doug drank, he became obnoxious.

A quick glance at the caller ID showed her father's number. As much as she wanted to, she knew it would do no good to ignore him. He would only show up at the office and cause a scene. She steeled herself and answered the phone. "What is it, Harvey?" She'd stopped calling him anything else years ago.

"Watch your attitude, Jane. Since when have you talked to me that way? And where the hell have you been?"

"At work. Where I still am, by the way. Why?"

"Doug called me. He says you're being unreasonable. What the hell's gotten into you?" Harvey Clarke cleared his throat, the phlegm causing him to spit. "He's a good man. You need to quit stalling and marry him. God knows you're not getting any younger, and he'll probably want kids. You're lucky he'll have you."

Janie gritted her teeth and counted to ten. Harvey always knew which buttons to push with her. "Did he bother to mention what happened last night?"

"He said you acted all high and mighty and treated him bad. That's no way to act with your fiancé."

"He came to my apartment drunk and practically attacked me. And he's not my fiancé."

Harvey coughed wetly. The years of smoking were ruining his lungs, but he wasn't about to give up the two-pack a day habit. "A man's got needs. It's your job to take care of him."

The cheap, disposable pen in Janie's hand snapped in two as she fought the urge to scream. "Doug talked to you about our sex life? I can't believe this."

"Calm down, Jane. The boy's trying to see what's wrong with you."

"Me? I suppose you think I should have let him rape me. After all, it's his right."

"It's not rape, you stupid girl. He's the man you're going to marry. At least I hope so. I'd like to see some grandkids before I die. I don't want to end up in the old folks home, all alone like my mother. It ain't right."

The disgusting thought of being tied to a man like Doug for the rest of her life gave Janie the courage to confront her father. "You've got a long wait, Harvey. I'm breaking up with Doug."

"What?" Harvey's exclamation caused him to go into a coughing fit. "You'll do no such thing. I worked hard to find you a man, and you're going to quit being such a little bitch and marry him."

"Like hell I will." Janie disconnected the call and turned off her phone. The exhilaration of finally standing up to Harvey's bullying was short lived. A creeping dread settled in and made her race to the bathroom, where she promptly vomited.

THE PARK'S AIR was choked with the heavy buzz of lawn equipment. Doug and his three-man crew were scattered around, each handling a different machine. He made the final two passes with the riding mower and drove it to the flatbed trailer. After guiding the vehicle up the ramp, he killed the engine.

A pickup truck with a city emblem on the side parked next to the trailer. The burly man behind the wheel got out and stretched. "Yo, Doug."

"Hey, Calvin. What's up?" Doug secured the mower and climbed off the trailer. "Does your yard need mowing?" He often cut his friend's grass, who then charged it back to the city as a business expense.

"Nah. Just came by to see if what I heard was true." Calvin's dark beard was thick, and several drops of tobacco juice glistened in the sun as he spit on the ground.

Doug brushed the grass from his hair. "What?"

"Bud said he saw your woman at Fern's this morning, having breakfast." He stared hard at Doug's chest. "Nope. Don't see 'em."

"What the fuck are you talking about?"

Calvin spit another stream close to Doug's foot. "He said she was with some manly-lookin' bitch. But knowing Bud's rotten eyesight, I figured you grew tits. 'Cause we all know that homely gal of yours ain't got no friends."

"You're full of shit. Is Bud sure she was with a woman? Could it have been her dad?"

"He's sure, all right. Says it looked like that broad who sings at Danny's."

"Fuck." Doug scowled and scratched his head. It wasn't like Janie to do things on her own. She'd starting growing a backbone lately, and he didn't like it one bit.

"You having problems?"

"No." But Doug couldn't understand what was going on with his girlfriend. The main reason he dated her was because their fathers both thought it was a good idea. She used to be an easy lay, at least until the last few months. For some reason, she starting finding excuses to not sleep with him, and he was getting tired of it.

"You sure?" Calvin hitched up his jeans and stuck his hands in the front pockets. He jangled the change, using the motion to scratch his crotch. "Guess if you're okay with it, that's all that matters. To each his own, I 'spose."

A nearby stick was perfect for Doug to take out his frustration out on. He snapped it in half, and threw the pieces at his so-called friend. "It's *not* okay with me, dammit. And as soon as we get done here, I'm going over to Janie's office and straighten her out."

DOUG STEPPED INTO the physician's waiting area and slammed the door behind him. He looked around and noticed only one patient and the receptionist in the room. He held a small bouquet of mixed flowers in one hand and turned his angry eyes toward the receptionist.

Laura McBride shrank back in her chair as he approached the desk. "May I help you?"

"Tell Janie I need to see her." He glared at the man waiting in the corner who gaped at him. "What?"

The receptionist's hand shook as it reached for the phone. "I'm sorry, who?"

Doug slapped his free hand on her desk. "Janie Clarke. She still works here, don't she?"

"Of course. But I don't think—"

"Tell her to get her scrawny ass out here."

She picked up the handset and dialed. "Janie? You have a visitor." Laura replaced the receiver and gestured behind him. "Would you like to take a seat, sir? She should be out in a moment."

JANIE STARED AT her phone once she hung up. She rarely had visitors at work. Unless she counted the times her father would show up, demanding she go to lunch with him. But Laura always mentioned Harvey by name. She straightened a few papers on her desk before heading toward the waiting room.

A man's voice could be heard before Janie opened the door. She steeled herself for the confrontation, recognizing Doug's gruff tones immediately. Her heart began to pound when she walked through the door. His tense posture put her on immediate alert. "Doug? What are you doing here?" Janie crossed to where he stood in order to keep her voice low. The last thing she wanted to do was share their problems with the other occupants of the room.

"I came to talk some sense into you." Doug thrust the flowers toward her. "Here."

Janie took a step back. "That's really nice of you. But you shouldn't be here." She glanced over her shoulder to Laura. "I could lose my job, getting personal visitors."

"Bullshit. That's not what this is about, is it?" Doug shook the flowers at her. "Take these damned things."

"No."

"Why the hell not? I paid good money for them." He threw the bouquet at her feet. "Fine. See if I give a damn. They were your old man's idea, anyway."

"What does my father have to do with you being here?"

Doug kicked the flowers out of the way and stepped closer to Janie. "He wants what's best for you."

"Please, don't." Janie backed farther away until she bumped into the door. "I really can't talk right now." She swallowed her fear and tried another tactic. "Can we meet after I get off work?"

"I guess." He took her arm. "I'll be at Danny's. You seem to like it there." After another hard squeeze, he released her and his expression softened. "We'll have a couple of drinks and talk all this out. It'll be okay."

Janie turned her head at the last moment and his kiss hit her cheek instead of her lips. She gave him what she hoped was a sincere look. "That sounds nice." She rubbed her arm and watched Doug leave. His behavior only served to reinforce her resolve. Although her father would make her life miserable, she was determined to break things off with Doug. Embarrassed, she picked up the discarded flowers and shared an apologetic smile with Laura then slipped through the door to the office.

IT WAS LATE afternoon at Danny's and only three patrons were in the bar. Still in his work uniform, Doug seemed determined to drink his way under the table in the shortest amount of time possible. The table where he sat was located in the far corner of the room. To help Ray out, Sam had taken Doug's drinks to him. His belligerence got worse as the day wore on. She placed his beer on the table and removed the empty glass. Before she could move away, he grabbed her wrist.

"Hold it." He raised his bleary eyes and focused on Sam. "Why aren't you singing?"

"Not enough people. No sense in entertaining an empty room." She tried to shake off his grip. "Look, buddy. I think you've had enough."

Doug tightened his hold. "I don't give a damn what you think. Ray's never complained." He slowly looked her up and down. "What is it with you, anyway? You trying to be a man?"

Sam pried his fingers loose and took a step back. "Not hardly. I'm perfectly happy being a woman."

"Don't act like no woman I've ever seen." He picked up the glass, already damp with condensation and drank from it as if he were dying of thirst. A small amount of foam covered his upper lip and he wiped it away with the back of his hand. "Why are you here?"

"Trying to make some money by singing a few songs." Sam shook her head and walked away when he turned to focus on his drink. He wasn't the first who questioned her arrival in town. She got tired of answering the local's questions, but didn't want to antagonize the people she tried to get tips from. Sam returned to the bar and placed the empty glass close to Ray. "Shouldn't you be cutting that guy off? I can't believe he's still conscious."

Ray glanced over at Doug. "Nah. He does that every now and then. Doug has a place nearby, so I know he's not driving. He gets pretty obnoxious, but doesn't do any harm."

She climbed onto a stool and hooked her feet on the lower rung. "It's your bar. Can I get a coke?"

"Sure." Ray filled a glass and set it in front of her. "Thanks for passing out drinks, by the way."

"No problem." Sam spun her stool around and watched the room. The more she helped out around the bar, the more cash Ray passed her way. It worked for both of them. He didn't have to fill out the necessary paperwork for an employee and she made extra money. She checked her watch. It was five-fifteen and the bar began to fill with the after-work crowd.

The arrival of a particular woman caught Sam's attention. She watched as Janie stopped inside the door and looked around the room. A smile lit Sam's face when she assumed she was trying to find her. She was about to get up from her seat when Janie hitched her purse strap on her shoulder and went to Doug's table.

JANIE PULLED OUT a chair across from Doug and sat. "Sorry I'm late. Andrea kept bringing me files to put away." She placed her purse in an empty chair and was surprised when she noticed Sam standing next to their table. Her heart beat faster at the thought of Doug finding out she knew the unusual woman. "Can I help you?"

"Actually, that's what I wanted to ask you. Would you like something from the bar?" Sam tucked her hands into her front pockets as she waited patiently for Janie's order.

"Um, sure. A light beer, please." Janie turned away, effectively dismissing the singer.

"Be right back."

Janie couldn't help but watch her walk away. She was so focused on Sam that she didn't hear Doug. His angry growl got her attention. "I'm sorry, what?"

He grabbed his glass and drained it. "I *said*, it's about damned time you got here."

"I told you—"

"I heard you." He turned and waved his empty glass toward the bar. "Worthless dyke."

"What?"

Doug glared at her. "Are you even listening to me?" He looked up when Sam placed two glasses on the table.

"Anything else I can get you?" Sam didn't seem perturbed in the least. Her gaze was focused on Janie. "Miss?"

Janie slowly shook her head. "No, thank you." She raised her glass in salute. "This is fine."

"Okay. Wave if you need anything." Sam left the table as quickly as she had arrived.

Doug finally gathered his thoughts. "You know her?"

"What?"

He grabbed her arm. "I heard about you two having breakfast together this morning. Since when do you hang out with someone like her?"

"We weren't hanging out. She happened to come into Fern's while I was there, and there weren't any tables available. I had a spare chair, so she sat with me. End of story." But her hand shook as she set her glass on the table.

The explanation seemed to appease Doug. He released her and took a deep drink from his beer. "Just don't make it a habit."

She bristled at his comment. Her newfound courage peeked out again. "I can eat with whomever I please. It's not a crime to share a table with someone besides you."

Doug almost spit his beer across the table. He sputtered and wiped his mouth. "I don't like your attitude, Janie. You're my girlfriend, and it makes me look bad when you do something like that."

"You don't own me."

"I will once we get married." He dug for his wallet and dropped several bills on the table. "Come on. Let's get out of here."

"No."

He stood and reached for her. "Don't argue with me. I said let's go."

Janie scooted away from him but didn't stand. "I'm not going anywhere with you." She sat up straighter and took a deep breath. "It's over, Doug."

"What do you mean?"

"Exactly what I said." She lowered her voice. "I don't think we should see each other anymore."

Doug seized her arm and pulled Janie to her feet. "I don't give a good goddamn what you *think*. You're my girlfriend, and you're going to be my wife."

"Doug, stop it. You're hurting me." Janie squirmed ineffectively. She tried to pry his fingers away. "Please, let go."

"No!" He jerked her closer. "I don't know what's gotten into you lately, but it's going to stop right now." He was about to drag her away from the table when someone touched his shoulder. Doug turned and scowled at the intruder. "Back off, bitch."

Sam hadn't planned on getting involved, but she couldn't stand by while the drunken man assaulted Janie. "Hey, come on. Let me buy you a drink. No sense in getting all bent out of shape."

He released Janie and narrowed his eyes. "I don't need you getting into my business, faggot. Get out of my face."

"No harm, bud." Sam saw movement behind the man and tried to keep him talking. "Let's go over to the bar and I'll get you that drink." She tipped her head toward the other side of the room. "Maybe two."

While Sam occupied Doug, Janie took the opportunity to make her escape.

In his drunken state, Doug allowed himself to be led to the bar. "Yeah, sure. She ain't going nowhere." He had no idea Janie had already left.

Chapter
Six

JANIE CALLED IN sick the next morning. She was afraid Doug would show up at the clinic, and she wasn't in the mood for another fight. She knew there'd be hell to pay for leaving him at the bar. The hard knock on her door scared her. She peeped through the security glass and fought the urge to hide.

Harvey Clarke beat on the door. "Jane, I know you're in there. They told me you didn't come to work today." He pounded his beefy hand on the wood. "I'm not leaving, Jane. Open up."

She unlocked the door and opened it slightly. "What is it, Harvey? I don't feel much like company."

He appeared to have come directly from work. His security guard uniform was wrinkled and a greasy stain on his chest showed the remains of the previous evening's meal. "Don't sass me, girl. Let me in."

Janie opened the door wider and allowed him inside. She followed her father to the living area, where he dropped his considerable bulk onto the red floral sofa. She resigned herself to his company. Harvey would leave when he was ready, and not a moment before. "Would you like a cup of coffee? I recently made a pot."

"Might as well." He stretched one arm across the back of the sofa and propped his scuffed shoes on the oak coffee table. "Put plenty of cream and sugar in it."

She rolled her eyes and went to the kitchen. If she wasn't so fond of her grandmother, Janie would have left Piperton years ago. She often dreamed of making a new start in a larger city. But as long as Lucille was alive, she wasn't going anywhere. Janie knew she was the only visitor her grandmother had and the thought pained her. She hurriedly made two cups of coffee and returned to Harvey. "Careful, it's hot."

"No shit." He took a cautious sip before setting the mug on the table. "Doug called me."

"I figured as much." Janie perched on the edge of the wingback chair across from him.

Harvey studied his daughter. "He's pretty upset. Says you got all nasty with him yesterday. What's up with that?"

"I'm through with Doug, Harvey."

"Why? You got someone better?"

Janie shook her head. "No. But—"

"Damn it, Jane. It took me forever to find a man who would even look at you. At least Doug isn't particular."

"No, he's a jerk."

Harvey got to his feet so quickly that the coffee almost toppled over. "That's enough out of you. He's a hardworking man who would take care of you."

She placed her coffee on the table and stood as well. "I don't need taking care of. Especially by someone like him. Doesn't it bother you that he almost raped me?"

"Quit being so dramatic. You've always stretched things out of proportion." He pointed a finger at her. "I told Doug you'd apologize. He's waiting for your call."

Janie crossed her arms over her chest. "He's got a long wait. If you're so keen on Doug, why don't *you* marry him?" The slap was unexpected and knocked her back into the chair. Janie covered her cheek with one hand and blinked away the tears. The shock on her face was evident. Harvey had rarely raised a hand to her since she became an adult.

"I've had about all of your smart mouth I can take. Don't give me no more lip, girl. Your mama listened to her daddy until I took her over, and you'll listen to me until you're married to Doug. That's how it's always been, and that's how it's gonna be."

"Why? What's the big deal, Harvey? Why now?" Janie's voice was quiet.

"Do you have any idea what it looks like, you not being married? I need a way to pass along my line. You need to hook up with Doug and start giving me some gran' kids before you dry out and become completely useless." Harvey pulled his pants higher on his waist and headed for the door. "You'll call him and hope to hell he'll take you back." he turned at the door and looked at her. "Now get yourself cleaned up. You look like shit." He slammed the door behind him.

SAM SAT IN the diner, picking at her lunch. Worrying about Janie kept her sleepless the night before. She knew it wasn't any of her business, but she couldn't help but be concerned about the shy woman she had spoken to the previous day. Although they had only recently met, there was something about Janie which made Sam want to protect her. She stuffed a cold fry into her mouth and chewed.

The bell over the door rang as three men came into the restaurant. Doug and his crew congregated around a table in the center of the room. He raised his hand and snapped his fingers at the waitress. "Hey, babe! Bring us three specials, will you?"

The waitress gathered three glasses of iced tea and placed them in front of the men. She tried to slip away but Doug swatted her on the rear. "Dana, you get cuter every day. How about going to dinner with me sometime?"

She muttered something and hurried back to the kitchen. Whatever she said must have amused the two men with Doug, because they both roared with laughter.

Doug turned red. "Her loss." He poked one of the other men. "What's the matter, Chuck? Jealous?"

"Nah." Chuck took off his filthy baseball cap and scratched his thinning hair. "I thought you had a girlfriend."

"Well, sure. But no sense in making all the other women suffer, right? There's more than enough of me to go around." Doug looked around the near-empty room and spotted Sam by the window. He stood and adjusted himself. "Be right back, guys."

Sam noticed him coming and closed her eyes. She jumped slightly when he rapped his knuckles on her table.

"Hey."

She opened her eyes and looked into his face. "Hi."

Doug sucked on his teeth and studied her. "Haven't seen you in here before. You waiting for anyone?"

"Uh, no. Just wanted lunch." Sam noticed how the muscles in Doug's arms flexed as he opened and closed his fists.

"Good." He leaned over until his face was only a few inches from hers. "I heard you had breakfast with my girl. Don't do it again." Doug straightened and chucked her on the shoulder. "Thanks for the drink yesterday."

Sam nodded, thankful he couldn't read her mind. The thoughts she'd had of his "girl" weren't the kind he'd appreciate. "Sure." She held her breath until he went back to his own table, then released it slowly.

The sight of Janie hurrying down the sidewalk caught Sam's attention. She quickly left enough money on her table for her meal and a tip, then got up. A short glance at Doug and his cronies assured her they hadn't noticed Janie, so she waved to the waitress and left the café.

It took Sam half a block before she caught up with Janie. The other woman was walking fast, yet her head was dipped low. Sam jogged up beside her. "Hey."

Janie ignored Sam. She continued to walk, although she did adjust the dark prescription sunglasses that partially hid her face. She shouldered her purse and continued on.

Sam touched her arm. "Are you all right?"

"Please, leave me alone." Janie's voice was apologetic, but she didn't slow down.

"Look, I'm sorry if I did anything to cause you trouble with your boyfriend. I only — "

Janie shook off her hand and spun to face Sam. Her glasses slipped down and she hurriedly tried to slide them back in place. "I appreciate your help last night, but I'm fine."

Sam removed Janie's glasses and noticed the discoloration beneath her left eye. "Did he do this?"

"Don't be silly. Doug would never hurt me." Janie took her glasses and placed them back on her face. "If you don't mind, I have some things to do." She edged by Sam and continued on her way.

"Right." Sam put her hands in the front pockets of her jeans and headed toward the bar.

SAM HAD VOLUNTEERED to mop the floor for Ray since it was too early for the bar to be open. The mindless work kept her from thinking about Janie. Or at least she thought it would. She couldn't understand why she cared so much what the other woman thought about her. It wasn't as if they were friends. She shook her head in disgust. She was so engrossed in her thoughts that she didn't hear Ray calling her name. The damp rag that hit her in the head caused Sam to spin around. "What was that for?"

Ray waved the phone in the air. "Call for you. Didn't you hear me?"

"No. Sorry." She leaned the mop against a table and walked to the bar. She handed the towel to Ray and took the phone from him. "This is Sam."

"Hey, Sam. Dell here. Got some good news for you. I've finally cleared some space, and I can take a look at your car."

"That is good news. I've got a slight problem though. It's not running, so I can't bring it to you." She picked at a scratch on the bar with her fingernail.

"No problem. I can tow you over."

She closed her eyes and calculated how much cash she had left. "How much would that run? I'm a little strapped at the moment."

Dell cleared his throat. "Tell you what. I'll throw in the tow for free. Least I could do since you've had to wait so long for me to look it over. I'll even bring over that tire you need, and put it on before I move the car."

"You're a lifesaver, Dell. Thanks." Sam hung up the phone and gave Ray a relieved smile. "Things are looking up."

"Yeah? You finally getting that old heap fixed?" He constantly teased her about the rusty Chevy.

She removed the apron from her waist and tossed it on the bar. "Yep. Now, if you'll excuse me, I'm going out to my 'old heap' and wait for Dell." She walked out the back door, his laughter still ringing in her ears.

Ten minutes later Dell drove up in his tow truck. He got out of the cab and stood next to Sam. "Well, looks like you've pissed off lots of folks. That thing's a mess."

"No, that's how it's always looked." Sam put her hands on her hips while he laughed. "Hey, it's gotten me where I needed to go, up until now."

"True. You usually can't kill these old things." Dell patted the fender. "Let me get another tire on it, then I'll hook it up and head on over to the shop. Want to come with me? Then I can tell you what it's gonna run you."

"Sure."

It didn't take Dell more than ten minutes to change the tire and hook up the Chevy. He and Sam sat in the cab of his truck silently, both absorbed in their own thoughts. He wheeled the rig into the parking lot of the shop. "You can go on into the office. It shouldn't take me long. There's fresh coffee, if you're interested."

Sam hopped out of the truck and dusted off her jeans. "Great. Thanks a lot, Dell."

"No problem." He went about his business, while she walked into the office.

Looking around the tiny area, Sam saw the coffee maker and proceeded to make herself a cup. She sat on one of the three available chairs and propped her feet in another. After taking a sip of the strong brew, she picked up a copy of the newspaper and flipped through it.

Half an hour later, Dell came into the office and noticed Sam's posture. Her chin was resting on her chest and her eyes were closed. "Looks like you made yourself at home."

Startled awake, Sam got to her feet and placed the paper on the table. "Uh, yeah. Sorry about that."

"Ain't nothing to be sorry for. It took a little longer than I expected." He fished a red shop towel out of the back pocket of his greasy overalls and wiped his hands. "Got some bad news for you, though. The engine's a goner, and the exhaust system is rusted through, too. It'd be a hell of a lot cheaper to find something else."

"Damn." Sam took out her wallet. "How much do I owe you?"

"Tell you what. Give me fifty for the diagnostics, and I'll even haul it to the wrecking yard for you."

She fished two twenties and a ten out of her wallet. "Thanks for the help, Dell. You got a spare garbage bag? I need to clean out my stuff."

After taking her belongings out of the car, Sam stepped into the sunshine and hefted the two black trash bags over her shoulders. She headed to the east, hoping to find the YMCA the mechanic had told her about.

Fifteen minutes later, one of the bags split, dropping Sam's clothes to the sidewalk. She tossed the other one next to it. "Shit."

"Looks like you've in a bit of trouble," a woman's voice called from the nearby doorway.

Sam put her hands on her hips and turned to see who was speaking. "No kidding."

The woman appeared to be in her mid-fifties, her gray hair cut close to her head. She held up a finger. "Hold on. I'll be right back." She disappeared behind a glass door that advertised a women's exercise facility, then returned a few minutes later, holding an old suitcase. "This would probably work better, dear."

"Uh, yeah, I guess so. But—"

"It's too damned hot to be standing out here arguing. Clean up your mess and then come inside." The woman left the suitcase on the walkway and disappeared into the building.

Not sure what she was in for, Sam did as she was told. She hefted the old case and stepped through the door, exhaling as the cool air hit her damp back. She set her baggage next to the door and walked to where the woman stood behind the counter. Upbeat music could be heard in the background, and three women were making the circuit of the exercise stations in one of the two large rooms. "Thank you for the suitcase. I'll get it back to you as soon as I find a place to stay."

"Take your time." The woman held out her hand. "Name's Betsy Haley. You looked like you needed a friend out there."

Sam shook her hand and smiled. "Sam Hendrickson. And you're right. I was just looking for the YMCA."

"What do you want with that nasty old place? Nothing but a bunch of horny old men hang out there." Betsy eyed the young woman across from her. "Looking for a place to stay?"

"Yes, ma'am. My car died, so I'm stuck here until I can earn enough to get something else. And I can't afford to spend much on a place to sleep." Sam normally didn't spill her woes to a stranger, but there was something comforting and almost familiar about the woman.

"Not from around here, are you?"

Sam chuckled and shook her head. "No, ma'am. I was just passing through."

Betsy eyeballed Sam over the top of her glasses. "You got a job?"

"Sort of. I've been singing at Danny's, and I was going to check the newspaper for something else."

"Uh-huh. You mind doing janitorial work?"

"Ma'am?"

Betsy sighed and shook her head. "Quit calling me that. You're making me feel old. My name's Betsy." She cut Sam's apology off with a wave of her hand. "I've got a room upstairs you can use, if you'll clean it out. Then I could use a hand with the general maintenance around here. I can't pay much, but if you help out around here, I won't charge you rent. You'll still have time to find another job."

"That's really kind of you, but why? You don't know me."

Betsy leaned across the counter and lowered her voice. "I understand what it's like to be in a strange place all alone." She straightened up. "Besides, you remind me of myself at your age."

Sam brushed her hair out of her eyes. "Thanks, Betsy. If you'll show me where to put my junk, I'll get started." She enjoyed the laughter from the older woman, as she followed her around the exercise area and through a door at the back of the room.

TWO DAYS LATER, Sam parked a green sedan in the parking lot of the local grocery store. The nineteen seventy-five Oldsmobile Delta Eighty-Eight was the size of an aircraft carrier, but the engine ran smooth and the price was right. The interior of the car looked brand new, and the engine had less than twenty thousand miles on it. A friend of Betsy's was willing to take payments on the old car until it was paid for, as long as Sam didn't mind also doing her yard work and a few odd jobs around her house. Sam thought it was a steal at eleven hundred dollars.

She hoped her daytime job at the store wouldn't interfere in her other endeavors, but the manager she had interviewed with had assured her it wouldn't. The part-time work was the only job she could find. At minimum wage, it would take her a long time to pay off her debts unless she continued to sing at night. She left the windows down on her car and hurried into the store, tying a red apron around her waist.

Half an hour later, Sam was methodically straightening cans of beans, when she noticed Janie at the end of the aisle. Intrigued as to why she wasn't at work, Sam stopped what she was doing and headed toward her.

Janie picked up a box of instant potatoes and placed it in her hand-held basket. She turned to grab a bag of rice and saw Sam. "Um, hi."

"Hey." Sam slid her free hand into the back pocket of her jeans. She didn't know why she was always so nervous around Janie. "I figured you'd be at work."

"No, I took the day off." Janie dropped the rice into the basket. "What are you doing here?"

Sam pointed at her apron. "I work here. Just started today, as a matter of fact."

"That's nice. Well, I'd better finish up." Janie began to walk toward the chips and crackers aisle, with Sam following behind. She took a box of saltines and placed it in her basket. "I didn't realize you were still here."

Holding up a large bag of chips, Sam shrugged. "I'm supposed to make sure everything's neat." She set the bag in its proper place and gave Janie an embarrassed grin. "Somebody's gotta do it."

An older couple at the end of the aisle stopped and watched Sam and Janie.

Janie's face flushed at the attention. "Why can't you leave me alone?" Her voice was loud. "I could never be friends with someone like you."

The biting comment hurt. Sam adjusted another bag roughly on the shelf. "Excuse the hell out of me." She stomped away and turned at the end of the aisle. "You don't have anything to worry about." She brushed by the people who had been watching them and headed for the aisle she'd been working on before.

Ten minutes later, Sam heard her name over the store's

loudspeaker, directing her to report to the manager's office. She shook her head and walked slowly down the aisle. She opened the door to the office and saw the manager sitting at his desk. "Did you need to see me?"

"Yeah." He sat up straighter in his chair and waved his hand. "Close the door, will you?"

Sam did as he asked, getting a sinking feeling in the pit of her stomach.

"Look, Sam, I just got a customer complaint about you." The manager brushed at the greasy comb-over across the top of his head. "I know you're new in town, but you can't go around harassing our customers."

She glared at him. "Who complained? And what was it I supposedly did?"

"Hey, don't get all bent out of shape. I know a gal with your obvious...inclinations can't help herself when there's a woman around, but we can't have that sort of thing going on here."

"What did she tell you?"

He gave her a perplexed look. "She? No, it was Mr. Simms. He said you got into an argument with a lady on the chip aisle." Lowering his voice, the manager asked, "You can tell me. Was she hot? I know it's hard to control yourself sometimes, being how you are, but—"

"For your information, it was a total misunderstanding." Sam untied her apron, wadded it into a ball and tossed it on his desk. "Forget it. You're not worth the trouble. I quit." She turned around and left, slamming the door behind her.

JANIE WAS ON her way home but couldn't stop thinking about Sam's parting words. Her guilt at her own behavior was augmented by curiosity. Nothing made sense to her anymore. Only a few short weeks ago, she was, if not content, at least resigned to her existence. Her life was mundane, but comfortable. Now all sorts of new thoughts filled her mind.

She drove her late-model Ford Escort past her apartment. She decided to visit her grandmother. Seeking Lucille's counsel was second-nature to her. She'd always been able to talk to her about anything, and she needed her Nana's wisdom now more than ever.

Within minutes the nursing home came into view. Janie wheeled carelessly into the parking lot. Usually meticulous, she took up two spaces and didn't even bother to lock her car after getting out. She hooked the strap of her purse on her shoulder and hurried inside. Halfway down the hall, she paused. How would she broach the subject to her grandmother?

She knocked timidly on Lucille's door, relieved to hear her grandmother's entreaty.

"Come on in."

Janie stood still for a moment, unsure of herself.

"Janie? Come here, honey." Lucille held out her arms and embraced the upset woman. "Tell Nana all about it."

Janie shuddered in Lucille's arms. "I...I...he—" She broke into tears.

"There, there. Everything's going to be all right." Lucille lifted Janie's chin and noticed her bruised face. "What happened?"

Wiping her eyes, Janie managed to pull herself together. "It's all such a mess, Nana. I don't know what to do."

Lucille wiped at Janie's face with a dainty handkerchief. "We'll figure it out. Tell me how you got this mouse."

"Harvey—"

"My worthless, good-for-nothing son did this?"

Janie lowered her eyes. "I probably deserved it. We argued and I said something I shouldn't have."

"Pish-posh. No matter what was said, you *never* deserve this." Lucille traced below the contusion with her finger. "I swear, that man is a waste of skin. If I'd known the trouble he'd end up being, I'd thrown him out with the bathwater years ago." She patted Janie's unblemished cheek. "*After* he'd given me you, that is. Now, what set him off?"

"I broke up with Doug."

"Oh? But I thought you two were happy."

Janie sniffled. "Not really. I never loved him, Nana." She blew her nose on a crumbled tissue she pulled from her purse. "I didn't even *like* him most of the time."

Lucille's eyes filled with sympathetic tears. "Why on earth were you with him, then?"

"Harvey wouldn't have given me a moment's peace, otherwise. Besides, he *did* have a point. Who else could ever be interested in me? I'm plain, at the best of times." Janie ruffled her hair. "Look at me. I'm nothing special."

"That's where you're wrong, honey. You've always been a pretty girl. And you've grown into a beautiful woman." Lucille brushed Janie's hair away from her face. "I've never understood how someone as ugly as my son could have fathered such a lovely girl."

Janie had grown up believing her father. As a teen, she'd hidden behind her bookish looks, the straight hair and glasses easily disguising her natural beauty. Without self-esteem, she never cared how she dressed. Her closet was filled with frumpy skirts. The brown dress she wore today was characteristic of her life – dull, bland, and colorless. "Doug said the same thing as Harvey. I'll probably grow old alone." She started to cry again.

"It sounds to me as if you made a good decision. Any man who can't see what a fine woman you are doesn't deserve you." Lucille rubbed her granddaughter's back in a soothing motion. "You're better off without him."

"I wish I could be as sure as you, Nana."

"Don't worry." Lucille kissed her forehead. "When you least expect it, Mr. Right will drop into your lap."

Janie wasn't so sure. She wondered what her grandmother would say if she knew the thoughts that filled her head. She kept thinking about Sam, and how badly she had treated her. Maybe Nana could help her sort through her feelings. "I met someone."

"Really? What's he like?"

Janie shook her head. "It's nothing like that. She started singing at the bar by my office." She wiped her eyes with the heel of her hand. "Nana, she's so different. I've never met anyone like her before."

Lucille tried not to show her surprise on her face. "A woman? Well, okay. Why don't you tell me about her?"

"I'm not sure where to start. She dresses so, I don't know, manly. Tee shirts or tank tops, and work boots. And her jeans! They're so faded, and tight. And she carries a wallet in her back pocket." Janie lowered her voice. "It has a chain on it. Like a biker or something."

"Maybe she travels a lot, and it's the most comfortable way to dress."

"No, I don't think that's it. She's obviously," Janie whispered, "gay."

"And this bothers you?"

Janie stilled as she contemplated her answer. "At one time, it did, but not now. She's really nice, even though I've treated her less than kindly."

"Has she made any untoward advances?"

"No. In fact, she told me today that I didn't even have to worry about being her friend."

Lucille's eyes widened. "What precipitated that comment? Were you—"

"No! Of course not!" Janie studied her hands and began to shred the tissue. "I think she had been trying to be friendly, and I just didn't handle things right."

"Did it upset you?"

"It did, at first. But now, I'm not so sure."

"Well, I don't see that it would hurt. Everyone could use another friend." Lucille patted Janie's hand. "Now, go wash your face so you can join Mr. Michaels and me in the common room for the karaoke contest. We can sit in the back and make fun of all the tone deaf singers."

Chapter
Seven

SAM RAN HER fingers down the piano keys with a flourish. She nodded her acknowledgement of the crowd's applause as she stood. "Thanks, folks. I'm going to call it a night."

Several people voiced their displeasure. "One more," a woman at the bar yelled. "I want to hear some Reba."

"Sorry. My voice is about gone." Sam accepted a glass of water from Ray and drank half of it before placing it on the bar.

The woman wriggled on her perch. Her black hair was obviously dyed, as it was too dark for her complexion. She took a deep drag from her cigarette and blew the smoke Sam's direction. "I like the way you sing."

"Um, thanks." Sam scooted away from the woman, who was at least fifteen years her senior. She wasn't looking for any trouble, and this lady reeked of it. "I'm here most nights."

"I know." Slightly overweight, she adjusted her short leather skirt, showing more of her ample thigh. "I've been in here quite a lot." She raised her hand and casually loosened the three top buttons of her red satin shirt. "It's mighty warm tonight, isn't it?"

Sam glanced at Ray, who gave her the "you're on your own" look. She quickly drained her water glass and held it up to him. "Could I have another, Ray?"

"Sure." He looked as if he was trying not to laugh at her predicament.

The woman held out her hand to Sam. "I'm Camille. But you can call me Cami." She squeezed Sam's hand and didn't release it. Smiling slyly, Cami leaned over closer and whispered, "You know, I've never been with a woman."

With a hard jerk, Sam regained her hand and quickly tucked it into her front pocket. She wasn't naive, but the last thing she wanted to do was to get tangled up with a predator like Cami. "Uh, yeah. I wish you luck on that one. It's been nice talking to you, but I have a few things to take care of in the back." She hurried to the kitchen as if the room was on fire.

Cami ground out her cigarette and lit another one. She blew several smoke rings and shook her glass at Ray. "Hit me again."

After running a full sink of dishwater, Sam furiously scrubbed every dirty glass she could find. She wasn't about to go back into the bar as long as Cami was there.

Two hours later, Ray came into the kitchen and leaned against the counter. Every inch of the room gleamed. "You've been busy."

"Yeah, well. It needed to be done, and I didn't feel like singing anymore tonight. I hope that was okay." Sam finished sweeping and placed the broom in a nearby closet.

"Sure. I'll never complain about you cleaning. I've locked the place up, if you want to go back to the main room. You're safe."

Sam tossed the dishcloth at him. "Very funny." She retrieved the broom again and escaped into the bar.

Since Sam had already washed the majority of the dishes, it only took the two of them thirty minutes to get the bar ready for the next day's business. Once outside, Ray locked the front door and pocketed the keys. "Guess I'll see you tomorrow, Sam." He patted her on the back. "You look tired. Try to get some rest."

She watched as he walked down the sidewalk and out of sight. The clouds covered any hint of moonlight, and the humidity caused Sam to break instantly into a sweat. She shuffled down the alley toward her car. Since it was so late, she decided to forego staying at Betsy's. She didn't want to disturb the older woman's rest and felt comfortable sleeping in her car, as she'd done for years.

A sound at the end of the alley caused Sam to stop. She stayed in the shadows and peered ahead, glad for once of the security light that brightened the area behind the bar. At first, she thought she was dreaming. Leaning against the Oldsmobile was the last person she expected to see. She stepped out of the darkness, yet kept a good distance between them. It had been days since she'd seen her. "What are you doing here?"

Janie pushed off the Oldsmobile. "I wanted to apologize for how I acted the other day."

"Okay, fine. You've apologized." Sam was tired of Janie's constant change of heart. She felt like she was on a see saw, and she'd never liked the things. "No hard feelings." She moved past Janie to open the back door of the car. "Now, if you'll excuse me, I'm tired."

"But—"

Sam took off her shoes and threw them in the floorboard of her car. "You're blocking my bedroom window."

"What?"

Undoing her belt, Sam started to slip her jeans down her legs. "I'm going to bed."

Janie blushed as more of Sam's legs were unveiled. The smooth expanse of thigh held her interest much longer than it should have. She blinked and met Sam's eyes. "Um, sorry."

"S'okay." Sam stepped out of the jeans and tossed them in the floorboard as well. "Listen. It's late. Do you need me to walk you home?"

"No, my car's out front."

Sam adjusted the waistband on her boxer shorts and tucked her hands beneath her arms. She wasn't cold, but her confusion over Janie's sudden attitude change kept her off balance. "Alright. Hey, since we're speaking to each other again, want to get together for breakfast tomorrow?"

"I...I don't normally eat breakfast."

"I see." Sam knew a brush off when she heard one. "Never mind." She climbed into the back seat of the car. "Guess I'll see you around." She slammed the door and disappeared beneath an old blanket, leaving Janie standing alone.

JANIE CLOSED HER door and walked into the apartment. It was dark, and for the first time since she'd moved out on her own, she noticed the quiet. She tossed her purse onto a chair and headed toward the bathroom.

After putting on her nightgown, she wandered into the kitchen and poured herself a glass of skim milk. She placed the glass on her nightstand and climbed into bed. A quick glance at her alarm clock showed it was three-thirty, yet she was wide awake. She kept going over in her mind her conversation with Sam. No matter how she dissected it, she always ended up sounding like an insensitive idiot. She finished the milk and placed the empty glass on her nightstand. "I was a jerk. No wonder she was so angry with me."

Tired of where her thoughts were taking her, Janie picked up the remote control and turned on her television. Even with the satellite dish, there wasn't anything worth watching. She was about to turn it off again when she came across a series on one of the movie channels.

She stared at the program for fifteen minutes and gasped when she realized two of the women were roughly removing each other's clothes. Although she knew she should change the channel, she instead stared at the screen, transfixed on the way one of the women began to run her hands all over the other one's body. "Oh, my god." She sat up in bed, her mouth slightly open in shock. The more active the characters on the screen became, the warmer her bedroom felt. When one of them moaned, Janie felt a sensual heat burn in the pit of her stomach.

As both women continued to writhe and moan, Janie couldn't take her eyes from the screen. She'd never seen anything like it before. Her heart began to pound, and she started breathing heavily. Suddenly, it dawned on her what she was watching, and she quickly turned off the television. She covered her face with her hands, ashamed of her arousal.

With a shaky sigh, Janie switched off the lamp next to her bed and sat in the darkness, more confused than ever.

SAM CAME INTO the gym early the next morning. She looked around for Betsy, but the woman was no where to be found. She started toward the showers to see if she needed to bring down clean towels. The sight of the older woman, kneeling on the floor, scared Sam to death. "Betsy? What's wrong?"

The gym manager raised her head. "Thank goodness you're here. I was mopping the floor and my damned back went out. I've been stuck like this for almost an hour." She grimaced as Sam helped her to her feet. "Ugh. I knew I should have opened a video store."

"Damn, Betsy. You know this is my job. Do you want to go to the emergency room?" Sam guided her out of the locker room, bearing most of Betsy's weight. The woman was a few inches shorter than she, but outweighed her by thirty pounds or more. "I can run and get my car."

"No, I'll be okay. This happens more often than I care to admit." Betsy shuffled to her office and sat gingerly on the leather sofa. "I'd love you forever if you'd get me an icepack, though."

Sam nodded and popped out of the room, returning quickly with the requested item wrapped in a towel. "Is ice a good idea?" she asked, while she placed it at the small of Betsy's back.

"Yep. It'll bring down the swelling and I'll be good as new in no time."

"Okay, as long as you're sure." Sam stood near the sofa. "Is there anything else I can do?"

Betsy opened her eyes and exhaled slowly. "Aaah. That's feeling better already." She willed the pain away, to no avail. "Are you real busy this morning?"

"No. I'm pretty much free until four o'clock or so. What do you need?"

"Would you mind watching the gym for me? I know you're scheduled to work at the grocery store, but—"

"No, that didn't work out." Sam took the afghan from the back of the couch and covered Betsy's legs. "Holler if you need anything. I'll finish up the mopping and make sure there's enough towels out for the morning masochists."

Betsy held out her hand until Sam took it. "Thanks, kiddo. You're a lifesaver."

Sam squeezed her hand and stepped back. "No problem." She heard the bell over the front door. "Guess I'd better get out there. Hopefully they won't think I killed you and buried you out back."

"If anyone gives you grief, send them to me." Another sharp pain hit, and Betsy closed her eyes. "But wait until after lunch."

"You got it, boss." Sam left the door partially open, so she could hear if Betsy called her. She jogged to the counter and greeted the first customer of the day.

HOURS LATER, BETSY came limping out of the office. The building was empty and she looked around for Sam. She heard a noise in the showers and peeked inside.

With her back to the door, Sam briskly pushed the mop over the tiles. Her gray tank top was plastered to her skin, yet she kept a steady pace. She was barefoot and sang softly under her breath.

Betsy watched the younger woman work. "Nice job, Sam."

Sam was almost to the door when Betsy announced her presence. She spun around. "You scared me."

"Sorry." Betsy slowly straightened to her full height. "How about we lock the doors and grab some lunch? My treat."

"I don't have to be asked twice." Sam leaned the mop against the wall. "Let me get cleaned up first. I'm a mess." She started to take off her shirt, but paused.

Betsy tossed her a towel. "All righty. But don't take too long. I'm hungry." She shuffled away, chuckling under her breath at Sam's modesty.

THE MINUTE HAND on the wall clock finally hit twelve. Janie had been staring at it for half an hour, counting the minutes until she could take her lunch break. She took her purse from the lower drawer of her desk and slipped the strap over one shoulder. She walked by Andrea's desk. "I'm going out for lunch today, so I won't be around until one."

Andrea looked up from painting her nails. "Don't be late. You only get an hour, you know."

"I know." Janie turned away and left the office. She wanted to see if she could find Sam, and maybe offer to buy her lunch. Her flat heels clicked on the sidewalk as she headed toward Danny's. Ten minutes later, she stood in front of the bar. She tried the door, but it was locked. With a muttered curse, Janie went down the alley until she was at Sam's car. She peeked in the windows, but it was empty. Her stomach growled, so she gave up and went in search of lunch.

The closest place to eat was Fern's. From the outside Janie could see how crowded it was. She stepped inside and looked around for an empty seat. Hearing Sam's laughter caused her head to turn.

Sam sat across a table from an older woman, who Janie recognized. She had gone to the gym a couple of times in the past, until Doug found out. He'd teased and harassed her about going, until she quit and never went back. But she remembered how nice the owner had been. She never would have thought Betsy to be a lesbian. They seemed to be having a good time, and Janie felt an irrational stab of jealousy. Betsy had to be at least fifteen years older than Janie, which made her even madder. She turned and left the restaurant as quickly as she had come.

She brushed by several people who moved out of her way. "What's she doing with that old woman? Are they dating? My god, she's old enough to be Sam's mother." Janie continued to mutter under her breath while she walked. "What does she see in her? Am I that grotesque?

What's wrong with me?" She stopped when she realized she'd walked all the way home. "Damn." Her heart wasn't in the mood to return to work. Janie walked up the stairs to the second floor and called out sick for the rest of the day.

SAM SPUTTERED, ALMOST choking on the fry she had put in her mouth. "Stop. You're going to kill me." She took a drink of her iced tea to force the food down. "Where do you come up with all these stories?"

"Hey, I've been around for quite a while. You run a place like mine, you see all sorts of things." Betsy sipped her coffee.

"Sounds like it." Sam bit into her hamburger again and closed her eyes at the taste. The homemade patty weighed half a pound, and the vegetables that adorned the sandwich were crisp and fresh. "I'm going to gain a ton before I leave, if I keep eating like this."

Betsy tossed an olive slice from her salad at Sam. "Not likely. You've got a long way to go, kid. Now, you were asking how I got started running the gym. What's the matter, don't I look like someone who values physical fitness?"

The diplomatic thing to do would be to keep her mouth shut. But Sam had never been called a diplomat. "Honestly? No. I mean, you look great, for your age." She quickly bit her tongue. "Not that you're old, or anything. Just—"

Betsy howled at the look on Sam's face. "I think you should stop while you're behind. It's okay. I don't offend easily. But if you said something bad about my cat, there'd be hell to pay."

"You don't have to worry. I like cats." A devious look crossed Sam's face. "They taste like chicken, you know."

"What?" Betsy glared at her, until she realized Sam was pulling her leg. "I'll get you for that one. Besides, I haven't had a cat in years."

Sam shrugged, but didn't appear too worried. She went back to eating her lunch. "History, please?"

"Oh, yeah. When my husband and I moved here in seventy-one, we wanted to live in the downtown area, such as it was. The only place we could find that wasn't a total dump was the apartment above the gym. The old man who owned it was getting on and wanted to sell the whole building." She took another sip of coffee. "It was a lot different than it is now. There was a boxing ring, and the showers were nasty."

"It was an old-time gym?"

Betsy nodded. "Problem was, no one in town went in there anymore. We considered remodeling into something else, but Jack thought the place held promise." She sat quietly for a moment, lost in the memory of her deceased husband. "As soon as we opened, business was great. But when Jack passed after his heart attack, I almost shut down for good." She sighed and wiped a tear from her eye. "Twenty years ago, and it still seems like yesterday."

"I'm sorry." Sam usually felt uncomfortable when someone mentioned death, but all she wanted to do was give Betsy a hug and tell her everything was going to be all right. She stared at her plate, at a loss for words.

"Don't be, Sam. I didn't have as much time with him as I would have liked, but I cherish each moment I did." She gazed fondly at Sam. "You know, with your eyes and coloring, you could have been his daughter. Those smoky gray eyes and strong chin. He was such a handsome man."

Sam wasn't sure what to say to that, so she wisely kept quiet.

Betsy slapped the table. "Listen to me, going on like that. I've probably embarrassed you."

"No, not really. More like flattered." Sam spared a glance around the room and realized no one was paying much attention to them. Maybe the townsfolk were starting to get used to her. Sam hoped so. She was beginning to get used to the place. "You don't seem too concerned about being seen with me."

"I'm not."

"Why? I'm certainly not like everyone else." Sam looked up when the waitress filled her tea glass. "Thanks."

Betsy leaned back in her chair. "No, you're not. But, I'm not a believer in strangers, only in friends we haven't yet met. And you seem like a good person." She crossed her arms over her chest. "You *are* a good person, aren't you? I don't have to worry about you hitting on all my women customers, do I?"

Sam choked on her tea. "What?"

"See how silly it sounds?" Betsy held her hand out and waited until Sam took it. She rested them both on the edge of the table, not caring what anyone else thought. "I like you, Sam. I believe we'll be great friends."

"We already are, Betsy. I like you too." After Betsy released her hand, Sam went back to eating. The longer she stayed in Piperton, the more she began to enjoy it.

THE APARTMENT SEEMED hugely empty and lonely to Janie. She dried the bowl she'd used for her lunch and placed it in the cupboard. Cold cereal wasn't her usual meal choice but she didn't feel like anything else. She stared at the soapy water, lost in her thoughts.

Seeing Sam with another woman, no matter how innocent it might have been, left Janie feeling unsettled. Although she'd rebuffed the singer's attempts at friendship, she still didn't want to have to share her. Angry at herself, Janie pulled the plug in the sink and wiped her hands on a towel. "This is ridiculous."

She started straightening up her apartment when her cell phone rang. A quick glance at the caller ID caused her to answer. "Hello?"

Sandra's voice, rough and loud came through the line. "Hey, girl. What's up? I tried calling you at work but they told me you were sick. Are you all right?"

"I'm fine." Janie took the phone with her to the sofa. "I didn't feel like going back after lunch."

"Well, if you're sure." The flick of a lighter, followed by a cough, told what Sandra was doing. "Since you're not sick, want to go out tonight?"

The silent apartment she once treasured now felt oppressive. "Sure. Dinner?"

"And then someplace to guy watch. Unless Doug won't let you."

"He has no say in what I can, or can't do."

Sandra snorted, which turned into another hacking cough. "Since when?"

"Since I broke up with him." The fear the declaration once would have caused was replaced by pride. The longer she was away from Doug, the more she realized it was the right thing to do.

"You're kidding! When?"

"A few days ago." Janie sighed and touched her cheek. She hadn't gotten over Harvey's anger, and had done a good job of avoiding him.

"Are you sure? He always seemed so good to you."

Janie choked back a bitter laugh. "It did seem that way, didn't it? Believe me, he was far from it."

"What happened?"

"Let's just say his true nature came out when he drank. I really don't want to get into it right now."

"All right." Sandra was quiet for a moment, then she could be heard lighting another cigarette. "You still feel up for going out tonight?"

Janie looked around. The floors needed a good vacuuming, and she could spy dust on the furniture. But now she wasn't in the mood for anymore housework. "Definitely. Do you want to meet somewhere?"

"Why don't I drop by and get you. About six?"

"Sounds good. And Sandra? Thanks."

"No problem, hon. We single girls got to stick together." After cementing their plans, she hung up the phone.

Janie kicked her shoes off, curled her feet underneath herself and snuggled into the corner of the sofa. She looked forward to the evening. Sandra was always able to get her out of her funk.

OF THE SEVERAL bars in Piperton, Sandra chose Danny's. Janie reluctantly followed her inside. The cigarette smoke was heavy for a Thursday night, and she fought the urge to fan her hand in front of her face.

Sandra found a table not far from the piano and led Janie by the arm. "Come on. This is perfect."

Sam's low voice was hard to hear over the room's din, although Janie understood every word. She placed her purse at the foot of her chair. Her eyes watered at the thick smoke, which was made worse by Sandra's chain-smoking. Janie ordered a light beer from the waitress and was soon sipping the cold brew and listening to Sam sing. She leaned closer to Sandra when her friend tapped her on the arm. "What?"

"Nice voice." Sandra pointed at Sam. "She looks a little rough around the edges though, doesn't she?"

"I don't know what you mean."

Sandra pursed her lips and stared at Janie. "Please. If her tee shirt wasn't so tight, it would be hard to tell she wasn't a man. Kind of scary, if you ask me."

"Well, I didn't." Janie pulled her arm away and tried not to stare at Sam.

"Why are you so snippy?"

Janie forced herself to look away from the piano. "I'm sorry, Sandra."

Sandra struggled to keep the disgruntled look on her face, but failed. "Just for that, you get to buy the next round."

"Fair enough." Janie glanced at the piano again, in time to lock eyes with Sam. She smiled shyly, blushed then turned away.

The move didn't go unnoticed by Sandra. "Do you know her?"

"Yes. I mean, no." Janie's hand shook as she picked up her beer bottle. "We've sort of, uh, met."

"Where on earth would you have met someone like her?" Sandra propped her elbows on the table and rested her chin on one hand. A startled look came upon her face. "Oh, my god. Did she come on to you?"

Janie pulled the bottle away too quickly, and beer dribbled down her chin. She wiped at it with the back of her hand. "Of course not!" With a quick look around, she hunched forward to keep from being overheard. "It was nothing like that. We met at Fern's not too long ago and had breakfast together."

Sandra's voice rose. "You're kidding! You've *dated* her?"

"Shhh!" Janie slapped her hand over her friend's mouth. "No, it wasn't a date. It was crowded, and she asked if she could sit at my table, that's all." The feel of Sandra's tongue against her palm caused her to jerk her hand away. "Ugh. That's disgusting."

"Ha. Better get used to it, if you plan on seeing much of her." Sandra's eyes gleamed wickedly. "I hear they like —"

"Sandra!"

Taking pity on Janie, Sandra sat back in her chair. "Okay, okay. I'll be good." She waited until Sam glanced their way then waggled her fingers at her. "Maybe we should buy her a drink. You could introduce me."

A deep voice cut off Janie's reply. "I should have known you'd be here, Janie." Doug placed his hand on the back of Janie's chair. "Hey, Sandra."

Sandra gave him a cool look. Janie had explained over dinner the events that led to the breakup. "Hello."

Doug caressed Janie's shoulder and winked at Sandra. "You want to give us a few minutes alone?"

"Not particularly." Sandra stuck her tongue out at the rude man. "Get lost, Doug."

"Bitch." He returned his attention to Janie. "Come on."

Janie tried to pry his hand away. "Leave me alone. I'm not interested in anything you have to say."

"I think you are." He bent down and placed a sloppy kiss on her cheek, his breath reeking of alcohol. "Your old man said you were ready to get back together. He wants grandkids, you know."

Wincing under the pressure of his grip, Janie grabbed his thumb and pulled it back until he removed his hand. "Then maybe you two should get busy, Doug. Because I don't plan on having any children. Especially not with you."

"You bitch!" Doug took a handful of her hair and yanked. "I ought to take you outside and show you some manners." He started to pull her out of her seat when the bartender, Ray, tapped him on the arm.

"Hey, man. Why don't you leave these two ladies alone?" Ray stood by the table. "Come on over to the bar, and I'll give you a beer, on the house."

Doug shoved Janie away and looked as if he was about to spit on her. "Yeah, okay. I'll talk to you later, Janie. We've still got some unfinished business."

As soon as he walked away, Janie began to shake. She barely registered Sandra's arm around her shoulder as her friend led her out of the bar.

Once Sandra had Janie buckled into the passenger seat of the car, she locked the doors. "I'm going to run in and grab our things and pay our tab. Be right back." She hurried back to the bar, but Sam met her at the door and held the purses out to her.

"I figured you'd need these." Sam looked behind Sandra to see Janie sitting in the front seat of the car, with a blank look on her face. "Is she all right?"

"I think she will be. I need to run in and settle our tab. Would you mind staying with Janie until I get back?"

Sam nodded and walked to the car. She stood where Janie could see her, not wanting to frighten her further.

Janie noticed her immediately and rolled down her window. "What are you doing here?"

"I wanted to make sure you were okay." Sam squatted beside the passenger door and propped her arm on the open window. "Are you?

Okay, I mean?"

"I think so." Janie rubbed her shoulder where Doug had squeezed. She knew when she got home she'd see a bruise. "I'm sorry we ruined your singing."

Sam's fingers tapped a beat on the car. "Don't worry about it. I was pretty much done for the night, anyway."

"It's a little early, isn't it?"

"Yeah, but when the smoke is that bad, I have to stop sooner. It gets to me."

Without thinking, Janie rested her hand on Sam's arm. The warm skin soothed her spirit. The altercation with Doug was quickly fading into the back of her mind. "I can imagine how bad that gets. Being around Sandra's smoke is enough to make me choke."

"She seems nice."

"She's my best friend. We've known each other since grade school." When Sandra came out of the bar, Janie reluctantly removed her hand. "I'm sorry about the way I've been treating you."

Sam stood and brushed imaginary dirt from her jeans. "Don't worry about it." She was about to step away when Janie gripped her forearm again.

"I'd like to make it up to you. Can I buy you breakfast tomorrow?"

"Are you sure?"

Janie smiled at Sandra, who walked around to open the driver's door. She tightened her grip before letting go. "Yes. Is seven-thirty okay?"

"Yeah." Sam ducked her head to speak to Sandra. "If you need anything, I can be reached here at the bar, or over at Betsy's gym."

"Thanks." Sandra buckled her seat belt and lit up another cigarette. "Be seeing you around."

Sam stepped back as the car backed away from the curb. She rested her hands on her hips and watched the tail lights until they were out of sight.

Chapter
Eight

BETSY LIMPED SLOWLY to the front door of the gym. Her back had stiffened up overnight, and she was beginning to think she'd done more damage to it than she originally realized. The insistent knocking hadn't awakened her, as she had always gotten up before dawn. But she didn't open up until eight, and some moron was banging on her door at six forty-five in the morning. "All right, hold your horses. I'm coming." The familiar silhouette caused her to shake her head. She unlocked the door and swung it open. "Why are you beating on the front door? Where's your key?"

Sam came inside, a bundle of clothes tucked beneath her arm. "I'm sorry, Betsy. I left my key on my nightstand. I slept in my car, but I've really got to take a shower."

"At this time of morning? What did you do, fall in a pile of dog crap? You don't smell bad to me." Betsy trailed Sam to the showers. She was surprised when the younger woman began to strip off her shirt. "No, I don't think that's it. Do you have a hot date or something?"

"No," came the indignant answer, muffled by the tee shirt Sam was trying to remove. Her face appeared after the material came off her head. "Not exactly."

Betsy leaned against the doorway and crossed her arms. "Do tell." She became amused when Sam's face sported a dark blush. "Who's the lucky girl?"

Sam covered her breasts with her arms. "Betsy! I'm trying to get undressed, here."

"I can see. Nice abs, kiddo."

"Hey!" Sam quickly turned her back. "Do you mind?"

"Not a bit." After laughing at her friend, Betsy decided she'd tortured Sam enough. "Fine, be that way. But you're going to tell me what's going on before you leave." She shuffled toward the kitchen to get a cup of coffee.

Ten minutes later, Sam came out of the locker room, her wet hair slicked back against her skull. The usual tank top she wore was covered by an unbuttoned red shirt. Her feet were still bare, but she carried her boots in one hand, while her dirty clothes hung loosely in the other. She dropped the boots, with the roll of clean socks tucked neatly inside, by the small table where Betsy sat. "Sorry I was so grumpy."

Betsy waved her off. "Don't apologize. I shouldn't have been giving you such a hard time." She studied Sam's attire. "I don't think I've ever seen you wear a real shirt before. You clean up real good."

"Thanks, I think." Sam pulled out the other chair and began to put on her boots. "I *am* meeting someone for breakfast, but it's not really a date." She crossed one leg over the other and propped her foot on her knee, making quick work of the laces. "She's only a friend."

"Uh-huh. And you got all gussied up for this friend? Heaven help us if you went out on a real date. You'd probably show up in a tuxedo." Betsy laughed at the look on Sam's face. "Simmer down. The closest place to rent one is about thirty miles away. You don't have time."

Never one to take herself too seriously, Sam laughed. "I don't think this town is ready for a woman in a tux." She tied her other boot and stood. "Do I really look okay?"

Betsy pretended to look her over carefully. She tsked a couple of times and shook her head.

"What?" Sam looked at her crotch. "Is my fly open?" She checked the buttons, which were all closed. Betsy's laughter made her realize she was being teased. "That's not nice."

"I couldn't resist. You're too uptight for someone who's *not* going out on a date." Betsy struggled to her feet, groaning at the pressure on her lower back. "Could you do me a favor?"

Sam finished buttoning her shirt and tucked it in. "Of course. What?"

"Come back by after your *not*-date. I want to talk to you about something." She brushed an imaginary speck of lint from Sam's shoulder before handing her the keys. "Lock up when you leave, and let yourself back in. I'm going to lie down in the office for a while." She lightly tapped Sam's cheek. "Don't stress over this, Sam. Any girl would be lucky to share a meal with you."

"Thanks. Do you need any help getting settled?"

"Nope. But you've got to come back and give me all the juicy details. I don't have much of a social life anymore, so I'll live vicariously through you. Now hurry up. You don't want to leave your *friend* wondering where you're at."

JANIE STARED AT the café entrance and checked her watch again. It was only seven-twenty, a minute longer than it was the previous time she looked. She kept wondering if she was doing the right thing. Her mind didn't allow her a moment's peace the entire night, and she wasn't certain how she'd make it through the work day on no sleep. Now that it was getting closer to the agreed upon time, her stomach began doing flips. She was about to get up and leave when the bell over the door jingled.

Sam stepped inside the restaurant, standing still for a moment while she searched the room. When she spotted Janie, she smiled and made her way to the table. "I hope you haven't been waiting long."

"No, I just got here," Janie lied.

"Great." Sam studied the menu. "Do you have any suggestions?" At Janie's silence, she looked up. "Janie?"

Janie blinked and shook her head slightly. "I'm sorry. It's that I've never seen you dressed before."

"What?" Sam dropped the menu.

"I mean, wearing a shirt." Janie closed her eyes and blushed. "What I meant to say was, every time I've been around you, you're wearing either a tee shirt or a tank top. But you look really nice today."

"Thanks." Sam picked up the folded paper and started reading again, a pleased smile on her face.

"Sunrise skillet."

Sam raised her eyes. "Huh?"

Janie wanted to crawl under the table. Every time she opened her mouth, she kept saying something stupid. "One of the best things on the menu is the sunrise skillet." She pointed to a particular spot on the menu.

Sam read the description and waved to the waitress, who had been standing nearby. She placed her order after Janie and sipped her coffee. "Thanks for inviting me this morning."

"You're welcome." Janie raised her glass of iced tea in salute. "Thank you for being so nice to me, even when I didn't deserve it."

They made small talk until their meals arrived. After they'd been eating for a while, Janie pointed her fork in Sam's direction. "I saw you in here yesterday."

"Yeah?" Sam swallowed another mouthful and wiped her face with her napkin. "Why didn't you say hello?"

"You were with someone. I didn't want to intrude."

Sam had to stop and think for a moment. "You mean Betsy? She wouldn't have minded."

"Well, I wasn't sure." Janie pushed her food around her plate with her fork. "I didn't know how things like that worked."

"What things?"

Janie lowered her voice. "*Your* things. You know." She leaned over the table and whispered, "*Lesbian* stuff."

"Actually, we're only friends. She's not my type."

"You have a type?" Janie was truly confused. "I thought every woman was your type."

"Uh, no. Not by a long shot."

"Is it because she's so much older? Don't you like older women? I heard once that all you people do is have sex all the time. Does it really matter what someone looks like?"

The conversation was quickly deteriorating. Sam tossed her napkin over her plate, even though she wasn't finished. "Why the sudden interest in my love life?" she snapped. "Just because I'm gay, it doesn't mean I'm some sort of sex maniac. I'm no different from you."

"I didn't mean—"

"Look. I have feelings, like you. I want to find someone to settle down and spend the rest of my life with. Just because that someone is a woman, it doesn't make it any less real." Sam stood and dug her wallet from her back pocket. She took out several bills and tossed them on the table. "Thanks, anyway. I've lost my appetite."

Janie sat completely still, shocked at the turn of events. She realized most of the people in the room were staring at her. With as much dignity as she could muster, Janie took cash from her purse and placed it next to Sam's. She tucked her bag beneath her arm and left the restaurant, ashamed of ruining the morning with her questions.

SAM STOMPED DOWN the sidewalk, struggling to unbutton the shirt while she walked. At the door of the gym, she gave up and tugged it over her head and threw it to the ground. "Stupid piece of shit." She had to try several times to unlock the door because she was so angry that her hand was shaking. "Goddamn it!"

"Sam? Is that you?" Betsy called from the office.

"Yeah." Sam followed her voice and was soon standing in the doorway.

Betsy tried to sit up. "What happened?" Her back spasmed and she rested her head on the sofa once more.

Sam hurried into the room and knelt beside the couch. She gently placed her hand on Betsy's shoulder. "Don't worry about me. Everything's fine." The pain on her friend's face helped her remember what was important. "I think we should get you to the doctor."

"As much as I hate to agree with you, I believe you're right." Betsy gestured to the desk. "My phone book is in the top drawer. Would you bring it to me, along with my cordless phone?"

"Sure."

The nurse at the doctor's office was helpful, and before she hung up, Betsy had a nine o'clock appointment. She struggled to a sitting position on the couch. "Thank god it's not far. I don't think I can handle driving for long."

"You won't have to worry about it. I'll be glad to take you. Let me get my car."

"You'll do no such thing. I have a perfectly good car out back, if you don't mind driving it."

Sam hadn't known Betsy for very long, but she knew better than to argue with her. "If you don't mind me driving it, then sure."

Betsy allowed Sam to help her to her feet. "Let's go through the back. It's closer."

"No problem." Sam jogged to the front of the gym and locked the door. She hurried back and assisted Betsy to her car.

THERE WERE ONLY two other patients in the doctor's office when they arrived. Sam helped Betsy to a chair before going to the counter to sign her in. She was handed a clipboard which she dutifully took to her friend.

"Good god! Am I supposed to fill out that crap again? I did that the last time I was here."

Sam sat next to her. "She said you weren't in the system. How long has it been?"

Betsy considered the question. "Let's see. This is August, isn't it?"

"Yeah."

"I think it was nineteen ninety-two." Betsy sighed as she began to fill out the paperwork. "I don't know why they can't look for my file in the back." She finished and had Sam take the board to the desk. "Now that I'm done, you're going to tell me how your breakfast went this morning. I wasn't expecting you back so soon."

Sam stretched her legs out in front of her and crossed them at the ankle. "Not much to say. We ate, I left."

"What happened to that nice shirt you had on?"

"I took it off. It wasn't very comfortable."

Betsy eyed her carefully. "Uh-huh. Exactly what happened to put your panties in a wad?"

Sam stared at her feet, noticing for the first time how old and scuffed her boots were. "She basically called me a pervert, so I didn't see any reason to stick around."

"She didn't!"

"Well, not in those exact words, no. But that's what she meant." Sam crossed her arms over her chest and sighed. "Breakfast was her idea, not mine. I swear I wasn't coming on to her, or anything."

Betsy patted her leg. "I'm sure you weren't, hon. But tell me what she *did* say. Maybe you misunderstood."

"It started out okay. Although she thought you were my girlfriend." Sam laughed at the look on Betsy's face. "What's wrong with that?"

"Nothing. I figured you had better taste in women than some old broad like me." She tapped Sam's leg again. "Go on."

Sam sighed. "When I said you weren't my type, she asked me why. Seems she thinks that all lesbians are sex fiends who'll sleep with anyone and everyone."

Betsy's laugh caused the other people in the room to look their way. "Boy, does she have the wrong number. You're the biggest prude I've ever met." She leaned closer and lowered her voice. "I bet you turn out the lights before getting busy."

"Betsy!" Sam covered her face with her hands. "I can't believe you said that."

"It's true, isn't it?" Betsy didn't wait for an answer. "Seriously, I think the woman is misinformed. If she's lived here for long, she probably hasn't ever even seen someone who's gay, much less interacted with them. Did she explain what she meant?"

Sam's mumble was indecipherable.

"You *did* give her a chance to explain, didn't you?" When Sam ducked her head, Betsy slapped her leg. "Shame on you! That poor little thing was probably mortified when you stormed out. You need to call her and apologize."

"I don't have her number."

"That's no excuse."

Sam tried to change the subject. "You said earlier you wanted to talk to me about something. I'm hoping it wasn't my dating habits."

"No, not that. Although I'm sure I could give you a few tips." Betsy shifted slightly to get more comfortable. Her lower back felt like it was on fire. "I have a proposition for you, if you're interested."

"Okay. What is it?"

"First, I'd like to know if you're going to stay around for a while. You told me when we first met that you liked to travel. I realize you'll have to be here long enough to pay for that old heap of Estelle Parker's, but I mean, after that. "

"I don't know." She'd thought about staying, but the argument with Janie had shaken her. Although the constant moving from place to place was beginning to get old. "Piperton isn't such a bad place."

Betsy nodded knowingly. "That's true. And you're welcome to stay with me for as long as you want. I'm not getting any younger, you know. Would you like to manage the gym for me?"

The offer was a surprise. "But you don't know me that well."

"Sure I do. I've always considered myself a good judge of character, and I like you. If it makes you feel any better, I married my Jack after we'd known each other for only a week. So when I make up my mind about someone, I'm always right."

"But—"

A small nurse in mauve-colored scrubs interrupted them. "Mrs. Haley? The doctor will see you now."

Sam jumped to her feet to help her friend. "Here. Lean on me."

"I plan to." Betsy leaned into Sam's body. "Come back with me?"

"Sure." Sam looked at the nurse. "If it's okay."

The nurse nodded. "Of course. You can stay with your mother."

Sam started to correct her, when Betsy spoke up. Tweaking Sam was beginning to be one of her favorite pastimes. "She's a very good daughter. I don't know what I'd do without her."

Realizing she had lost, Sam helped Betsy down the bright hallway. A movement out of the corner of her eye caused Sam to turn her head. "You've got to be kidding me."

"What?" Betsy looked to see what she was talking about. A petite woman stood at the end of the hall clutching several file folders to her chest. If her startled look was any indication, she was surprised to see

Sam as well. She was vaguely familiar to Betsy, but she couldn't place her. "Do you know her?"

"It's her."

"Who?"

"*Her*," Sam enunciated slowly. She couldn't stop staring at Janie. The anger she felt toward the other woman had passed, leaving only resigned sorrow behind. "Come on. Let's get you into a room and comfortable."

Betsy held her ground. "I'll be fine. You go talk to her." She nudged Sam along. "And don't come back until you've straightened everything out." She took the nurse's arm and moved slowly into the exam room.

Sam tucked her hands into her front pockets, but didn't move. She tried to control her nerves as Janie stepped closer. She wanted to lash out at her, but the puffiness around Janie's eyes changed her mind. She realized Janie had been crying and didn't want to hurt her any more than she already had. "I'm sorry—"

"I'm so sorry—"

They both spoke at the same time but Sam was the first to recover. "I owe you an apology."

Janie shook her head. "I'm the one who made an ass of herself. I honestly didn't mean to hurt your feelings."

"I know. I shouldn't be so sensitive." Sam held out her hand. "Truce?" She was relieved when Janie grasped it and held on. "Can we try again? I'd like to buy you dinner."

"No." At Sam's crestfallen expression, Janie rushed to explain. "Let me cook dinner for you. Please."

"You don't have to do that."

Janie squeezed Sam's hand. "I'd like to. Oh. I forgot. You sing at night."

"I think I can skip one night. If you're sure you want to cook." When someone else came into the hall, Sam pulled her hand back to spare Janie from any embarrassment. She was surprised when it was captured again.

"How about Sunday? It's usually a quieter night, isn't it?"

Sam smiled. "Yeah, it is." She turned when the exam room opened and Betsy's nurse gestured to her. "I've got to go."

"Sure." Janie let go of her then tucked a strand of hair behind her ear. "I'll come by the bar tonight, so we can finish making plans."

"Great." Sam started to walk away. "If I'm not there, I'll be at the gym. It's over on Sycamore."

Janie waved to her. "I'll find you. Go take care of your friend."

BETSY CONTINUED TO curse as Sam drove back to the gym. "Damned quack. I don't know why I bothered." The doctor had told her she'd have to stay off her feet as much as possible for several weeks.

"He wanted an excuse for the big bill he's going to send. They're all alike."

"Don't worry, Betsy. It'll be okay." Sam steered carefully around a pothole. Betsy's car was an eighty-nine Plymouth Reliant, and the shocks had seen better days. "Is your offer still open?"

"Offer?"

"Yeah, you know. Managing the gym, and your undying love?" Sam winced as her arm was slapped. "Hey, no beating on the driver."

Betsy's chuckle died and she became more serious. "You're not offering because of my back, are you?"

"Nah." Sam parked behind the gym and turned off the engine. "I really am getting tired of traveling so much. Maybe wintering here will give me a chance to recharge."

"Are you sure it doesn't have to do with a certain little brown-haired gal? Don't think I didn't see that smile you had after you talked to her."

Sam got out of the car and opened Betsy's door. "We're friends. At least I hope so." She helped the older woman up and walked her carefully inside.

They stood at the foot of the stairs. Betsy shook her head. "I don't think I can make it." The back brace her doctor had given her impeded Betsy's movements. There was no way she'd be able to climb the stairs, at least not for a few days.

"Wait. I've got an idea." Sam hustled to the gym and returned a moment later, pushing Betsy's rolling office chair.

"Honey, I hate to break it to you, but that chair isn't going to get me upstairs."

Sam eased her into the seat. "No, but it'll get you up front easier. What if I move your bedroom down to your office? We've got everything else you'll need down here." She wheeled Betsy up front.

"That's too much trouble." But Betsy seemed to like the idea. "You can't move my bed by yourself."

"I'll get Ray from the bar to help. He won't mind." With the idea firmly entrenched in her mind, Sam left Betsy in the office, and went upstairs to see how hard it would be to move enough of the furniture to make Betsy comfortable.

HARVEY CLARKE PUNCHED the familiar number into the cordless phone. He was sick and tired of his daughter going against his word, and she'd repeatedly ignored his phone calls to her cell. The only avenue left for him was to call her work number. While he waited for someone to pick up, he dropped his body into the recliner and kicked off his shoes. He'd always hated the graveyard shift at the hospital, where he worked as a security guard.

With the phone propped on one shoulder, Harvey used his free hand to unclip his belt and loosen the button on his trousers, groaning in relief. He almost dropped the phone when a perky voice came on the line.

"Fourth Street Medical office, how may I direct your call?"

Harvey cleared his throat. "Good afternoon. May I speak to Jane Clarke?" He raised the tone of his voice higher than normal, hoping to sound friendlier.

"Of course, sir. Please hold one moment." The receptionist placed him on hold.

Less than a minute later, the classical music was replaced by Janie's voice. "This is Jane Clarke. How may I help you?"

"Janie, what the fuck do you think you're doing?" Harvey scratched at his belly where his slacks had dug into his pudgy flesh. "I've been trying to reach you!"

"I'm sorry, Harvey. But I've been busy. What exactly is it you need from me?"

He unbuttoned his shirt to get more comfortable. "Don't take that tone with me. You know damn good and well what I'm calling for."

Janie sighed. "If this is about Doug, don't bother. I'm not changing my mind about him."

"You sure as shit better change it, girl, because you're not getting any younger."

"We've already gone over this, Harvey. I know I'm thirty-seven years old. But that's no reason for me to stay with a jerk like him. It's over."

Harvey kicked the footrest of the recliner down and got to his feet. He stomped into the kitchen, opened the refrigerator door, and took out a can of beer. The phone went back on his shoulder so he could pop the top on the can. "Listen here. I've put up with your smartass mouth until now. You'll do as I say, and that's final."

"No, I don't think so." Janie's voice took on a more business-like tone. "If you'll excuse me, I have to get back to work." She hung up the phone without another word.

With a loud curse, Harvey tossed the cordless phone across the kitchen, getting a jolt of satisfaction when it slammed against the far wall and broke into pieces. "You arrogant little bitch. I'll have to do something about your attitude." He drained the beer and went to his bedroom to change clothes.

ALTHOUGH IT WAS not even four o'clock, heavy smoke filled the bar. Harvey spotted who he had come to see. He huffed his way to the bar and perched on the next stool. "Hey, Reg."

The man, thin and balding, turned to Harvey. "Harv. What brings you here?"

"We got to talk." Harvey pointed at his companion's glass and raised a finger. Moments later, he was nursing his own brew. He grabbed a handful of greasy peanuts from the closest dish and popped them into his mouth. "Your boy fucked up." Small bits of food dotted his lips and a stray particle hit the other man's face.

Reggie Howard took a deep drag from the cigarette hanging from his mouth before wiping at his jaw. "You sure about that? 'Cause that's not what I heard."

"Hell, yes, he did." Harvey chewed with his mouth open and smacked a few times. "If he hadn't attacked Janie, they'd probably be engaged by now."

"If that girl of yours wasn't so frigid, he wouldn't have had to take control." Reggie drained his glass and waved it at the bartender. "My friend's buying the next one."

Harvey cursed, but removed his wallet and dropped a twenty dollar bill on the counter. "Start us a tab."

The bartender, Fred, shrugged his shoulders and took the money. He returned quickly with two more mugs. "Happy hour, guys. Drink up."

Reggie took several sips before returning to their previous conversation. "Doug would be better off with a gal who's more receptive. Why should he saddle himself with Janie?"

"Pickin's are lean around here, you know that." Harvey fingered his nose, before dipping his hand back into the peanuts. "I want grandkids, Reg. Somebody's got to take care of me when I get old. I don't want to end up like my ma, stuck off in some old folks home."

"What about Janie? She's always been a good girl, as far as that goes. I bet she'll change your diapers when you can't keep from shitting yourself." Reggie's laugh turned into a rattling cough. He took a drink of his beer and quieted.

Harvey lit his own cigarette and blew the smoke toward Reggie. "That's what I thought, too. But she's been getting more uppity lately. I don't know what's wrong with her."

"It seems like a lot of trouble for grandchildren. Besides, I don't think Doug wants to be tied down."

"He don't have to stop seeing all his other women, you know. Hell, it's a man's nature to stay active." Harvey finished the peanuts and thumped the empty container in front of him. "Hey, can we get more?"

Fred grabbed a bowl from the end of the bar and slid it to Harvey. He then turned his back and continued to read the paper.

"Asshole." Harvey took a final drag from his smoke and ground it out in the overflowing ashtray. He returned his attention to the peanuts and ate as if it were his last meal. "Doug needs to try harder. Janie's not a strong woman, so it should be easy enough to get her back."

"But why Doug?"

Harvey lit another cigarette. "Because they have a history. She's never been one to try new things, and I don't think I have the patience to wait for her to get attached to another guy. Besides, do you want him living with you for the rest of your life? A man needs a woman to cook and clean for him. My girl's at least good at that. What do you say?"

"Okay, I'll talk to him. But I'm not guaranteeing anything." Reggie finished his beer and gestured for another. "Now that we've got that out of the way, let's get down to some serious business."

ONCE THE CLOCK struck five, Janie couldn't leave the office fast enough. She gave Laura a wave and hustled out the door. Friday was always her favorite day of the week. Although she didn't hate her job, it was always a pleasure to leave for the weekend.

Before she knew it, Janie was standing outside of Danny's. She checked her watch. Ten minutes past five. Sam usually didn't start singing until after six. Janie flushed when she realized she knew Sam's schedule so well. She shook off the embarrassing thoughts and walked inside.

She resisted the urge to cough as she was assailed by the low hanging cloud of smoke. A dozen or so people were already seated, and Janie knew from previous experience it would only get worse. She was about to go to the bar when she heard her father's distinctive laugh. A cross between a braying donkey and a wheezing goat, she cringed as the loud sound rang through the bar. She saw Harvey talking with Doug's father, Reggie. A nervous flutter began in her stomach. Whenever the two of them got together, it usually meant trouble.

Panicking, Janie turned and hurried out of Danny's. The last thing she wanted was a confrontation with the two men. Especially since they'd been drinking. Her mind reeled at the implications. They were most likely plotting to get Doug and her back together.

As she walked home, she thought about her relationship with Doug. They'd been introduced by their fathers who thought they would make a nice couple. At first, Janie enjoyed Doug's company. He was attentive and charming, and they shared similar tastes in movies and music. Six months into the relationship, a New Year's Eve party was the catalyst in changing everything. Although she didn't remember having much to drink, Janie woke the following morning, hung over and in bed with Doug. She hadn't been a virgin, but still felt unsettled by the circumstances.

From that time onward, Doug seemed to think they should jump into bed every time they had dinner at her apartment. She often went along to keep the peace, although the act didn't bring her much pleasure. Never in love with him, Janie stayed with Doug because it was expected, and because of her father's constant badgering to settle down.

Janie was almost home when she remembered why she went to the bar to begin with. Once inside her apartment, she tossed her purse on the sofa and looked up the phone number to Danny's in the phone book.

She dialed and was relieved when Sam was the one who answered. "Sam? This is Janie."

"Hey." Sam spoke loudly into the phone. "It's hard to hear you. Let me put you on hold for a minute and I'll pick up in the office."

The phone clicked and Janie waited apprehensively. She almost hung up, but Sam was back on the line before she could follow through.

"Sorry about that. What's up? I thought you were going to come by tonight."

Janie paced around her living room, trying to come up with the right words. "I was. I mean, I did. But when I got there, my father was sitting at the bar. And I didn't—"

"You didn't want him to see you talking with me," Sam finished for her.

"No. That's not it. Well, not exactly." Janie became flustered. "You don't understand."

"Yeah, I do. It's okay. Being seen with me would probably cause you trouble anyway." Sam cleared her throat. "See you around."

"Wait! Please don't hang up." Janie heard the hurt in Sam's voice and hated being the one who caused it. "I honestly want to see you. I promised you dinner, didn't I?"

Sam sighed wearily. "Yeah, but you don't have to. It's not that big of a deal."

"It is to me." Janie came to a decision. She was tired of doing what was expected of her and wanted to take control of her life. "Do you take a break anytime during the night?"

"Yeah. Usually about half an hour, a couple of hours into the set. Why?"

"Can we meet then?"

"I guess. But wouldn't it be easier to talk now?" The confusion was evident in Sam's voice. "I mean, we're already talking."

Janie laughed. "Yes, we are. But I'd like to be able to spend a few minutes talking in person."

"Okay. Do you want to come in around eight?" At Janie's silence, Sam continued, "I've got a better idea. Let's meet out back, by my car. It's quieter."

"That would be great. I'll see you then." Janie waited until Sam hung up before she held the cell phone to her chest and smiled. It didn't occur to her that seeing Sam was exciting her more than going out with Doug ever did.

HOT, SWEATY AND tired, all Doug wanted was to down several cold beers before going home for the evening. He trudged into Danny's and sat at the bar before he realized who was beside him. "Hey, Pop."

Reggie twisted his stool around. "Son. We was just talking about you." He gestured to the bartender. "Bring another round, and get my son a brew." He slapped Doug on the back, causing dust to float around them. "Damn, boy. You're filthy."

Doug picked up his beer the moment it was placed in front of him. "No shit. I work for a living." He swallowed half the glass before setting it down. "Damn, that's good."

Harvey leaned over the bar so he could see past Reggie. "Have you made up with Janie yet?"

"Hell, no. That little bitch doesn't want anything to do with me, Harv. I think you're going to have to find someone else to take her off your hands." Doug drained his mug and waved it at Fred, who filled another one and traded with him. "Thanks, man." A peanut hit him on the neck, compliments of Harvey. "What the hell was that for?"

"That's my daughter you're talking about."

"So? I've heard you call her worse." Doug slid another dish of peanuts toward himself and gathered a handful. "What are you two old farts up to, anyway? Did the old folk's home run you off, and you're trolling the bars for babes?" He snickered at his own joke.

Reggie cuffed him on the side of the head. "Watch it, boy. We're here trying to straighten out the mess you made."

Doug rubbed his head. "That hurt." It took a minute for his father's words to set in. "What did I do?"

"Screwed up a good thing, that's what."

"Huh?"

Harvey got off his barstool and moved to the other side of Doug. "All you had to do was keep Jane happy until you were married. But you fucked that up."

"It's not my fault your daughter is a frigid bitch." Doug flinched when Harvey whacked him on the shoulder. "Would you two quit beating up on me?"

"Listen, boy," Reggie snarled, "Harv wants grandkids, and you're his best bet. Hell, I'd like to have some young'uns around, too. God knows I can't expect Sue to take care of me in my old age. She'd probably suffocate me in my sleep if she could get away with it."

Doug nursed his beer. "I don't see why it has to be me, though."

While the three of them had been arguing, Sam sat at the piano and begun to play. Her voice drifted over the growing crowd, which rewarded her with polite applause.

Reggie stared at the singer for a moment before returning his attention to his son. "When are you gonna grow up and move out on your own? Janie will make you a nice wife, son."

Doug lowered his voice so only Reggie could hear. "Pop, I don't want to be tied down to Janie. She's been acting all pissy. And I sure as hell don't want to be a father."

"Being a daddy ain't that hard, boy. The woman does most of the work. You can still fool around on the side."

"I guess. But how am I supposed to get her back? She pretty much told me to fuck off."

Harvey dug a ten-dollar bill out of his wallet. "Take her out to eat. Women seem to like that sort of thing."

Reggie added his own advice. "Apologize. Hell, grovel if you have to. If you play your cards right, you might even get laid."

Doug took the money and crammed it into his pocket. "I'm not going to hold my breath," he muttered.

"That's my boy." Reggie thumped him on the back. "Go on home and get cleaned up. You got a woman to work on."

"Not tonight, I'm tired." But Doug pushed away from the bar and stood. "A nice hot shower would feel good, though."

Harvey stood also. "I'll walk you out. I need to get a couple of hours sleep before I go into work." He looked at Reggie. "You coming?"

"Not quite yet. I'm going to need more fortification if I'm going home to my wife." Reggie lit another cigarette. "Doug, don't waste too much time. The sooner you get her back, the better it'll be."

"I know. But I've got a date tomorrow night. I'll go see her Sunday."

"Fair enough." Reggie went back to his drink, while the other two left.

JANIE PACED BESIDE Sam's car. In the hours since she'd spoken to the singer, she couldn't get her out of her mind. She didn't know what about Sam intrigued her so. Maybe it was the way she dressed. Or maybe it was the fact she never cared what anyone else thought. Janie had never met anyone quite like her.

The back door to the bar opened. Sam grinned when she saw Janie. "Hey."

"Hi." Now that they were together, Janie felt shy. "Thanks for meeting me. I know you're busy."

"No biggie. I doubt the drunks will even know if I'm gone." Sam rested against the Olds and tucked her hands into her front pockets. "So, we still on for dinner Sunday?"

Janie nodded and crossed her arms beneath her breasts. "If you'd still like to come. I'm not a great cook, but I know my way around a kitchen."

"A home-cooked meal will be a treat." Sam scuffed her toe on the gravel. "And, if you don't mind me saying, so would getting the chance to spend some time with you."

"Even after the way I've acted?"

Sam looked at the ground. "You were only asking questions. I shouldn't have gone off on you. I'm sorry."

"Apology accepted, if you'll accept mine." Janie held out her hand. She was pleased when Sam accepted her offer. The rough feel of Sam's hand surprised her. "You're not only a musician, are you?"

"No, I do a little of everything. For instance, I'm helping out at Betsy's gym for a while. Between that and my tips at the bar, I've got it pretty good."

"I thought you worked at the grocery store, too."

Sam shrugged. "Nah, I quit. Wasn't enough hours or money. What is it you do at the doctor's office? If you don't mind me asking."

Janie lowered their hands but kept her grip. "Mostly filing. Although I've been doing a lot more insurance forms lately. It's not very important, but the pay's not bad."

Yelling from the front of the alley caused them to break apart. Both laughed self-consciously, but Janie was the first to regain her equilibrium. "Well, I guess I'd better let you get back to work." She turned to leave, but stopped. "I almost forgot. Do you have any food allergies, or things you don't like to eat?"

"Nope. That's one thing living on the road does. It keeps you from getting too picky." Sam took Janie's hand again. "I'm sure whatever you'll make will be wonderful."

Janie squeezed Sam's hand before letting go. "Guess I'd better let you get back to work. I'll see you Sunday?"

"Yep. Six o'clock, right?"

"Uh-huh." Janie started down the alley. "Bye."

Sam exhaled and rested against the car again as Janie walked away. She was looking forward to Sunday.

Janie was halfway down the alley when someone approached. When she saw who it was, her nerves went into overdrive. "Hi, Reggie."

He pulled up. "Janie. What are you doing here?"

"I was on my way home. Do you need a ride?" The last thing she wanted was to be cooped up in a car with Doug's father, but her sense of decency outweighed her discomfort.

"Nah. A long walk gives me more time before I have to face Sue." He stumbled away, muttering under his breath.

Janie spared him a final glance before hurrying out of the alley. The old man had always made her nervous.

Reggie noticed someone standing next to a car at the end of the alley. "Hey, don't I know you?"

Sam shook her head and pushed away from the Oldsmobile. "I don't think so." She ran her hands through her hair as she walked past him and noticed the heavy scent of beer. "You probably saw me inside. I sing."

"Oh, yeah." Reggie belched and weaved his way through the alley.

Chapter
Nine

SUNDAY DIDN'T START well for Sam. Since Betsy's incapacitation, she'd been spending nights at the gym, sleeping on the lumpy guest bed. They'd originally considered moving Betsy's bed to the downstairs office, but Sam and Ray decided it would be easier to assist the older woman upstairs.

Sam clinched her jaw to stop a yawn as she scrambled eggs for Betsy's breakfast. Three and a half hours of sleep hadn't been enough. She felt as if she'd barely closed her eyes when the alarm went off. She'd stayed late at the bar the night before, not by choice. Fred had dropped two trays of mugs, and it had taken over an hour to get all the glass cleaned up.

Working two jobs, three if you counted helping out in the bar, was beginning to wear on Sam. None of them were particularly difficult, but the time consumed left little time for anything else. Such as sleeping.

She spooned the eggs onto a plate and added a small helping of melon chunks. Betsy's small appetite belied her sturdy build, and it didn't take much food to satisfy her. Sam placed the plate, along with a cup of coffee, on a tray and carried it to her friend's room.

"Dammit, Sam. I told you yesterday to quit waiting on me." But Betsy sat up gingerly and straightened her covers to accommodate the tray. She happily dug into the meal with gusto. "Did you get any sleep at all?"

"Yes, I did. And you're welcome, by the way." Sam sat at the foot of the bed and watched her friend move the eggs around with her fork. "Stop bellyaching and finish it up before it gets cold."

Betsy popped a piece of melon into her mouth. "Fruit's *supposed* to be cold, kid."

"Smartass." Sam lay across the bed and propped her head on her upraised hand. "You'd starve if it wasn't for me."

"Nah. I'd live off peanut butter crackers and warm cokes."

"That's disgusting."

Betsy scooped up a forkful of eggs. "Don't knock it 'til you tried it. I can only imagine what your diet consisted of when you were on the road."

Sam gave her a superior look. "Fresh fruit, bottled water," she grinned, "and peanut butter crackers." She grimaced when a piece of fruit bounced off her forehead. "Yuck."

"So," Betsy smiled cheekily, "tell me about your date tonight."

"It's *not* a date."

"Uh-huh. Right. You'll probably try to sell me a bridge, next."

With a heavy sigh, Sam flopped onto her back and stared at the ceiling. "Honestly, I don't know *what* it is. She's confusing the hell out of me. Are all straight women so hard to figure out?"

"You're asking me?" Betsy finished off the fruit and wiped her mouth with a napkin. "Just because my clients are women doesn't mean I know what makes them tick. But if women are half as difficult to understand as men, you're in a world of hurt."

"Gee, thanks." Sam rolled over and faced her. "One minute she's all nice and friendly, then the next she's accusing me of being some sort of perverted sex fiend."

Betsy pushed the tray away. "Sounds to me like she's confused."

"She's not the only one."

"Hush." Betsy tapped her chin with the tip of her finger while she considered Sam's predicament. "What do you want from her?"

"Nothing. I'm not looking to convert her to the dark side, or anything like that."

"I know, hon. But what are you hoping for? A friend? A girlfriend?" Betsy chuckled as a naughty thought crossed her mind. "Someone to do the nasty with in the backseat of your car?"

"Betsy!" Sam blushed heavily. "I'd never — "

The older woman laughed at the look on Sam's face. "I'm sorry. You're just so easy to pick on."

Sam wiped her hand down her face in an attempt to calm herself. "I really would like to be her friend. I don't have too many of those, and I don't think she does, either."

"Mmm-hmm." Nodding thoughtfully, Betsy tried to get to the heart of the matter. "What would you do if *she* wants more than friendship?"

A blank look covered Sam's face. She hadn't considered that particular scenario. "I don't know. I guess it depended on how long I'll be here." She turned deadly serious. "I've never had a relationship only for sex. I'm not made that way."

"Good for you." Betsy held out her hand and waited until Sam took it. "Don't ever change, Sam. And as for how long you'll stay, I'd still like you to consider being my manager."

"But I don't know anything about running a gym."

"You've done pretty well so far. Besides, if you do, I can take a vacation. I haven't had one of those in forever."

Sam nodding in agreement. "All right. You've got a deal. Will I still be able to work part-time at the bar? The tips are getting better."

"Sure. Play your cards right, and I'll even show up and cheer you on."

"Cool." Sam rolled to her feet. "I've got a lot to do before tonight. Leave the tray on the bed and I'll be back for it later, okay?" She stopped at the doorway. "Should I take something to Janie? Wine, flowers, candy?"

Betsy laughed at the flummoxed look on Sam's face. "Quit worrying so much. It's not a date, remember?"

"Yeah, but—"

"Try a small bouquet of flowers. Those are always nice."

Sam grinned. "Yeah. I can do that." She saluted Betsy and sauntered out of the room, singing under her breath.

JANIE LOOKED AT herself in the mirror. On a lark, she'd gone on a shopping spree and the beauty salon Saturday afternoon. Her brown hair, which had hung limply past her shoulders, now barely touched them. Bangs brushed her forehead, and the washed-out brown was presently highlighted with streaks of blonde, giving her a more youthful appearance. The black-framed glasses, a style she'd had since high school, were gone. Now she sported a more stylish pair of oval-shaped wire frames. Not quite satisfied with her appearance, Janie applied a minute amount of lipstick and stepped out of the bathroom.

On her way through the living room, the smell wafting from the oven caused her to smile. She had fretted over the menu all day Saturday until something Sam had said gave her an idea. One of Janie's specialties was meatloaf. It was also something that was better cooked at home than in a restaurant. She only hoped Sam would think the same. Janie made another pass through the apartment, looking for anything out of place. She'd cleaned until late Saturday night, now the furniture gleamed and the wood floors glistened.

She was putting the finishing touches on the table setting when there was a knock on the door. Janie nervously fingered her hair as she hastened to the door. She took a deep breath and turned the handle.

Sam stood uncertainly, a small spray of wildflowers in one hand. Her jeans were pressed, her boots shined, and the powder blue shirt contrasted nicely with her tan. "Did you do something different to your hair? You look fantastic."

"Really?" Janie fluffed her hair self-consciously. "I...I thought a change would be nice."

"It looks great on you." Sam held the flowers out to Janie. "I wasn't sure what to bring. I hope these are okay."

"They're beautiful." Janie took the bouquet. "Come in. Dinner should be ready in about ten minutes."

"Great." Sam followed her inside and surveyed the apartment. "You've got a great place."

Janie gestured to the living area. "Thank you. Make yourself comfortable. I'm going to put these in water." She left the room, her nose stuck in the flowers.

Sam wandered around the room, checking out the photographs. Many were of a younger Janie, usually in the company of an older woman. She noticed with some satisfaction that not one picture of Doug could be seen. A particular shot caught her eye, and she picked up the frame and studied it.

"I was a dorky kid," Janie explained as she came into the room. She went to stand by Sam. "Maybe someday I'll grow out of it."

"Actually, I was thinking how cute you were." Sam replaced the picture and turned to Janie. "And you grew into a beautiful woman."

Janie blushed. "Hardly." She fussed with her new dress. Much brighter than most of her clothes, the pale yellow picked up the new highlights in her hair. "I'm average, at best."

Sam shook her head. "We don't know each other very well, but I know one thing for certain. You are a beautiful soul." She touched Janie's cheek. "Don't base your self-worth on the small-minded people in this town." Suddenly realizing how close they were, she stepped back and quickly changed the subject. "It smells good in here."

Even after they moved apart, Janie could feel Sam's touch on her face. She led the way to the sofa, where they each took a corner. She turned and tucked one sandaled foot beneath her. "I hope you'll like it. Meatloaf is one of the things I can make well."

"I'm looking forward to it." Sam shifted so she could look at Janie. "Thank you again for inviting me."

"Don't thank me until you taste it," Janie joked. "Harvey, I mean, my father constantly complained my cooking was too bland." His tendency to cover everything with hot sauce had always been a sore spot with her.

The urge to touch Janie again was driving Sam crazy. She jiggled one leg nervously. "You call him by his first name?"

"I have since I was a teenager." Janie felt she needed to explain. "We don't get along. He's never been much of a father to me."

"I'm sorry." Sam motioned to the pictures. "Is that your mom?"

Janie finally smiled. "No, my grandmother. My mother left when I was fifteen." At the pitying look Sam gave her, Janie hurried to explain. "My Nana is great. She's always been there for me. I don't know how someone as sweet as she is could have a son like Harvey." She played with the hem of her dress. "What about your family?"

"I'd never known my father, and my mother was a teenage drug addict. She left after I was born and my grandmother raised me. To this day, I have no idea where she is, or if she's even alive." Sam propped her left ankle on her right knee to get more comfortable. "Gran did the best she could, even though she wasn't in the greatest health."

"I'm sure she's very proud of you."

Sam's eyes dropped to Janie's hands. "She died ten years ago. That's when I took off on the road." She cleared her throat and forced a smile onto her face. "Sorry about getting so maudlin."

"Don't apologize. The only way we're going to get to know each other is to talk. And it's nice to have a friend to talk to."

"Is that what we are?"

Janie nodded. "I'd like to think so." She held out her hand.

"Me too." Sam took her hand, but startled when a buzzer went off in the kitchen.

"Oops. Dinner's ready." Janie reluctantly let go of Sam and stood. "Why don't you sit at the table?"

Sam got to her feet and followed Janie. The table was covered with a blue satin tablecloth, and was set with white china. Four dark cherry, spindly-legged chairs surrounded it. "Do you need any help?"

"Nope." Janie pushed her toward a chair. "Get comfortable, and I'll bring everything out." She hustled to the kitchen and returned quickly with a salad, then left to get the rest of the meal.

Sam watched as Janie brought each dish. In addition to the salad, there was a bowl of green beans, another of mashed potatoes, and finally the meatloaf. Once Janie had everything placed, Sam pulled out her chair for her.

"Thank you." Janie couldn't remember the last time someone was so chivalrous. Doug had stopped treating her like a lady after they'd slept together the first time. She placed the cloth napkin in her lap and watched Sam carefully sit. "Don't worry. The chairs are a lot sturdier than they look. Nana gave them to me. She'd kept the set in storage until I moved out of Harvey's."

"It's nice." Sam mimicked Janie's actions and waited to see what she'd do next. She felt completely out of her element. "Where's your grandmother now?"

Janie served them each helpings of food while she spoke. "She lives in the Spring Gardens Nursing Home. I visit her as often as I can."

"I bet it's great having her so close by." Sam waited until Janie picked up her fork before doing the same. She realized she was being watched. "What?"

"You can eat, you know," Janie teased gently.

Sam took a forkful of meatloaf and placed it in her mouth. The flavors hit her tongue and she was unable to hold back a moan. "Oh, my god. This is fantastic." She quickly took several more bites.

"I'm glad you like it." Janie started eating as well, although at a much slower pace.

They were silent as they ate, both using the meal as an excuse to contemplate the evening so far. The only sound was the clink of silverware against plates, and the occasional sip of tea.

Sam wiped her mouth before taking another drink. She sneaked a glance at her hostess. The new hairstyle was perfect for Janie, and apparently gave her a newfound confidence. Her eyes sparkled beneath her new wireframe glasses. "You really look beautiful tonight."

"Excuse me?"

"Damn." Sam covered her face with her hand. "Did I say that out loud?"

Janie's smile covered her face. "I'm afraid you did. But thank you."

With an embarrassed shrug, Sam picked up her glass. "And you cooked a fantastic meal."

"Thank you again." Janie was about to offer dessert when there was a knock on the door. "I'll be right back."

From her vantage point, Sam could see the door. She was as surprised as her hostess when Janie opened the door.

Janie fought the urge to slam the door closed. "Doug? What are you doing here?"

He thrust a large bouquet of roses in her face. "These are for you." Using his shoulder, he pushed the door open wider. "I thought we could—" Seeing Sam at the table, he threw the flowers on the floor. "What the fuck is *she* doing here?"

"Having dinner." Janie's hand shook where she held the doorknob.

For her part, Sam wasn't sure what to do. She was afraid if she stood, he'd think she was confronting him. The last thing she wanted to do was start a fight in Janie's apartment. The terrified look on Janie's face changed her mind. She got to her feet and held out her hand. "Hi, I'm Sam."

Doug clenched his fists, ignoring her offer. "I know who the hell you are. You're that queer that sings at Danny's. How do you know my fiancée?"

"Your what?" Janie's ire came to the top. Having Sam with her gave her confidence, and she took his arm and tried to lead him to the door. "I broke up with you, Doug. And I've *never* been engaged to you." She started to pull him away. "Now I'd like for you to leave."

"But she's a dyke! You're not safe, Janie."

Janie tugged him along. "She's my friend, Doug. Go home."

He was so in shock that he never realized when she guided him out of the apartment, until the door slammed in his face. "Hey!" The deadbolt locked into place. "Well, fuck!"

Inside, Janie turned to Sam. "I'm so sorry."

"It's not your fault." Sam met her halfway across the room. When Janie began to cry, she pulled her into her arms and held her. "It's okay."

"Why can't he leave me alone? It's not as if he loves me." Janie sniffled but didn't try to move away. She felt safe for the first time in a long time, and was in no hurry to draw away.

Somehow they gravitated to the sofa, where Janie continued to huddle in Sam's embrace. They sat quietly for a while, until Janie broke the silence. "Can I ask you a question?"

"Sure."

"How, um, when did you know that you were, uh, gay?" Janie kept her head on Sam's chest, afraid to look her in the eyes.

"I think I've always known. I mean, when I was younger, I didn't have a name for how I felt. But I've always been attracted to girls. Guys were who I hung out with, but I never felt anything but friendship for them."

Janie raised her head. "Was it hard? Growing up?"

"Not any harder than for you, I guess. At least until high school. That was a bit rough." Sam chuckled disparagingly. "A girl dressed like me wasn't exactly well-received."

"What happened?"

Sam sighed. "The usual. I was called names, pushed around, and teased. Got into my share of fights, too. Lost most of them. Gran wasn't too happy about that."

"I'm sorry." Janie snuggled down and hugged Sam. "I wasn't much better when we first met."

"Well, it turned out okay." Sam rested her chin on the top of Janie's head. "You're probably going to get a lot of flack from him tomorrow."

"I don't care." And, to her own surprise, Janie found that she didn't. Her worst fear had happened, and she survived. She was looking forward to having Sam as a friend.

UPSTAIRS, OVER THE GYM, was dark and quiet. Sam closed the door carefully, trying not to make a sound. She tiptoed into the living room carrying her boots, picking her way around the furniture in the dark. She was almost to the sofa when the light flicked on.

Standing at the door to the hall was Betsy, leaning on a cane. "Coming in a bit late from your non-date, aren't you?" She took note of the boots Sam held in one hand. "Curfew was one o'clock," she teased, pointing to the clock over the bookcase. "It's almost two."

"Curfew?" Sam plopped on the couch and dropped her boots. "Have you been mixing your pain pills?"

Betsy shuffled to sit next to her. "Nah. Just having some fun with you." She made a point to look Sam over carefully.

"What are you doing?"

"Making sure your clothes are right-side out."

Sam edged away from her. "Of course they are. Why wouldn't they be?"

"Seeing's how late you got home, I thought maybe you overslept and dressed in a hurry."

"Huh?"

Betsy swatted Sam's shoulder. "Never mind."

It finally dawned on Sam as to what she was insinuating. "For god's sake, Betsy. It was only dinner."

"Dinner that lasted until almost breakfast, I might add. What exactly were you doing all evening?"

"Talking." At her friend's disbelieving look, Sam hastened to add, "Honestly, that's all." She leaned against the back of the sofa. "She's a nice person."

Betsy wasn't convinced. "And there was *no* hanky panky going on? Not even a smidgen?"

"No." Sam reconsidered. "Unless you count," she paused, "no, you're probably not interested." She tried to stand but was hauled down by her belt.

"Wait a cotton-pickin' minute, kid. I want *all* the details." When Sam kept silent, Betsy wasn't above pleading. "Come on, Sam. I'm an old woman. Don't tease."

Sam laughed and settled down again. "Teach you to pick on me. Seriously, though, we only talked. Well, and hugged." Her grin turned cocky. "The cuddling on the couch was nice, too." While Betsy sat with her mouth hanging open, Sam took the opportunity to jump up and race to the bathroom to change for bed. "Ha!"

"You brat!" Betsy struggled to stand and moved slowly toward her bedroom. She paused at the bathroom door. "You *will* tell me all about it over breakfast."

"Maybe," Sam sang through the door. She laughed louder when Betsy rapped the door with her cane. "Goodnight, Betsy."

Betsy hobbled down the hallway. "Good *morning*, Sam," she yelled, snickering to herself.

After undressing, Sam stepped out of the bathroom and moved quietly toward the guest room. She snuggled under the clean sheets. Even the discomfort of the old bed couldn't wipe the smile off her face.

She linked her hands beneath her head and stared at the ceiling. The evening had gone better than she could have ever hoped. Janie was a marvelous cook, although the food paled in comparison to the hostess herself. The new hairstyle, along with the yellow sundress, made Janie glow. Sam had always thought she was attractive, but the new look made her realize what a lovely woman she truly was.

Sam sighed. Even Doug's interruption didn't ruin the night. After they'd moved to the couch, they spent several hours enjoying each other's company. They talked more about Sam's sexuality, Janie asking quite a few good questions that Sam was more than happy to answer. She even spoke of the beatings she received in high school once she came out. Janie had been shocked, but very supportive. Sam felt as if they'd cemented their friendship. Anything else was pure wishing on her part, but Sam couldn't help it. She felt more comfortable with Janie than she had anyone else in her life.

Sam closed her eyes, wondering what the future would bring.

UNABLE TO SLEEP, Janie found herself in the kitchen washing the dinner dishes. She had planned on leaving them until morning, but once she was in bed, her mind kept whirling over the evening and she was unable to nod off.

As apprehensive as she had been before Sam arrived, she hadn't expected to enjoy herself so much. But Sam had surprised her. She was warm, witty, and even though seven years her junior, very easy to talk to. Their conversations ranged from silly to serious.

Janie ran the scrub sponge over a plate then rinsed it in hot water. She looked at the china dish and remembered how complimentary Sam had been on her cooking. She hated to keep comparing her to Doug, but it was hard not to. His only comments during meals at her apartment had been innuendos about sex. It was nice to spend a meal with someone who had no hidden motives. Being able to have an intelligent conversation was a treat.

The only blemish had been Doug's unexpected arrival. She had been terrified of a confrontation. Doug's temper, which had always been fiery, had become violent with the more alcohol he consumed. It was another reason she'd finally decided to break away from him. But Sam had handled things well, and she had surprised herself by throwing Doug out.

What happened afterward brought another smile to her face. The tender way Sam held her touched Janie deeply in places she didn't know existed. She wiped her hands on a dishtowel and sighed. She could almost feel Sam's arms around her; almost hear the beat of her heart. It was one of the nicest evenings she'd ever had and she couldn't wait to repeat the experience.

Humming to herself, Janie left the kitchen and headed to her bedroom. She knew what her dreams would hold.

Chapter
Ten

THERE WAS A decided spring in Sam's step as she brought Betsy her breakfast. "Good morning. I hope you like omelets. I was feeling creative." She situated the tray and sat on the edge of the bed.

"You're certainly chipper for someone who stayed out half the night." Betsy tucked the napkin under her chin and concentrated on her plate. "What did you put in this, anyway?"

"It's a surprise." Sam pointedly ignored Betsy's first remark. Nothing could ruin her good mood. Not even her friend's teasing.

Betsy poked at the eggs with her fork. "Looks like you cleaned out my refrigerator."

"Someone had to. Things were beginning to crawl to the front and jump." Sam snagged a piece of fruit and popped it into her mouth.

"Stop stealing food off an invalid's plate. It's not nice." But Betsy started on the omelet, humming happily as she ate. "Not bad."

"Thanks." Sam pulled her socked feet on the bed and put her arms around her upraised knees. "What's on our agenda today?"

Betsy swallowed and sipped on her coffee. "I'd like to write up a business contract for you. I'd rather get it done sooner, than later. Besides, I can't do much else."

"Sounds like a plan." Sam started to get up, but changed her mind. "Can I ask you something?"

"Sure."

"Do you think, I mean, could it be possible," Sam struggled for the right words. She exhaled heavily and impatiently brushed her hand through her hair. "Damn."

Betsy continued to eat, the only sound being her fork as it scraped the plate.

"Ugh." Sam looked into her friend's eyes, which twinkled with amusement. "It's about Janie. Last night was," she sighed, "amazing. I mean, we didn't do anything, except eat and talk, but we got along so well. Am I making any sense?"

"It sounds like you had a nice time." Betsy tried to be careful with her words. "I take it she's more comfortable with you being a lesbian?"

"She seems to be. But I guess I won't really know until we see each other in public." Sam propped her chin on her knees. "Am I reading too much into last night?"

"I don't know. I wasn't there." Betsy pushed the tray away and sat up straighter. "You didn't make out on the couch, did you?"

Sam's mouth dropped open and her eyes got wide. "Of course not!" Her face pinkened. "We did kind of snuggle, though."

"Excuse me?"

"It wasn't what you think. Janie's ex-boyfriend showed up and upset her. I was only trying to make her feel better." Sam turned thoughtful. "We spent the rest of the evening on the sofa. She could have moved away any time, but she didn't. Do you think that means something?"

Betsy patted Sam's foot. "I think it means she felt comfortable with her new friend. Don't read any more into it. I'd hate to see you get hurt."

Tired of the conversation, Sam got off the bed. "Don't worry, I'm pretty tough." She took Betsy's tray. "I'm going to get the dishes cleaned up then I'll start on the showers downstairs."

"Okay, hon. Don't wear yourself out." Betsy waited until Sam was almost out of the room. "And you're about as tough as a wet paper towel. Be careful."

"Yes, mom." Sam edged out of the room, barely dodging the pillow Betsy flung at her.

THREE HOURS LATER, Sam put the vacuum away. After she'd mopped the gym, she came upstairs and did some light housework, much to Betsy's surprise. The older woman had asked Sam to help her make it downstairs, where she could keep an eye on the customers.

Betsy's voice rang through the intercom from the gym. "Sam, could you help me with something, please?"

With a tired sigh, Sam trudged down the stairs to see what her friend needed. She pulled up short when she saw who stood at the counter with Betsy. "Janie?"

"Hi. I was telling Betsy how I wanted to rejoin her program, or maybe something else." The pink tinge to Janie's cheeks gave her away. "I was on my lunch break, and remembered you talking about the gym."

Sam glanced at Betsy, who looked like the cat who swallowed the canary. "That's great. Although I don't know what—"

"I was telling Janie how I'm planning on starting up an aerobics class. One of the gals who comes in says she used to teach one before she moved here."

"Really? Funny, you haven't mentioned it to me before." Sam had a sneaking suspicion Betsy was trying to play matchmaker. "When are these alleged classes beginning?"

Betsy shook her finger at her. "Don't get smart with me, kid." She turned to Janie. "As soon as I call Pamela and give her the okay we should be able to start. Maybe you'd like to pass the word around."

"Of course. The women at work are always talking about getting some exercise. This would be perfect." Janie looked at Sam. "Do you work out?"

"Ha." Betsy winked at Sam. "That one doesn't have time to exercise, or so she tells me."

Sam crossed her arms over her chest. "You keep me too busy, you mean." She directed her next comments to Janie. "If you don't mind me saying, you don't look like you need to work out, either."

Janie smiled shyly. "I'd actually like to put on some muscle. I hate feeling so run down and tired all the time."

"You came to the right place then," Betsy assured her. "As a matter of fact, since you'll be my first aerobics customer, I'll give you the gym membership for free. All I ask is that you tell your friends."

"You don't have to do that. I can pay."

Betsy patted her hand, which was resting on the counter. "Pay the aerobics instructor her fee. We're good."

Janie didn't look convinced, but she kept silent. She switched her attention to Sam, who still appeared peeved. "You don't mind me coming in from time to time, do you?"

"Of course not. It'll be nice to see more of you." Sam heard the words and realized how it sounded. "I mean, nice to see you here." She tried to ignore Betsy's chortling. Her friend was getting too much enjoyment out of her discomfort. "Have you had lunch? I was about to run out and get ours, and I could grab yours, too." She shook her head at herself. "Your lunch, I mean."

Betsy howled. "My god, Sam. I didn't know a person could turn that particular shade of red." She popped open the cash drawer and took out a twenty dollar bill. "Here. Fetch us all some hamburgers, if you don't mind."

Sam glared at her as she took the money. "Yes, ma'am. So Janie, what would you like?"

"I, um," Janie appeared at a loss. She hadn't planned on having lunch today. "You don't have to—"

"Burger and fries it is." Sam started out the door. "Mustard or mayo?"

Janie grinned. "However you like it will be fine. I'm easy."

Betsy was about to say something, but Sam's warning finger caused her to cover her mouth with one hand. She waited until Sam was out the door before bursting into laughter.

THE GYM'S OFFICE was the perfect place for the trio's impromptu picnic. Betsy had commandeered the chair behind the desk while Sam and Janie were each parked in folding chairs across from her.

Betsy watched the two interact, doing her best not to smirk. She wondered if they had any idea how cute they were. Seeing them together, she could plainly see the mutual attraction. Whether they would ever do something about it, she didn't know. But it couldn't hurt to give them a tiny nudge in the right direction. She finished chewing a French fry before speaking. "Janie, how long have you lived in Piperton?"

Janie appeared startled at the question, but quickly regained her composure. "All my life. I've never even traveled out of town."

"My, that *is* something, isn't it? Why, by the time I was your age I'd lived in four different states. My Jack was a wanderer at heart. We tended to move around a lot, but I wouldn't change a minute of it." Betsy nibbled on another fry. "Have you ever thought about traveling? What if your husband was transferred somewhere else?"

"That's never going to be a factor. I've had my fill of men for a while. Although it does sound exciting to see more of the country."

Sam finished her soda and set the can down on the desk with a thump. "Travel isn't as exciting as you might think."

"Oh? And you've spent all those years on the road because?" Betsy couldn't wait to hear Sam's explanation.

"Never found a reason to stay anywhere," Sam admitted quietly, her eyes never leaving Janie.

A hopeful look crossed Janie' face. "What would be a good reason?"

It was if they were the only two people in the room. Sam's answer was for Janie, in more ways than one. "Friends," her voice softened, "family."

"Oh." Janie reached for her hand, but the bell over the front door rang, breaking the moment.

Betsy cursed and began to rise. "No one shows up all day, but they arrive in time to interrupt our lunch."

Janie stood. "I've got to run anyway. Do you want me to see what they need?"

"No, that's all right. It's probably Pamela. She usually comes in on Mondays, and I might as well see if I can work up a deal with her about starting some aerobics classes." Betsy came around the desk and surprised Janie with a hug. "Come by anytime. The back door's always unlocked."

Sam's embarrassment over her earlier confession was apparent on her face. She searched her mind for something to say. "I'm glad you came by."

"Me too." Janie followed her instincts and gently grasped Sam's forearm. "I enjoyed last night."

"So did I." Sam's eyes closed when Janie's hand slid down to hold hers. "Janie, I—"

"Shh." Janie kissed her on the cheek and moved away. "I'll try to come by the bar tonight." She squeezed Sam's hand before leaving.

HOT, STALE AIR circulated around the repair shop courtesy of an ancient industrial floor fan. The wrench Reggie was using on the lawnmower engine slipped and caused his knuckles to scrape against the metal. He cursed and brought the injured knuckles to his mouth and sucked on them to clean the wound.

"That's disgusting, Pop." Doug handed his father a filthy shop rag. "At least use something more sanitary."

Reggie glared at his son as he snatched the cloth out of his hand. "What's crawled up your ass today? I figure you'd be in a better mood after getting Janie back."

"I don't want to talk about it." Before Doug could turn away, his father's greasy hand stopped him. "Watch it. I don't want grease all over me."

"A little dirt never hurt anyone. Did you go see her?"

The pout that crossed Doug's face was his answer. He headed for the office adjacent to the shop. Even though he spent his workday in the sun, his favorite place was at his desk in front of the air conditioner. When Reggie followed him inside and closed the door, he scowled. "Would you leave me the fuck alone?"

With a tired grunt, Reggie sprawled in the ratty chair. "Not until you tell me what happened."

"She's not interested, okay? Leave it at that."

"Nope."

Doug looked in the center drawer of the desk and brought out a paperclip, which he opened and used to clean the dirt from beneath his nails. "I showed up, gave her the flowers, and she told me in no uncertain terms we were done. End of story."

"And you gave up?"

"Look old man, she had someone else there all right? Even I know when to let it go." Doug dropped the clip on the desk and slammed his hands on the top. "You and Harvey can just get the hell over it. I'm done."

"I never figured I raised a quitter."

Furious, Doug leapt to his feet and his chair slammed back against the wall. "Damn it! She's made her decision. Leave her alone."

Reggie stood, put his hands on his hips and shook his head. "You've turned into a whiny-assed piece of shit."

"Fuck you." Doug shoved by his father and stormed out of the office. Eager to get away from Reggie's interrogation, he decided to join his afternoon mowing crew, the midday heat be damned.

JANIE DIDN'T MAKE it by Danny's Monday night, but it didn't keep Sam from putting on a good show. Her music reflected her mood. Every song was upbeat and the few people in the bar seemed to enjoy the evening. Many sang along to several tunes and by the end of the night Sam's tip jar was full. She played two encores before finally giving her voice a rest. She thanked the audience and headed for the bar, where Ray had a glass of ice water waiting. "Thanks."

"Sure." He glanced at his watch. "It's barely ten. Are you calling it a night?"

"I think so. I've got some things to take care of at the gym before morning, unless you need me to hang around here and help."

Ray acknowledged a customer two stools away and filled a mug with draft beer. He exchanged the drink with the cash left on the bar and looked around the room. "No sense in you staying. Crowd's starting to break up." Mondays were notoriously slow. He waved to a couple leaving. "Y'all be careful heading home."

Sam finished her water. "I can come in early tomorrow and take care of the floors, if you want."

"That'd be great. Fred's off and I'd appreciate all the help I can get. Are you still sleeping in your car out back?"

"Only if I'm too tired to drive home." She caught her slip. It was too soon for her to consider Betsy's place hers. "I mean, I don't want to wake Betsy by coming in at all hours. Why? Do you need me to move it?"

"Nah, it's fine where it's at. I'm only worried about you being back there alone."

She picked up a tray of dirty glasses. "I've been sleeping in my car for years, in places a lot worse than here. Haven't had anything happen to me yet." Sam shifted the tray to make it easier to carry. "I'll do these before I leave." Considering the conversation over, she took the tray to the kitchen. The small room was still clean from earlier, so it didn't take her long to get everything washed and put away.

A short time later she went through the back door, hearing the metallic snick of the lock as it closed. A moment too late, she saw a silhouette in the darkness leaning against her car. It was too big to be Janie and Sam began to get nervous at the realization of who it was.

"It's about time you got here," Doug called out. "I saw you head to the back fifteen minutes ago."

Sam suddenly regretted not accepting a door key from Ray weeks ago. She hadn't wanted the added responsibility, since at the time she didn't think she'd be staying for long. She noticed Doug's muscled arms and inwardly cringed. Sam knew she was no match for him. His work outdoors kept him strong. She quickly figured the distance between him and the mouth of the alley. He was too close, and running in her heavy boots was out of the question. Her only chance was to reason with him. "Yeah, sorry about that. I had to do a few dishes before leaving." She edged closer to the alleyway. "What can I do for you?"

He pushed off the car and started toward her. "I never thought I'd see Janie spending time with someone like you."

"It's not—"

"She's not like you." He continued closer, causing her to change direction. "Janie's a gentle woman who's lived here all her life and she's very trusting."

Sam held out her hands to keep him back. "Yes, I know. She was the first person outside the bar to even speak to me."

"That's how she is."

As Doug moved within a step of her, Sam backed up too quickly and her boots slipped on the gravel, causing her to fall onto her rear. "I don't know what you think is going on, but we barely know each other."

He bent and took a firm hold of her upper arms. "I don't believe you." Even as Sam struggled, he had no trouble lifting her to her feet. "Janie's not the type to make friends easily." His face was inches from hers. "I'd hate to see her get hurt."

"I understand," she managed to say through her fear. "But I swear to you—"

"Would you shut the fuck up?" He shook her. "I'm trying to make a point here."

She didn't seem to listen. "It was only dinner, nothing else." Sam squirmed until she was able to get out of his grip then stumbled away. With distance between them, she found her normal attitude returning. "Janie's a grown woman and I don't see why she can't choose her own friends."

"That's what I was talking about." Doug scratched his head. "This isn't going right."

Sam rubbed her left arm, where his fingers had dug in particularly hard. "Why are you here?"

He tucked his hands into his front pockets. "Last night, when I saw you in her apartment, sitting at her table like you belonged there, it was more than I could take. I always thought we'd be together for a long time. Maybe settle down and get married. Hell, even her old man wants us together."

"What about what Janie wants? Isn't that important?"

"Yeah. You know, I didn't sleep at all last night. I kept thinking about you and her."

Even though Sam could say the same thing, she didn't think it was wise to admit it to him. But she felt a need to explain. "We didn't—"

Doug cut her off. "When we first met, Janie was my friend. But I can tell she hasn't been happy for a long time." He looked embarrassed. "What I'm trying to say is, I'm sorry."

It was the last thing Sam thought she'd ever hear from him. "What?"

"I've been acting like an ass lately. Our fathers have been putting a lot of pressure on me. I've done some things I'm not proud of and I gotta live with that. As soon as Janie will talk to me, I plan on apologizing to her too." He held out his hand. "If she wants to have you as a friend, I've got no say in the matter." His face grew even more serious as their hands clasped. "But if you do anything to hurt her, I'll kill you." Doug released her hand and stared at Sam for a long moment, as if trying to see why Janie would have anything to do with someone like her. He shook his head, turned and walked away, leaving a stunned Sam behind.

Sam exhaled shakily as her knees threatened to collapse beneath her. "Damn."

THE DOOR TO the clinic opened and Janie stepped onto the sidewalk. She was followed by a gray haired, middle-aged man, who locked the door and pocketed the keys. His blue suit coat was draped over one arm, and his red tie was loosened. They began to walk toward the small parking lot to the west, their shoes thudding softly into the quiet evening.

"Thank you for staying tonight, Janie. I didn't feel comfortable being alone with Ms. Taylor." Dr. Richmond placed one hand on the small of her back without thought, guiding Janie around a pothole.

The office computer system had crashed around nine o'clock that morning, and it took the technician they'd called well into the evening to get it back online. During the course of the day, the woman constantly flirted with the doctor, who was in charge of the clinic. For the sake of propriety, he'd asked for volunteers to stay after work. Janie had agreed, since the other women were either married, or found excuses to leave.

Janie surreptitiously checked her watch. It was ten-fifteen, probably too late to catch Sam at the bar. "It wasn't a problem, Ted. I would have hated to try and explain to your wife why you stayed late at work with a woman you didn't know."

"I was thinking the exact same thing. Speaking of Sharon, she was asking the other day when you'd be coming back over for dinner." He stopped next to a white Lexus sedan. "I think she wants to set you up with her cousin."

The thought of a blind date was not appealing to Janie. "She heard about Doug and me breaking up, didn't she?"

"Possibly." He tossed his coat into the back seat. "But don't let that deter you. We'd love to have you. I'll even do what I can to keep you safe from Sharon's matchmaking." Ted looked around the parking lot, which was completely vacant. "Where's your car?"

"I walk to work when the weather's nice." Janie glanced at her watch again. "I'll see you in the morning."

"You had plans, didn't you?"

She shrugged. "No, not really. I was going to see a friend after work, but the plans weren't set in stone."

"Still, I feel bad. Is there some way I can make it up to you? At least let me drive you home." He stepped around the car and opened the passenger door. "Please?"

There was no good reason to refuse, yet Janie hung back. She thought about stopping by the gym, to see if Sam had gone home. "Thank you, but—"

"If you don't agree, I'll follow you home," he threatened with a smile on his face. "I'd hate to look like a stalker."

"It's really not necessary. I've been walking home for years," she argued, even as she climbed into the car. As she sunk into the soft leather seat, Janie couldn't help but release a sigh.

Ted hurried around the car and got behind the wheel. "Thank you for humoring me. Sharon would never let me hear the end of it, you know. Especially considering the late hour."

Peering through the side window, Janie relaxed. She'd call Sam first thing in the morning. "No. Thank you. It would be silly to walk at night."

They shamelessly gossiped about the others in the office during the drive. Dr. Richmond's wife spent a lot of time at the clinic, unofficially managing the office. She knew all the sordid details where the ladies were involved, and delighted in sharing with her husband. If Sharon didn't have to take care of her elderly mother, she would most likely be there full time.

It wasn't long before Ted parked in front of Janie's building. As she stepped from the car, he leaned across the seat to be heard. "Thanks again for your help. Since you were there so late, why not take tomorrow off? Let the others clean up the files for a change."

Janie almost declined, but reconsidered. It would be the perfect opportunity to spend more time with Sam. She felt bad when she hadn't been able to call and tell her she wouldn't be at Danny's tonight. Maybe she could make it up to her by cooking lunch. "Thank you, Ted. I'd enjoy having a free day."

"Great. I'll see you Wednesday, then. Goodnight." He drove off after she closed the door and went inside the building.

She was barely inside the apartment before she kicked off her shoes. They skittered across the wood floor and ended up beneath her coffee table. Janie ignored the urge to pick them up, instead stubbornly striding past them on her way to her bedroom. After getting out of her work clothes, she went into the kitchen and opened her refrigerator. She wasn't hungry, since Dr. Richmond had pizza delivered to the office for dinner. But a snack sounded good, so she grabbed an orange.

On her way back to the bedroom, she heard a knock at her door. She set the orange on the kitchen table hoping it was Sam. Janie didn't bother to see who it was, instead swinging the door open with a smile.

Doug mirrored her smile. "Hi, Janie."

"What are you doing here?" Belatedly she realized she was clad only in a cotton nightgown. She crossed her arms over her chest. "It's late."

"I know, and I'm sorry. But I was driving by and saw your light on, and I wanted to talk to you." Unlike his last visit, Doug seemed content to stand in the hall. "I promise it won't take long."

Against her better judgment, Janie stepped back and motioned him in. After she closed the door, she gestured to the sofa. "Have a seat. I'll be right back." She hurried into the bedroom, returning clad in her robe.

He looked uncomfortable on the sofa, sitting on the edge with his hands hanging off his knees. At Janie's return, he looked at his feet. "I saw your friend tonight."

"Sam?" Janie sat on the chair opposite, placing as much distance between them as possible. "Is she okay?"

"I guess." He raised his head and looked her in the eyes. "I met her out behind the bar." He seemed genuinely sad. "What do you see in her?"

The question sparked a nervous fear in the pit of Janie's stomach. Could he read her mind? "What do you mean? We barely know each other."

"That's what she told me, too. But I didn't believe her." He stood and began to pace. "Is she the reason you don't want to see me anymore?"

"Of course not," Janie vehemently denied. "I think you know things were getting bad between us for a long time."

Doug rubbed his knuckles, seemingly not listening. "I've seen them on television and the movies, but never thought to see one here." He continued to walk back and forth across the room.

The more the agitated Doug paced around the room, the more nervous Janie became. "Please sit down, Doug. You said you came here to talk?"

He scratched the top of his head but did as she asked. "I thought you loved me."

Did she? Janie looked into her heart. "I cared for you, Doug. But I honestly don't think I ever loved you. At least not like I should have."

"We had some good times, though, didn't we?"

"Yes, we did. At least in the beginning." Janie became more comfortable with the conversation when she realized he was sober. "But things deteriorated after we started sleeping together."

Doug sighed. "I thought you wanted it."

"You never asked."

"Yeah, but after New Year's —"

Janie adjusted the folds of her robe. "I don't remember much about that night." It still bothered her, waking up beside him with no memory.

"To tell you the truth, neither do I," he admitted. "But you never said anything, so I thought you were okay with it."

"I know, and that's my fault. I thought it would be easier to go along than to fight about it." She felt guilty about leading him on. "I should have never let it get that far."

He flopped against the back of the sofa. "We were going to get married."

"No, we weren't." Janie noticed the dejected set of his shoulders. "What's the big deal, Doug? It's not like you were faithful to me."

"You knew?"

She laughed ruefully. "In a town this size, *everyone* knew."

"I'm sorry." He sat up again and scooted to the edge of his seat. "I'm sorry for a lot of things, Janie. That's what I came here to say." Doug got to his feet and knelt in front of her. "I was a rotten bastard, and I hope you can find it in your heart to forgive me someday." He raised one of her hands and kissed it. "I did care for you." He stood and gave her a sad little smile. "See you around."

Janie stared at the closed door long after Doug left. Just when she thought she had people figured out, something like this came out of the blue. She'd have to ask Sam tomorrow about what he had said to her.

Chapter
Eleven

THE ANNOYING RING of her cell phone woke Janie from a sound sleep. She peered blearily at her alarm clock and wondered who was calling her at seven-thirty in the morning. She flipped the phone open as she sat up in bed. "Hello?"

"Miss Clarke? This is Helen at Spring Gardens."

The woman's words jolted Janie into full wakefulness. "Is it my grandmother? Is she okay? What's wrong?"

"She's fine, physically. But we're worried about her emotional well-being."

Janie was tempted to crawl through the phone and shake the woman, unless she began to give better answers. "Could you please tell me why you called?"

The woman became snippy. "Of course. As I was trying to say, there was a bit of trouble last night—"

"Oh, god."

"Please, Miss Clarke. If you'll allow me to continue." The woman sighed dramatically. "Mr. Clarke came by to see her last night, and—"

"Harvey? What did he want?" Janie swung her legs over the side of the bed and put her feet into her slippers. She had a feeling she was going to need a pot of coffee to get through the day.

"I'm not certain, and Mrs. Clarke wouldn't say. But they had quite an argument. Even the residents in the media room heard them."

Janie filled the coffee maker with water. "Dammit. He never visits unless he wants something. Are you sure she's all right?"

"She wasn't harmed, if that's what you mean. But after he left, she stayed in her room and didn't come out for dinner. She won't speak to anyone, and hasn't joined us for breakfast, either. And she missed bingo last night." The woman's tone told of her worry. Lucille was one of the most social of their residents, and never missed an activity.

"I'll be there in half an hour. Thanks for calling." Janie closed her phone and stared at the coffee pot, which now percolated noisily. With her grandmother's well being at the forefront of her mind, she completely forgot about contacting Sam.

Within twenty minutes Janie was showered, dressed, and on her way to Spring Gardens. Her mind whirled. She couldn't figure out why Harvey had gone to visit her grandmother. He never bothered sending her a card on her birthday, and holidays were no different. She wondered if he'd found out about his mother's "nest egg". Lucille paid her own way at the home. She wasn't wealthy, but due to smart investments, she had been able to stretch her husband's insurance benefits for years.

After parking, Janie took her usual path down the hallway, only to find her grandmother's door closed. With a frown, Janie tapped on the door. When there was no answer, she knocked louder.

"Go 'way! How many times do I have to tell you busybodies to leave me alone?" Lucille's voice rang out quite clearly. She sounded perturbed, but otherwise fine.

Janie ignored her and opened the door slowly. She noticed her grandmother staring out the window. "Nana?"

The mechanical whine of the chair echoed in the room as Lucille spun around. "Janie. I didn't want them to bother you." She met Janie halfway and embraced her.

"It's no bother, and you know it. The woman on the phone told me you had a pretty good fight with Harvey."

"To put it mildly." Lucille wheeled toward the bed and moved the brightly colored afghan blanket out of the way. "Might as well get comfortable, since you're here." She waited until Janie was settled before explaining the previous night's activities. "You've changed your hair. And got new glasses."

Feeling her face heat, Janie studied her lap. "Yes, on Saturday."

"You look wonderful. So, about yesterday. Your father demanded I talk some sense into you. He's under the notion you're going to die an old maid, and he'll be left alone in his doddering years." The twinkle returned to her eyes. "I told him, in no uncertain terms, that you could have a dozen children and he'd still be alone." She laughed at her own joke. "That's when he got all pissy and started yelling. I couldn't let him have *all* the fun, so I yelled back."

Janie rolled her eyes. She could only imagine the ruckus they caused. No wonder the nurse who called her was so upset. "If you enjoyed yourself so much, why are you hiding in your room?"

"I'm not hiding. I was tired of all these little snot-nosed do-gooders fawning all over me. I figured if I laid low for a while, they'd go back to pestering someone else."

"Okay." Janie picked at the afghan. "If Harvey's so worried about me, why did he talk to you?"

"I asked him that very same thing."

"And?"

Lucille wagged her finger at Janie. "Don't get sassy. He seems to think I'd, and I quote, 'talk some sense into you'. Like you don't have a brain of your own."

The last thing Janie wanted was her grandmother in the middle of her ongoing feud with Harvey. "As much as I hate to admit it, he does have a point. You're one of the few people I trust anymore." She began to gnaw on a fingernail, but stopped when Lucille snapped her fingers at her. The bad childhood habit always reappeared when she was nervous. "But nothing anyone can say will make me go back to Doug."

"He hurt you that badly?"

Janie wasn't going to tell her about the night Doug came to her apartment and attacked her. It was in the past, and all it would do was upset Lucille. "No, he didn't hurt me. I finally realized we were only together to keep our fathers happy. I never loved him."

"So you've told me before." Lucille's tone changed from concerned to curious. "How's it going with your new friend?"

A blush heated Janie's skin. "Her name's Sam." She looked into her grandmother's eyes. "We've become pretty good friends."

Janie thought her grandmother seemed momentarily uncomfortable, but dismissed it when her Nana's voice still sounded upbeat. "That's wonderful. Tell me more about her. Last time you were here, all you did was describe what she looked like."

"Well, she's very sweet. As a matter of fact, she's helping Betsy at the gym when she's not singing at the bar."

"Betsy?"

Janie nodded enthusiastically. "Yes. She's probably old enough to be Sam's mother, and she's really nice. They're starting aerobics classes next week, and I'm going to join."

"Really?"

"I can't wait. A couple of women from work will be there also. I think it's going to be a lot of fun."

"Will Sam be running the class?"

Janie snorted in laughter.

"What?"

Janie had a hard time picturing her friend in workout leotards. "Nana, I don't think Sam is the aerobics kind. She came over for dinner the other night, and we had a really nice time. But when Doug showed up, I thought things were going to get nasty."

"What happened? Did they get into a fight?"

"No, but I was afraid they would. Doug was really obnoxious, but Sam didn't let him goad her into anything." Visions of ending the evening together on the sofa passed through Janie's mind. "And afterward, well, it all worked out."

Lucille rested her hand on Janie's knee. "I'm glad. She sounds like a very good friend."

"She is." Janie suddenly remembered what she originally planned for the day. "I was going to see about cooking her lunch today."

"Shouldn't you be at work?"

Janie shook her head. "I worked late last night, so Dr. Richmond gave me today off." She squeezed her grandmother's hand. "Would you like to come home with me for the day? I'd love for you to meet Sam."

"No, not today. I've got to try to smooth things over with the staff, or they'll tiptoe around me all week. Maybe another time."

"All right." Janie stood and kissed her on the cheek. "I'll hold you to it."

JANIE WAS ON her way to find Sam when her cell phone rang. She glanced at the readout and wasn't surprised to hear Andrea's voice, realizing the opportunity for a day off was too good to be true.

Andrea sounded frantic. "Jane, thank god. Where are you?"

It was amazing to Janie that when it counted, Andrea had no trouble remembering her name. "I'm in my car. Why?"

"The shit has really hit the fan around here. We can't find the records you were supposed to enter yesterday."

"Of course you couldn't find them. The computers were down all day, remember?" Janie stopped at a red light and drummed her fingertips on the steering wheel.

"Yes, I remember. But you were here all evening. What were you doing?"

Janie sighed. "I was waiting for the computers to come back up."

"Did it take all night?" Andrea's voice turned sly. "Or were you enjoying Dr. Richmond's company?"

"He's married, for god's sake." Janie wanted to strangle the annoying woman.

Andrea giggled. "Like *that* matters. Are you coming to work today?"

"No. Dr. Richmond gave me the day off."

"And you said nothing happened," Andrea teased.

Slowly losing patience, Janie ground out her next words. "That's exactly what I said, Andrea."

"Well, that's not fair. I'm not about to enter all these files by myself."

"You don't have to. Leave them and I'll take care of them tomorrow." Once the light was green, Janie started through it. She couldn't believe how childish Andrea was being. "I've got to go." She hung up the phone and tossed it on the seat beside her. "Of all the stupid—" she had to swerve as a car tried to back out of a parking space in front of her. "Watch it, jerk!"

She'd barely made it a block before the phone rang again. Flipping it open, she growled, "What?"

"Oh, I'm sorry," Sam apologized quietly. "I didn't mean to bother you." She hung up the phone, much to Janie's dismay.

Janie cursed and checked the log on the phone. Sam had called from Danny's, so at least now she knew where Sam was.

Within minutes, Janie wheeled into a parking space not far from the bar's entrance. It was still too early for them to be open, but she tried the handle anyway. It was locked. She rattled the knob in irritation. "Dammit! Won't one thing go right today?" Not to be deterred, she went to the back of the building and rapped on the delivery door.

It seemed like forever before the door opened and Ray appeared. "Can I help you?"

"I'm looking for Sam. She called from here a few minutes ago."

"Oh, yeah. She left."

Janie felt like crying. "Do you know where she went?"

"Nope. She didn't say."

"If you happen to talk to her or see her, could you please ask her to call Janie again? It's important."

Ray shrugged. "Yeah, sure." He closed the door.

Staring at the cracked wood, Janie felt like kicking the door in frustration. She turned and noticed Sam's car parked nearby. She walked over and looked inside, finding it empty. "So much for that idea."

Determined to find Sam, she went back to her own car. She decided to try the gym. It took her less than five minutes to get there. She parked illegally out front and hurried inside.

Betsy was at the counter. "Well, hello there."

Janie flashed her a fond smile. "Hi. Is Sam around?"

"No, I haven't seen her. I thought she was at Danny's." Betsy came out from behind the counter.

"I came from the bar, and she's not there, either." Tears of frustration welled in Janie's eyes but didn't fall. "Do you have any idea where she might be?"

"I'm sorry, no. What's the matter?"

Janie lowered her eyes in shame. "I thought she was someone else when she called and I snapped at her. She hung up before I could apologize." She raised her head. "Please, if you see her, let her know I'm trying to find her."

"Sure, no problem. Hey, it's about lunchtime. Want to go upstairs with me? I was going to have a sandwich."

"No, I can't." Janie was flustered. "I really have to find Sam."

Betsy gave Janie a much-needed hug. "You do that. I'll have her call you if she comes in."

"Thanks." Janie turned and left as quickly as she came.

Refusing to give up, Janie continued to search for Sam. "Where are you?" Her phone rang and she quickly answered it. "Sam?"

"No, this is Andrea." She paused. "Who's Sam?"

"Never mind. What do you want?"

"Jane, we need you to come in. Dr. Retzburg is on a tear and we've got to get the files in order ASAP."

Janie exhaled heavily. "I can't. I'm not dressed for work, and I have some other things to take care of."

"I don't care how you're dressed. This is an emergency," Andrea stressed.

"Fine. I'll be there in ten minutes." Janie wanted to pound her head on the steering wheel in frustration. Things were not going her way.

SAM HAD FOUND the darkest, quietest corner of the library and was trying to read the newspaper to take her mind off Janie. She didn't know what she did to incur Janie's wrath and her heart crumbled at the thought.

She was afraid something like this would happen. Especially when she hadn't heard from Janie since Monday afternoon. Trying to be friends was one thing, but wanting something more was pure foolishness. To get more comfortable, she pulled her knees up to her chest and wrapped her arms around her legs. She angrily wiped a tear from her cheek.

The newspaper fell to the floor, its pages fanning out beneath her chair. Sam propped her chin on her knees and stared into space. She couldn't figure out what exactly went wrong. Everything seemed fine when Janie left the gym after lunch.

Her eyes closed and she fought off the urge to cry. This was precisely the reason she never got too close to anyone, never stayed in one place very long. It hurt too much. The last meaningful relationship she had was four years ago in Austin. She thought she'd found a kindred spirit. Nora was a grad student she'd met in a bar near the university and they'd hit it off immediately. She'd spent almost six months with her, so sure in the relationship she'd considered finding a permanent job and residence. But Nora's girlfriend, whom she'd forgotten to mention, returned from a year's studying in California. Nora dumped Sam without so much as an apology or goodbye, and Sam took the fastest highway out of the capital city.

Now, here she was, in almost the same situation. At least she and Janie hadn't gotten physical, other than the one night of cuddling. The thought made more tears run down her cheeks. The loss of Janie as a friend hurt more than anything.

Sam's watch beeped and she glanced at the time. She needed to get back to the bar and ready things for the evening. With a heavy heart, she gathered up the scattered newspaper and left the library.

JANIE'S AFTERNOON DIDN'T go any better than her morning. After she arrived at work, she was inundated with file requests. Many of the files had been lost when the computer crashed, so she spent the majority of her day re-entering the data. It was almost five-thirty when Dr. Richmond came by her desk.

"Janie? I thought you were taking today off?" He noticed the large pile of folders stacked in her out-box.

"I was. But Andrea called me. She was going nuts, screaming about lost histories and demanding doctors. I thought it would be easier to come in today and get a start on things."

He loosened his tie. "She does have a tendency to panic at the drop of a hat," he agreed. "But it's past quitting time, so find a stopping place and go home. The paperwork won't go anywhere."

"I will."

Fifteen minutes later, she followed his advice. Her car was one of the last in the parking lot so it wasn't hard to find. Before she could drive off, her cell rang. She quickly snatched it up, hoping it was Sam. "Hello?"

"Hey, girl. What are you doing tonight?" Sandra sounded well on her way to being drunk, and it wasn't even six o'clock.

"I'm leaving work, why?"

The phone was muffled and Sandra could be heard saying something to someone else. She was soon back, giggling. "Meet me at the bar. I have someone you've *got* to meet."

Janie wasn't in the mood to socialize. All she wanted was to find Sam, but maybe she could do both. "Which bar?"

"The one you like to hang out at." Sandra lowered her tone. "You know, the one with the *lesbian* singer."

"Okay. I'll be there in a couple of minutes. But you have to buy the first round."

Sandra giggled again. "I already have. And the second, and the third, and the —"

"I get the point. Bye." Janie closed her phone. She was glad she hadn't changed from her casual clothes to go to work. The navy cotton slacks and matching short-sleeved blouse were more comfortable for an evening out.

The closest parking space was a block away. Janie grumbled as she got out of her car, thinking she might as well have gone home and walked. Once inside she had no trouble finding Sandra.

The blonde was at a table close to the piano, and she wasn't alone. Her laughter could be heard over Sam's singing. "Play something happier, will you? This shit is boring," she yelled, laughing at something her companion said.

Janie walked to the table and sat in an empty chair. She tried to make eye contact with Sam, but the singer stared at the piano keys while she sang a depressing ballad.

"Janie! I'm so glad you're here," Sandra loudly exclaimed. "Whatcha drinking?"

"I think I'll get a coke." Janie started to stand, but the man sitting close to Sandra got to his feet first.

"I'll take care of it." He was tall, muscular and his dark hair and eyes went well with his deep tan. He held out his hand and waited until Janie took it. "I'm Terry Humphrey. Sandra's told me all about you, Janie."

"It's nice to meet you, Terry. Have you known Sandra long?"

He winked. "Long enough." Turning his attention to Sandra, he chucked her under the chin with his index finger. "How about you, babe? Want another?"

Janie interrupted Sandra's answer. "Maybe she'd be better off with a cup of coffee," she suggested.

Sandra waved her hands, one of which held a lit cigarette. The ashes scattered across the table. "Hell, no! We're celebrabating. Ain't we, Terry?"

"Sure are, sweet thing. Another beer coming up." He gave Janie a sly smile before going to the bar.

Once they were alone, Janie leaned across the table so she wouldn't be overheard. "Don't you think you've had enough? You can barely sit up."

"I'm fine." Sandra pointed toward the bar. "Isn't he cute?"

"I suppose. Where did you meet him?"

"Saturday, at the flea market." Sandra took a deep drag from her cigarette. "He was selling the saddles he makes. And god is he good in bed! Whew!" She fanned her face with her free hand. "I think he's the one."

The admission surprised Janie. She knew Sandra was a free spirit and fell in "like" at the drop of a hat, but she'd never heard her talk like this before. "How can you be sure? You haven't even known him a week."

"Honey, we haven't been apart since we met. He's perfect." She grinned lasciviously. "And he's hung like a stallion."

"Sandra!" Janie looked around. "I can't believe you said that."

Terry returned and placed the drinks on the table. "Here you go, ladies." He swung his leg over his chair and sat. When Sam started another sad number, he yelled to voice his displeasure. "Come on! We're trying to party here," he yelled.

Sam looked up long enough to see Janie at the table. Her voice faltered, but she quickly found her place and continued.

Sandra didn't want to feel left out. "Yeah, what he said. We want some dancing music!" Her voice carried clearly over the piano.

Ashamed and embarrassed, Janie could do nothing but sit idly by while her companions heckled Sam. She could feel the eyes of the other patrons on them and tapped Sandra's arms to quiet her.

"Hey, butch! The ladies want some decent music," Terry added.

Sam jabbed the keys on the final notes and stood. "I'm done." She fled the room, ignoring the requests that rang out behind her.

Janie had heard enough. "You two deserve each other." She grabbed her purse and got up from the table. She didn't know who she was more upset with—Sandra and her boyfriend, or herself. She knew she should have said something while they harassed Sam. She only hoped she could catch up to her and explain.

Someone else watched Janie leave and decided to follow. He made sure no one noticed as he slipped out behind her.

Once outside, Janie heard a scuffling in the alley and followed the sound. "Sam?" When she saw Sam rest her arms onto the roof of the car and lay her head down, Janie moved closer. She touched Sam's shoulder and turned her around. The tears on the other woman's face broke her heart. "I'm so sorry."

"Don't be." Sam tried to pull away. "It's pretty much what I expected."

"What do you mean?"

Sam broke free and leaned her hip against the car. "I thought we were friends. But you're worse than the rest of them. At least they have the guts to be jerks to my face."

"No, it's—"

"You have no idea what you do to me, do you? Sometimes you act as if I have the plague, and other times," she ran her hand through her hair, trying to think of how to put her feelings into words. "Other times you seem to be attracted to me. These mixed signals are driving me nuts."

"What do you want from me?" Janie paced back and forth, the glare of the nearby light pole casting her shadow against the car. "I'm not like you. I have to live here."

Sam pushed off from where she had stood against the fender. She wanted to grab Janie and shake some sense into her. "You don't *have* to do anything you don't want to. These people don't own you."

"That's where you're wrong."

"I don't need this. You've obviously changed your mind about being friends. Again." With a heavy sigh, Sam turned and started to walk to the other side of the car. Janie's hand on her arm stopped her. "What?"

"Don't leave me." Janie tightened her grip. "Please." When Sam's eyes locked with hers, she felt lightheaded from an overpowering emotion. "In such a short time you've brought more into my life than I could ever imagine. I don't know what will happen to me if you go."

The plea melted something in Sam's heart. There was no way she'd be able to walk away from the feeling that being in Janie's presence evoked. But she was too proud to be pulled back and forth. "Do you want a relationship with me?"

"I...I'm not sure. I mean, I know I feel *something* for you. My god, Sam. I can't even close my eyes without seeing you." Janie tugged on Sam's arm to bring her closer. "But I've been taught all my life that what I'm feeling for you is wrong. It's hard to reverse that kind of thinking." Her eyes darted around to make certain they were alone in the alley. "Please be patient with me."

"Believe it or not, this is new to me, too." Sam pulled Janie into her arms and kissed the side of her head. "I'd wait for you forever, if I knew I had a chance."

Janie's arms tightened around Sam's waist. "You have more than a chance. I do care about you. It's just hard."

Sam had heard the same excuses before from other women. She

hoped it was different this time. Tears of frustration fell from her eyes.

"Oh, honey." Janie cupped Sam's face in her hands and tenderly wiped the tears away with her thumbs. Her heart broke at the pain she caused.

The light touch on her face felt so good, Sam couldn't help but lean into it and close her eyes. Soft breath against her skin, followed by the slightest touch of Janie's lips against hers, surprised Sam so much she almost fell. When a tongue tentatively touched her lower lip, Sam moaned. She opened her mouth and staggered against the car when their tongues danced together for the first time.

Janie's eyes grew large as she realized what she had done. She stumbled away back several steps. "Oh, my god. I can't believe I did that." She looked around nervously. "I shouldn't have—"

"Why not? There's nothing wrong with a simple kiss." Sam moved toward her. "I certainly don't regret it."

"No." Janie held her hands out in front of her. "This is wrong." She turned and ran out of the alley, leaving a confused Sam behind.

In the shadows, a hidden figure gripped the lid of the trash can he hid behind. He could feel the metal bending beneath his fingers.

Chapter
Twelve

IT TOOK HALF an hour for Sam to come back to her senses after Janie left. She shook her head to clear it and returned to the bar. After a wave to Ray, she headed toward the back room, pointedly ignoring Sandra's table.

Ray followed her into the kitchen. "Hey, you all right?"

"Yeah." Sam started the hot water into one of the deep, stainless steel sinks. "Sorry about running out on you like that." Once the sink was filled to her satisfaction, she filled the other with hot water as well. In one sink she added soap, the other a disinfectant solution.

"No problem. You lasted longer than I would have." He looked over his shoulder at the main room, making sure no one went behind the bar. "It's getting close to the end of summer, so I've decided to start closing up earlier during the week."

Sam dipped her hands into the steaming water, not reacting to the heat. "Sounds like a good idea to me. There's never many after ten, anyway."

"True." Ray leaned against the doorframe and crossed his arms over his chest. "Listen, I've been thinking. You told me the other day you were going to stick around for a while, right?"

"Uh-huh." Sam concentrated on the dishwater.

"Ever since you started singing, you've brought in more business, and I really appreciate it. I also appreciate you helping out around here."

She shrugged. "Part of the deal, remember?"

"Yeah, well. What I'm trying to say is I'd like to make it more official. Why don't you stay after closing and fill out the paperwork? You'd get a steady check, plus all your tips."

Sam finally turned to look at him. "You want me to work here full-time? As an employee?"

Ray grinned. "Why not? You're already doing more than Fred, and he's been here for five years. What do you say?"

"Do I get to wear one of those snazzy things?" she asked half-joking, referring to the dark blue tee shirt which bore the bar's name over the left breast. The thought of finally belonging somewhere intrigued her. It would also supplement the small income she was getting from Betsy. Although the papers had been signed to make her a manager in the gym, she still refused to take much money from the older woman.

"Of course."

Sam wiped her hands on a towel and came over to shake his hand. "Sounds great. I might even quit sleeping in my car." The running joke between the two of them was friendly, but she knew he was concerned about her welfare. It was one of the reasons she was glad she had a room above the gym.

"Even better." He tilted his head toward the bar. "Guess I'd better get back to work. The papers are on my desk in the office."

"Pretty sure of my answer, weren't you?"

"Yup." Ray jumped away when Sam tried to pop him with her towel. "Get them all filled out, and leave them on the desk."

Sam laughed and went back to the dishes. Now if she could get her personal life to fall into place things would be perfect.

JANIE WAS HALFWAY home when she remembered she'd driven to the bar. She wasn't quite ready to face Sam again so she continued on her way. Her mind wouldn't give her any peace as she kept going over and over what happened in the alley.

They'd kissed. Or, more truthfully, *she'd* kissed Sam. She hurried up the stairs to her apartment while the implications set in. The only consolation was that Sam looked as surprised as she had been. "What was I thinking?" Janie opened her door and went inside, tossing her keys on the table.

"I wasn't thinking. That's the problem." She went into the kitchen and took a bottle of light beer from the refrigerator. After taking several swallows, she walked mechanically into the living room and sat on the sofa. She fingered her lips and swore they still tingled from touching Sam's. "It was nice, though."

She kicked off her shoes and curled her feet beneath her. The only light in the room was from a floor lamp in the corner, which she kept on all the time. She was so shocked by what she'd done that she hadn't bothered to turn on any others.

Janie had no idea how long she sat there before she realized she was still holding the beer. Two-thirds full and now at room temperature, she scowled at the bottle and got up from the couch. Her joints were stiff from sitting for so long, and she limped to the kitchen to dispose of the drink.

After washing her hands, Janie returned to the living room and looked at the clock. It was close to eleven. She had the irrational urge to go back to the bar and talk to Sam. She also wanted to explain why she had been a no-show on Monday.

Her mind made up, she grabbed her purse and left the loft. It was a nice night, and the walk would allow her time to organize her thoughts.

WITHOUT SAM SINGING, the bar cleared out early, and Ray took the opportunity to lock up at ten. He told Sam he'd post a sign announcing the new hours.

Sam finished sweeping the floor and put the broom away. She double-checked the restrooms while Ray closed out the cash register. They both completed their tasks at the same time and met at the front door.

Ray took a spare key from his pocket. "Since you're an employee now, take this."

"I don't know." Sam hesitated. "That's a big responsibility."

"I trust you." He took her hand and placed the key on her palm, then closed her hand over it. "Besides, I know where you live," he teased.

Sam tucked the key into the front pocket of her jeans. "Thanks, Ray. Guess I'll see you tomorrow." She followed him out the front and waited while he locked the door.

Ray looked around the quiet streets. "You going to the gym tonight?"

"Yeah. I want to tell Betsy the good news. I'll even drive over there, if it'll keep you from worrying so much."

"It would, thanks." He clapped her on the shoulder. "See you in the morning, Sam."

Sam laughed at his protective streak and headed down the alley. She was almost into the light when a heavy weight slammed into her back and knocked her face down on the ground.

"You think you're so smart, don't you?" A menacing voice growled.

She tried to get up, but the firm foot between her shoulder blades didn't allow her to move. "What are you talking about?"

"Coming into town, acting like you own the place," the voice continued, seemingly not listening to her. "Flaunting your unnatural ways, not giving a damn who you bothered."

"I don't—" Sam's breath was cut off when the foot stomped hard.

"Shut up, bitch. It's high time someone taught you a lesson in manners."

The pressure eased, but before Sam could roll over, she was kicked in the ribs. Gasping for air, she made it onto her side. She wrapped her arms around her stomach in an effort to protect herself. "What—" Another kick brought tears to her eyes.

"I saw everything, you know." The assailant slammed his foot into her face, knocking her onto her back.

Sam struggled to see through the blood falling into her eyes. She could barely make out a shadow above her. "Why are you doing this?" she choked out.

"We don't need your kind here. Everything was fine until you came along." He picked her up by her shirt and punched her in the face. "You should have left her alone." His fist smashed into her twice more then he threw her to the ground. "You filthy whore. Maybe if you couldn't make any more money, you'd leave." He kicked her right arm away from her body and crushed her hand with all his weight. "Get the fuck out of town, because next time I see you, I'll kill you. And if you go to the cops, maybe I'll teach little Jane a few things, too."

Sam screamed at the blinding pain. She was unable to move as she was kicked again and again. His threats rang in her head as she mercifully lost consciousness.

JANIE TALKED TO herself as she walked, trying to come up with the right words. "Sam, I really like you." She groaned. "No. Too simple. Sam, I liked the kiss. No. Too forward." She kicked at a stone on the sidewalk. "Sam, I'd like to try and see where this could go. Good grief, how pathetic is that?"

A dark truck sped down the street, but Janie was too caught up in her private conversation to pay much attention. "Maybe I should start with an apology. Explain why I didn't come by to see her Monday evening, and tell her why I was so bitchy on the phone." She nodded. "Yes, that'll work." She noticed the parking spaces around the bar were empty as she walked up to the door.

It was locked, and no one answered when she knocked. "Well, that's great." She looked at her watch. It was a few minutes after eleven. Too early to close, at least she thought so. With a heavy sigh, she started down the alley to see if Sam was at her car.

Janie saw a form curled into a fetal position. Her heart caught in her throat and she ran the rest of the way. She fell to her knees next to the body. "Sam?" Cautiously she touched Sam's shoulder. "Hey."

Sam moaned in response. When Janie's hand closed around her upper arm, she tried to get away. "No." Her voice was rough and she gagged on the blood in her mouth.

"Shh. It's only me." Janie scooted to the other side of Sam in order to see her better. "Dear god. Who did this to you?" She dug into her purse and brought out a crumpled tissue. After only a couple of dabs, she could tell it was futile. There was too much blood. "I'm calling an ambulance."

"No," Sam pleaded. She struggled onto her back and cried out at the pain it caused.

Janie's hands were shaking as she reached for her. "You need medical attention. I don't—"

Sam cradled her right hand against her chest. "No money."

"Honey, they have to treat you." Janie noticed Sam's hand. It was scraped and misshapen. "Oh, no." She could tell it was broken, and she wondered how Sam would be able to support herself if she couldn't play the piano, or any of the other odd jobs she did around town.

Sam tried to sit up. "Gotta get out of here."

"You're not going anywhere, except to a doctor." Even as she argued, Janie helped Sam upright.

"Can't. He'll find me." Sam coughed and spit a mouthful of blood to the side. "Shit."

Janie heard the fear in Sam's voice. "Who? Do you know who did this?"

Sam shook her head, closing her eyes at the pain the movement caused. "Couldn't see, too dark." She paused to catch her breath. As much as her swollen eyes would allow, she looked into Janie's face. "He saw us."

"Saw us? What do you—" The realization slapped Janie in the face like a physical blow. "He saw me kiss you? Is that why he did this?"

"Yeah, I think so." Almost in slow motion, Sam got to her knees. "Jesus." She bent forward with her arms around her torso. "Fuck, that hurts," she ground out.

Janie eased her arm around Sam's back. "Stay still. You could be bleeding internally." When Sam struggled, she held her close. "Stop, please. If you won't go to the hospital, at least let me take you home. I don't want you to be alone."

"Not safe." But even as she spoke, Sam leaned against her. She was quickly losing the energy to argue.

"You're coming with me, and that's final. Will you be okay here while I run get my car?"

"Yeah." Sam allowed Janie to help her lie back on the ground. Her eyes closed, but the tension never left her features.

Janie stroked her cheek before getting up. "I'll be right back." Her footsteps echoed in the darkness as she ran.

In less than a minute, Janie maneuvered her car through the alley. She parked as close to Sam as she dared, letting it idle while she hurried around and opened the passenger door. She knelt beside the injured woman. "Sam? Hey, come on. Let's get you out of here."

Sam gritted her teeth as Janie helped her rise to a sitting position. The pain was making her nauseous and she fought off a wave of vertigo as she struggled to her knees. "Fuck."

"Dammit, Sam. Let me call an ambulance." Janie staggered under Sam's weight as she helped her into the car. "This is ridiculous."

Remembering her assailant's threats, Sam shook her head. "No." She winced as the movement brought renewed agony to her battered body. "Drop me off at Betsy's. I'll be fine."

Janie buckled Sam's seatbelt and climbed behind the steering wheel. She slammed the car into reverse, grumbling under her breath. The gravel clattered beneath the wheels and she hurriedly backed from the alley. She slipped the car into gear and headed down the deserted street.

Less than a block away, Janie stopped at a traffic light. She took the opportunity to check on Sam, who was slumped against the door. She seemed to struggle for every breath, which frightened Janie. She made a quick u-turn toward the hospital.

Sam turned her head away from the window. "This isn't the way to the gym."

"I'm taking you to the hospital." Janie stopped at the red light. She tapped her fingers on the steering wheel, anxious to be under way once again.

"No!" Sam opened the car door. "I can't go to the hospital," she gasped, almost falling out of the car.

"Sam!" Janie shoved the car into park and hurried around to the other side. She carefully lifted Sam back into the seat and closed the door. Once she was also buckled in, she turned to face Sam. "You need medical attention. Please let me take you to the emergency room."

Tears leaked from Sam's swollen eyes as she held her injured hand against her chest. "No, please. I can't."

Her empathy overruling her good sense, Janie turned right at the next street. "It's going to be all right. No hospital, I promise."

SAM WOKE AND struggled to see through the slits her eyes had become. The room was dark and unfamiliar. She wondered where she was, before her senses came back and she remembered the earlier events. The only light came from a nearby doorway, and from what she could see, the bedroom was tastefully decorated. The bed was firm although the pillow top mattress kept it from being uncomfortable. Opposite the bed was a light oak entertainment unit, which housed a television and several additional components. Framed prints adorned the walls as well as personal pictures scattered about the room. On the nightstand was a single lamp and alarm clock. She tried to sit up but pain caused her to cry out.

"Hey, stay still." Janie came out of the bathroom carrying a small basin. She cautiously sat on the side of the bed and placed a damp cloth across Sam's brow. "How are you feeling?"

"Been better." Sam closed her eyes again at the light touch. "What time is it?"

"Around three in the morning." Janie's hand stilled when Sam winced as the cloth touched a scrape on her left cheekbone. "Sorry."

"How did I get here?"

Janie wiped at Sam's face. She'd cleaned it earlier, but it was something to do to keep her hands busy. "You don't remember?"

"No."

"I got you into my car and brought you." Janie dabbed at a gash on Sam's cheek that still slowly oozed blood. "Climbing the stairs was a little tough, though." Her back still ached from having to bear most of Sam's weight. She was heavier than she looked.

"I can't stay here."

"You're not going anywhere."

"It's not safe," Sam argued. She tried to raise her hand, but found it wrapped in a towel. "What—"

"I think it's broken." Janie didn't need to be a doctor to know that much. "I wish you'd let me take you to the hospital."

"Can't."

Janie sighed. "I'm sure they'll let us work something out financially. I have some money saved—"

"No!" Sam coughed, which caused waves of pain across her head and body.

"You are so damned stubborn." Janie hadn't given up, but she had another idea. If Sam wouldn't go to the doctor, she'd have one come to her. "I'm going to get you something to drink." She left the cloth on Sam's forehead before leaving the room. Janie grabbed her cell from her purse and went into the kitchen. A quick scroll through her phone numbers and she found what she was looking for. She only hoped it wouldn't backfire on her.

The phone rang twice before being answered by a sleepy voice. "Hello?"

"Ted? I'm terribly sorry for bothering you at this hour, but I could really use your help."

"Are you all right, Janie?" Another voice could be heard in the background. "I don't know, Sharon. Hold on." He spoke to Janie. "Are you in trouble?"

Janie looked toward her bedroom. "Not me, but a friend. She's been beaten pretty badly, and I've got her at my house."

"Why at your house? If she's injured, she should be in the emergency room."

"I've tried. But she's scared the man who did this will find her."

He could be heard getting dressed. "Have you called the police?"

"No, she wouldn't let me do that, either."

"Is she a criminal?"

Janie felt insulted at the question. "Of course not. She's new in town and doesn't trust many people."

Ted said something else to his wife then returned to the conversation. "I'll be there in ten minutes."

"Thank you." Janie shut her phone and paced around the kitchen. She was afraid of what Sam might say once Ted showed up. What if she told him Janie kissed her? What would he think of Janie then? She quickly poured a glass of water from the container she kept in the refrigerator and took it to the bedroom. She'd worry about Ted once he got there.

TWO HOURS LATER, Dr. Richmond stepped out of Janie's bedroom, carrying a small valise. He met Janie in the living room, where he'd banished her after he arrived.

"How is she?"

"Resting. I gave her some pretty strong stuff for the pain." Ted sat on the end of the sofa. "You're right. She's extremely stubborn."

Janie hovered nearby, torn between talking to him and checking on Sam. "But will she be all right?"

"She should be, barring any unforeseen complications. Her hand is a mess. From what I can tell, two of her ribs are at least bruised. I put four stitches in her cheek, and three more over her eye. Although it's swollen, I don't believe her nose is actually broken. I know you said she was beaten, but why? She wouldn't say." He patted the couch. "Come on. I can tell you're about to drop."

She did as he asked, but stayed perched on the edge of her seat. Janie trusted Ted, but was still afraid of him knowing the truth. "She was jumped behind Danny's after she got off work."

"Was it because she's gay?"

Janie almost fell off the couch. "How did you know?"

Ted sighed. "I may live in a small town, but I'm not naïve. This has hate-crime written all over it. You should call the authorities."

"And tell them what? That someone took offense to a lesbian living in Piperton? Just what do you think they'd do about it? I'm sure a lot of them feel the same way." Janie's exhaustion only added to her disgust. She'd seen people she thought she knew show their true colors, and was ashamed to be associated with them. "I don't want her to go through any more pain, physical or emotional."

"You care for her." It was a statement, not a question.

Janie lowered her eyes. "She's my friend."

"Then she's very lucky." Ted stood and picked up his bag. "Bring her into the office tomorrow. I want to run some x-rays and put a cast on her hand. And keep an eye out for blood in her urine. She's got some nasty bruising on her back which concerns me."

"But—"

"Don't worry about the fees. She told me she'd pay me even though I told her I was here as a favor to you. So I agreed to let her work off any bills once she's back on her feet." He lowered his voice. "Although I'm sure we'll have a fight about the amount, I plan on keeping the charges to a minimum."

She followed him to the door. "Thank you so much for coming. I don't know what I would have done without you. And please apologize to Sharon for me. I'm going to owe you both for a very long time."

Ted took her hand in his. "No need. It gives me a chance to brag that I still make house calls. Don't worry about work, either. I'm sure they can survive without you for a few days."

Once he was gone, Janie dragged her living room chair into the bedroom and placed it next to the bed. She didn't want to leave Sam alone and sleeping on the bed was something she wasn't quite ready for.

SAM'S THRASHING ABOUT woke Janie at nine am. She was in the throes of a nightmare and Janie was afraid she would injure herself further. She kept talking in soothing tones until Sam settled down again.

Now fully awake, Janie went into the bathroom to shower. She kept the door open to listen for Sam, and was drying off with a towel when she felt someone watching her.

Sam leaned against the door, clad only in her tee shirt and boxer shorts. She held her broken hand closely to her chest as she averted her eyes. "I'm sorry. I, um, have to go to the bathroom."

"No, it's okay." Janie fought down her embarrassment and hurriedly wrapped a towel around her body. "Do you need any help?"

"I think I can manage." Sam still couldn't look at her. The image of Janie's wet, naked body was seared into her mind forever. "I can wait until you get dressed, though."

Janie took her robe from behind the door. She covered herself and tied it tightly. "No need." She put her arm around Sam's waist and helped her into the bathroom. "Call me when you're ready to come back to bed. No arguments."

"Yes, ma'am." Sam stayed against the bathroom sink until the door closed behind Janie. She came out five minutes later, sweating and weak. Before she took more than a step, Janie was beside her.

"I thought I told you —"

Sam struggled to catch her breath. "I wanted to do it myself." She allowed Janie to guide her to the bed. "Stupid, I know."

"I'm glad you agree with me." Janie fussed over her, trying to get the blankets straight. Once Sam was tucked in to her satisfaction, she took a good look at her. The bandage covering her cheek appeared clean, but what she could see of her eyes were glassy. Janie touched her forehead and wasn't surprised to feel heat. "You're burning up."

"Yeah. I don't feel too great." Sam started to relax until she remembered something. "I need to get out of here."

"Why? Are you afraid?"

Sam tried to keep her eyes open. "I'm scared shitless."

Janie felt like crying. In that sickening moment when she found Sam lying in the alley, she'd realized how much she meant to her. And now she wanted to leave. It wasn't fair. "I can't say that I blame you."

"No, you don't understand." Sam tried to sit up, but her trip to the bathroom had worn her out. She fell back to the bed with a pained gasp. "It's not about me. What if he decides to come after you next? I couldn't bear that."

"I've lived in this town my entire life. You said he talked about me, so I have to know him. No one I know would hurt me." Janie stroked Sam's cheek. "But maybe you'd be better off away from here."

Sam relaxed at the gentle touch. "Is that what you want? For me to leave?"

"No."

"Then I guess I'll stay. At least for now." Her eyes opened as far as they could and she tried to focus on Janie.

Janie leaned down and pressed her lips to Sam's, mindful of the bruising.

Once she moved away, Sam smiled as much as her split lip would allow. "You're not going to run off again, are you?"

"No. I'm through running." Janie meant it in more ways than one.

DOUG RUBBED HIS eyes with one hand as he walked into the shop. He'd overslept, and hoped he wouldn't run into his father this morning. The last thing he wanted to do was fight about Janie, and Reggie wouldn't let the subject drop. He headed toward his office and was relieved when he saw that the room was empty. With a wide yawn, he set the Styrofoam coffee cup on the desk and dropped heavily into his chair. While sipping his coffee, Doug flipped through the spiral notebook he used to keep up with appointments.

Ten minutes later, Reggie shuffled into the room and plopped into his usual chair. Hung over from the previous evening, he snatched Doug's coffee and took a deep pull, choking from the taste. "Damn, boy. Got enough sugar in that?"

Doug looked up from his planner. "That's what you get for grabbing it." He leaned back in his chair and stretched his arms over his head. "You're dragging in later than usual."

"So? Didn't know I was punching a clock 'round here." Reggie coughed and reached into his shirt pocket for his cigarettes. He shook one out of the pack and lit it, inhaling with near reverence when the nicotine invaded his lungs.

His son scooted farther away from the desk and waved his hand in front of his face. "Do you have to do that in here?" When Reggie ignored him, Doug flipped on the air conditioner. "Ornery old fart." He glared at Reggie. "Hey, what did you do to your hands?"

Reggie left the cigarette hanging from his lips and looked at his hands. "I dunno. Probably skinned 'em up when I was working on that piece of shit mower you picked up." Doug paid next to nothing for non-working machines, then expected him to bring them back to life. He hated working for his son. "Cheap bastard," he grumbled under his breath.

"What?"

"Nothin'." Reggie got to his feet. "I got stuff to do."

Doug watched him leave. He rolled his eyes and went back to the notebook. If it wasn't for his mother, he'd have never hired the old man.

SAM GRIPPED THE arm of the wheelchair with her good hand. She hated feeling so weak. "This is completely unnecessary. I can walk."

"Too bad. Just sit there and enjoy the ride." Janie wheeled her through the back door of the medical clinic. It was shortly after noon, and only Dr. Richmond and Tammy, his nurse, were in the office. Everyone else had gone to lunch.

Tammy met them in the hall. She was around the same age as Ted and had been his nurse since the clinic had opened. "You poor thing." She took the chair away from Janie. "Let's get you checked out. Janie, Dr. Richmond says you're welcome to wait in his office."

"But I thought she'd stay with me," Sam argued, apprehensive about being around people she didn't know.

"You'll be fine, hon. I promise we won't do any surgery without your consent." When Sam stiffened, Tammy laughed. "Kidding." She winked at Janie before guiding Sam into an open door at the end of the hall.

Still peeved at what she perceived to be a snub, Janie huffed and headed for Dr. Richmond's office. She trusted him completely, but her concern for Sam overrode her other feelings.

His was a corner office, and had windows that looked out into the street on one side, and into the parking lot on another. Janie stared at the street, watching the cars and pedestrians go by. Her mind wandered while she waited. Now that she had acknowledged to herself her feelings for Sam, she wasn't sure what to do next.

In what seemed like hours but was less than one, Dr. Richmond returned to his office. He carried a folder and sat in one of his guest chairs. "Sit down, Janie."

She moved away from the window and perched on the edge of her chair. "How is she?"

"Sam's very lucky. Two of her ribs are cracked, but somehow she escaped internal injuries. She should heal fine."

Janie heaved a sigh of relief. "What about her hand?"

"I've set it, but I wanted her to have it checked by an orthopedic surgeon. She refused, which didn't surprise me."

"Will she be able to use it again? She plays the piano beautifully."

His eyes conveyed his understanding. "I hope so, but I can't make any guarantees."

"Thank you. I know this was all a bit unorthodox, but I was at a loss as to what to do. Where is she?"

"Tammy's helping her get dressed. Try to keep her still and quiet for a few days, if you can. Rest is the best thing for Sam right now." He stood and was surprised when Janie got up and gave him a hug. "Don't worry. She's in good physical shape, which will go a long way in her healing."

Janie released him and stepped back, embarrassed by her uncharacteristic actions. "I don't know how to thank you."

"You already have, several times. Does she have a place to stay?"

"No, not really. Well, she has been staying at the gym over on

Sycamore." Janie's eyes got wider and she covered her mouth with her hand. "Damn. I forgot about Betsy."

Ted took her arm and escorted her out of the office. "Is that her, um, girlfriend?"

"No, Betsy is the owner of the gym. She's old enough to be Sam's mother." Janie chuckled at what Betsy's reaction would be when she found out someone thought she was dating Sam. "I'd forgotten all about her. She's got to be frantic by now."

"Would you like to use the phone in my office to call her?"

Janie shook her head. "I'll use my cell. She'll recognize the number." She had her hand in her purse when Tammy came down the hall, pushing a quiet Sam in the wheelchair.

Tammy stopped near them. "Here you go." She tapped Sam lightly on the shoulder. "Now you behave and don't give Janie a hard time."

Sam was too exhausted to argue. She held out her good hand to Ted. "Thanks again, Doc. As soon as I can, I'll work out something with you, if that's okay."

He gingerly shook her hand. "Take your time. I'm not going anywhere." He gestured to the small paper bag that sat on her lap. "And take all your medicine, too. I'll see you in a week to remove your stitches."

With Tammy's help, Janie got Sam buckled into the passenger seat of her car and got away from the office before anyone saw them. She stopped at a light and took the opportunity to look at Sam. Her head rested against the seat and she appeared to be asleep. Although Ted had assured Janie to the contrary, she was worried for Sam. The light turned green and her cell phone rang. She fumbled in her purse, trying to answer before it woke Sam. "Hello?"

"Janie, this is Betsy. I'm sorry to bother you, but I'm trying to find Sam. Have you seen her?"

Janie kept her voice low. "I was going to call you when we got home. She's with me."

"Thank goodness. Like I said, I normally wouldn't have called, but Ray from the bar was looking for her."

"I'm sorry. I should have called sooner." Janie pulled into a parking lot so she could talk. "Something happened last night, and —"

"Oh, honey. You don't have to tell me a thing. You're both consenting adults." Betsy sounded embarrassed. "But you might tell Sam to contact Ray. I think he was expecting her this morning."

"You think, that we, I mean," Janie sputtered. "No, that's not it at all. Maybe it would be better to talk in person. We're about five minutes away. Could you meet us in the back?"

"Well, alrighty. I surely can."

Janie promised to explain everything once they were there and closed her phone. She wasn't looking forward to seeing Betsy, because she knew the older woman would be upset she hadn't been notified before now.

A short time later, Betsy didn't disappoint. They stood behind the gym, and Betsy fussed over Sam. They left her in the car while they talked, and it didn't take Sam any time at all to fall asleep again.

"I wish you would have called me, Janie. I would have been over there in a flash. It couldn't have been easy to take care of her alone. It must have been hell for you."

"You're right. It was one of the worst things I've ever been through. And I would have called you, if I hadn't been so focused on Sam. I'm sorry." Everything finally caught up to Janie and she began to cry.

Betsy pulled Janie to her. "There, there. You did a fine job. I wouldn't have been much help anyway, not with this bum back I've got." She rubbed Janie's shoulders and held her while she cried. "That's right. Let it out," she encouraged.

After getting it out of her system, Janie finally stepped back and wiped her face. "Thanks. It's been a rough day."

"Quite all right. I can see you're worn out. Why not help me get her up to her room? Then you can run home and get some rest."

"No, it's okay. I only wanted to come by and let you know what happened, and maybe pick up a few of Sam's things."

Betsy wouldn't be deterred. "Sam can stay with me. She's already got a room here, and I can get Pamela to help with the gym, so I can keep an eye on her."

"Well—"

"No, I insist. You have to work and I'll bet you haven't gotten any rest. And I'm sure your place is a bit small for two, right?"

Janie couldn't come up with one good reason why Sam shouldn't convalesce at Betsy's. But she could think of a million more why she wanted Sam with her. "No, actually it's fine. My boss has given me some time off, so it won't be a problem at all." And she couldn't stand the thought of not seeing Sam. She felt responsible for her injuries. If she hadn't kissed her, Sam would have never gotten hurt. Even if only to herself, she had to admit there was more to it. Sam was important to her.

They were both silent, each studying the other. Betsy had the look of someone who knew more than she was letting on. She finally glanced over Janie's shoulder at Sam, who was dozing in the front seat of her car. "Are you really okay with this?"

"More than okay. I promise to take good care of her."

"I know you will." Betsy gave her a hug. "I'll run upstairs and get a few of her things." She paused before going into the building. "You be sure and take care of you, too. And be careful. I don't trust whoever did this not to try something else."

Janie felt the same way. She'd be looking over her shoulder for a long time to come. But if they tried to hurt Sam again, they'd have a fight on their hands.

Chapter
Thirteen

FOR THE NEXT couple of days, Sam spent most of her time in bed. The medication Dr. Richmond gave her kept her too sleepy to do much else. She'd only wake long enough to eat, take more medicine and make the occasional trip to the bathroom. By Saturday, she was feeling more like herself.

Janie brought a glass of water into the bedroom. "You need to take your meds." She handed the drink to Sam, along with two pills. "Go on, I can see you're hurting."

"I'm tired of feeling drugged up all the time." Sam placed the tablets on the nightstand. She patted the bed. "Come on. I'll survive."

"I don't know. I have a lot of things to do, and —"

"And the world won't stop turning if you slow down and take a break. Even as doped up as I've been, I know you've been going non-stop for days." Sam held out her left hand. "Please?"

Janie took her hand and allowed herself to be tugged onto the edge of the bed. "You do look like you're feeling better."

Sam gave her a crooked smile. "Yeah, and I have you to thank for it." She rubbed the top of Janie's hand with her thumb. "If I haven't said it before, thank you. I don't know what would have happened if you hadn't come along." She brought Janie's hand up and kissed her knuckles.

Janie blushed and lowered her eyes. The feel of Sam's lips on her skin caused a pleasant tingle in the pit of her stomach. She pulled her hand free. "I've got some things I need to do."

"Wait, please. I need to know something. The other night, in the alley. Why did you kiss me?"

It wasn't a subject Janie wanted to delve into, especially sitting this close to Sam. "I don't know."

"That's not an answer."

Janie abruptly stood. "It's the only answer I have. Don't you think I haven't asked myself the same thing?" She took several steps back and crossed her arms over her body. "Don't you know I feel responsible for what happened to you? If I hadn't kissed you, you wouldn't be lying there right now."

"It's not your fault."

"Yes, it is. He saw us, saw me," Janie choked back a sob, "saw me kiss you. We both know it's what set him off."

Sam struggled to sit up. She held her broken hand against her stomach and swung her legs off the bed. "You were just faster. Believe me, I was about to do the same thing to you."

"You were?"

"Oh, yeah. I've wanted to kiss you for days." Sam got to her feet and walked slowly to Janie.

"You have?" Janie couldn't seem to form any coherent sentences, especially with the way Sam was looking at her. She stood frozen as Sam began to stroke her cheek with her fingertips.

"Mmm-hmm." Leaning closer, Sam brushed her lips against Janie's. For a moment, she was afraid she'd gone too far, until she felt Janie return the kiss. She put her left hand on Janie's hip and tugged until their bodies touched.

Janie moaned when Sam deepened the kiss, until she felt her nipples tighten in response. Horrified, she jerked away. "Oh, god."

Sam saw the panic in Janie's eyes. "Go ahead, take off again. Are you that afraid of being alone with me?"

"I'm not afraid." But even as she said it, Janie backed away. "I just remembered we needed a few things from the store."

"Yeah, right." Sam brushed her hand angrily through her hair, and sucked in a pained breath when she grazed a sore spot.

"Are you okay?"

"I'm fine. Just go." Sam stormed into the bathroom and slammed the door.

Janie was so mad she wanted to scream. Instead, she stomped into the living room and picked up her purse. "I'll be back soon," she yelled, before jerking the front door closed with as much strength as she could muster.

SHE KNEW THE car didn't deserve her ire, but Janie pounded the steering wheel anyway. "I've never met anyone who was so overly sensitive and cranky." She whacked the wheel again, startled when the horn blew. "Dammit!"

Before she had a chance to think about where she was going, Janie pulled in front of the gym. She considered leaving, but she needed someone to talk to. Maybe Betsy could help her sort through her feelings. She opened the door to the gym, and when Betsy turned to look at her, Janie almost changed her mind and left.

"Hello there. Come on in." Betsy stepped around the desk and gave the younger woman a hug. "How's Sam? She getting around more?"

Janie blushed, remembering just how well Sam was getting around. "Uh, yeah. She's doing better."

"Good. And how are you doing? Is something wrong?"

Wasn't that the million dollar question? Janie looked around at the women milling about. "Do you have a minute? I could really use a friendly ear."

"Certainly." Betsy kept her arm around Janie and led her toward the back. "Let's go into my office, so we can have some privacy." She closed the door behind them and motioned toward the sofa. "Make yourself comfortable. Do you want something to drink?"

"No, thank you." Janie sat on one end of the couch, while Betsy took the other. "I'm not sure why I'm here."

Betsy was silent, but her face wore a friendly expression.

"She's driving me crazy. One minute things are going along just fine, and the next we're fighting."

"What are you fighting about?"

Janie looked embarrassed. "It's kind of hard to say."

Betsy nodded knowingly. "Ah. I see."

"You do?"

"Sexual tension."

"Excuse me?" Janie squeaked. "S...s...sexual—" She couldn't finish.

"Tension. My lord, woman. When the two of you are together, it's so thick you could cut it with a knife."

Janie covered her face with her hands. "That's impossible. No."

"Oh, yes. Big time."

Could it be true? Janie knew she felt things. One touch from Sam and parts of her body came alive that she hadn't realized existed. "I'm scared, Betsy. I'm thirty-seven years old. Isn't it a little late to be feeling like this?"

"Like what?"

"When I'm around Sam I feel like an inexperienced kid. I kissed her," she blurted out.

If it surprised Betsy, she didn't show it. "Oh? When?"

"That night." Janie didn't need to elaborate on what night. "I'm the reason she got hurt. That man, the one who beat her, told Sam he saw us." She looked at her lap, where her fingers twined nervously. "She could have died because of me."

"No." Betsy covered Janie's hands with one of her own. "Some sick son of a bitch attacked Sam. We both know what kind of town this is. A woman like her was bound to stir someone up, sooner or later."

"But it was her friendship with me that drew attention to her."

Betsy chuckled. "Hon, have you looked at Sam? She draws plenty of attention to herself without anyone else's help." She squeezed Janie's hand. "Don't take the world's responsibilities on your shoulders. If bigots are intent on causing trouble, nothing anyone says or does will stop them."

"I still feel like she'd be better off if we weren't friends." Just saying the words brought a lump to Janie's throat. The mere thought of losing Sam make her feel sick.

"What does Sam say?"

"I don't know. We haven't really talked about it."

"Uh-huh." Betsy let go of her hand and leaned back. "Don't you think she should have a say in who she wants to be friends with? Why did you kiss her?"

"Um." Janie's face reddened. "I'm not sure."

"I think you are." Betsy's smile was gentle. "You'd feel better if you talked about it."

Janie sighed. "Maybe." She paused to sort out her thoughts. "I know this sounds crazy. But I feel like she understands me more than anyone ever has. She doesn't judge me, or try to force me to do things I don't want to. And she's so... I don't know how to explain it. Gallant, I think." Janie laughed at the thought that Sam was more chivalrous than the majority of the men in Piperton. "She's always treated me like I was special. And I don't think it's sexual. I mean, she doesn't act like she's being nice to me just to get me into bed."

"No, I can't see Sam playing games, especially sexual ones. Could *you* ever be interested in her that way?"

"I don't know." Janie decided to be truthful. "Actually, I do. Sometimes she just looks at me, or touches me, and my insides ignite." She blushed. "But I'm not sure I could ever do anything about it."

Betsy took Janie's hand again and looked into her eyes. "Well, you need to think long and hard about what you want from Sam. We both know that under that 'I don't give a damn attitude', she's extremely vulnerable. The last thing she needs is to become a failed experiment."

"I wouldn't do that to her," Janie promised. "She already means too much to me." Now all she had to do was decide if that was enough.

BORED, SAM SLOWLY wandered around the apartment. Her entire body ached, but she was tired of lying around in bed. Janie had been gone for over two hours, and Sam felt horrible for the way she'd acted toward her. Yes, she could feel something between them. And Janie *had* kissed her back. But could she lay her heart out again? The last time almost killed her emotionally. And she hadn't cared for Nora half as much as she already did for Janie.

She walked into the kitchen and peered into the refrigerator. Nothing appealed to her, so she went back to the living room and sat on the sofa. She spent almost two full minutes there before getting up to pace the room. She took the opportunity to look at the pictures scattered about. The one that intrigued her most was of Janie as a teen. She was wearing a graduation cap and gown, and stood between a man and a woman. The man wore a security uniform and stood with one arm gripped tightly around Janie's shoulders. The woman, Janie's grandmother, looked at her with love. But it was Janie's expression that bothered Sam. On what should have been a happy occasion, her eyes were dull and there was a resigned look on her face. Sam wished she could go back in time and bring a smile to the younger Janie's face. She realized what she was thinking and laughed at herself. She'd probably been ten or eleven at the time the photo was taken.

The rattling of the front doorknob caused Sam to turn away from the photo. Janie came in, juggling several grocery sacks. Sam hobbled toward her. "Let me help you."

Janie's head jerked up as she kicked the door closed. She seemed surprised to see Sam. "You're dressed?"

"As much as I can be." Sam winced as she took one of the bags from Janie. Her ribs didn't appreciate the effort, but she could tell Janie did. "Thanks for the sweats." It had taken her ten minutes to pull the gray pants on, but she hadn't felt comfortable walking around in her underwear, even though the boxers were more than adequate.

"You can thank Betsy for those. She hoped they wouldn't be too large." Janie hurried to the kitchen and placed the bags on the counter. "I meant to ask you, why do you wear men's underwear? Or is that none of my business?"

Sam started taking items from the sack and setting them on the counter. "No, it's okay. I only wear them because I sleep in my car so much. Boxers cover more than regular underwear."

"Oh. Right. That makes sense."

They worked together to put away the foodstuffs, and were soon back in the living room. Janie waited until Sam sat on one end of the sofa, before taking her own seat on the other end. "You look tired."

"Yeah, I guess I am, a little. I never knew getting clothes on would be such hard work." A dull pain throbbed between Sam's shoulder blades and she shifted to get more comfortable. The move made her ribs ache and she bit back a groan.

Janie saw the pain on Sam's face. "You need to go back to bed."

"Not yet."

"Sam —"

"I'm fine." Sam didn't want to argue with Janie again. "I'm sorry for this morning."

Janie scooted closer. "Me too." She took Sam's hand in hers. "I'm sorry I left in such a hurry. It wasn't you I was afraid of. It was me."

"What do you mean?"

"I'm feeling things for you I've never felt before, and it scares me."

"Why?" Sam squeezed Janie's hand in encouragement. "What kind of things?"

Janie lowered her eyes to their linked hands. "You know. *Things*." She sighed. "I've always thought there was something wrong with me. Doug did, too."

"What does he have to do with this?"

"He always said I was frigid, and I thought he was right. Sex never did anything for me." Janie took a shaky breath and raised her head. "But when you kiss me, I feel," she bit her lip. "Alive."

Sam felt a surge of hope at Janie's admission. "Then why are you scared?"

"Because I've always been told what was 'normal' and what was 'right'. And two women, well, that was always, most definitely *not* right."

"I see." Sam's heart shattered into a million pieces. She tried to keep it from showing on her face. "Can," she cleared her throat, "can we still be friends?"

"I hope so."

When Janie slid closer and cupped Sam's face with her hands, Sam's eyes grew wider and filled with tears.

"But I want more."

As Janie's lips pressed to hers, Sam tasted salty tears. Whose, she wasn't sure, because they were both crying. The tender kiss patched her wounded heart. Although painful, Sam pulled Janie into her lap as they continued to explore each other. Unable to breathe too deeply, she finally had to stop for air. "Damn," she wheezed, as Janie continued to cover her lips and face with gentle kisses. "You're good at that." Frigid was not a word she'd use to describe Janie. The passion she invoked left Sam trembling with desire. But her heavily beating heart caused her head to pound. "Baby, stop."

"Don't want to," Janie murmured, her lips trying to cover as much of Sam's neck as possible. "You taste so good."

The words shot a jolt of desire to Sam's stomach, and lower. "Janie, hold on. We can't." Her words were taken away as Janie claimed her mouth once more. For a moment, Sam didn't think about the consequences, until she moved wrong and a fierce pain knifed through her ribs. "Ow."

Janie froze. "Oh, honey. I forgot. I'm so sorry."

"It's okay. I'm fine." Sam closed her eyes for a moment and took several shallow breaths. "But I think we'd better slow down for a while."

"As much as I hate to admit it, I know you're right. Okay." Janie kissed the tip of Sam's nose. "For now." She rested her head against Sam's with a contented sigh, and both women quietly absorbed the new feelings that the contact brought.

BY TUESDAY, SAM came to the realization that she was going to have to leave the apartment. As much as she enjoyed spending time with Janie, she knew it was only a matter of time before their heavy make out sessions escalated into something more. Neither one of them was ready for such a step. She also feared the longer she stayed, the easier it would be for her assailant to find her. Sam's greatest concern was for Janie's safety.

The perfect opportunity to discuss their living arrangement came after lunch. Janie got into an argument with Andrea about when she'd be returning to work.

"No, as I've told you before, Dr. Richmond said I could take as long as I needed. I haven't used my vacation days for this year." Janie gave Sam an apologetic smile, before going to the bedroom to finish the call. She closed the door and raised her voice. "Look, Andrea. I really don't give a damn what you want. I'll be back at work when I'm ready, not a minute sooner." She pulled the phone away from her ear, even as the other woman continued to rave. "I'm hanging up now. Have a nice day." She disconnected the call and stuffed the cell into the back pocket of her jeans.

Sam raised her eyes from the magazine she had been reading when Janie came back into the room. "Everything all right?"

"Yes. Just the office manager being her usual charming self." Janie sat next to Sam on the sofa. "How are you doing?" She used the motion of moving Sam's bangs from her eyes to check for fever.

"I'm okay." Sam brushed Janie's hand away. "I'm doing a lot better. In fact, it would probably be a good idea for me to go back to Betsy's."

"Why? Don't you like it here?"

Sam held Janie's hand close to her chest. "That's not the point. You need to be able to sleep in your own bed so you can go back to work."

"I've been doing fine on the sofa." Janie pulled her hand back and stood. She crossed her arms over her chest. "Have I done something to upset you?"

"Of course not." Sam slowly got to her feet and reached for Janie, who backed away. "Hey." She continued to move toward the other woman, until Janie was standing against the wall by the kitchen. Sam cautiously touched Janie's cheek with her good hand. "I didn't mean to upset you, but I can't stay here indefinitely."

Janie leaned into the touch and closed her eyes. "I know, it's just that—" Her argument died when Sam's lips pressed against hers. She moaned and placed her hands on Sam's hips to draw her closer. When Sam started to nip the skin on her throat, Janie tipped her head back to allow her better access. Her body felt on fire, and she was barely aware of Sam unbuttoning her top. A warm hand squeezed her breast and she realized how far they'd gone. "Sam, wait."

"Janie—" Sam started to lift Janie's breast from her bra when she heard her. She blinked and stumbled back, fear and shame crossing her features. "Oh my god. I'm so sorry." She exhaled heavily and shook her head. "See? I can't control myself around you."

Closing her shirt, Janie couldn't help but smile. "I'm not complaining, Sam."

"I know. But this is exactly the reason why I should go. I don't think either one of us is ready to go any further right now." Her grin was sheepish. "God knows I want to, but—"

"It's okay." Janie laughed. "How about you sit and relax, and I'll get your stuff packed up."

BETSY WATCHED AS Janie fussed over Sam, who was lying on the bed in the guestroom. Sam looked totally disgusted as Janie raised the comforter and tucked it beneath her chin.

"I'm not an invalid, you know," Sam grumbled.

Janie smirked. "I know. But look me in the eye and tell me you don't love the attention." She leaned over and whispered in Sam's ear, "As for not being an invalid, that's why you're staying here now, remember?"

"Nice blush you're sporting there, kid," Betsy teased. "I think I'll give you two a little privacy. Janie, come into the kitchen when you're done." She closed the door, still chuckling.

Sam hooked her good hand behind Janie's neck and slowly pulled her closer. "It's going to be weird, not seeing you when I wake up." Their lips touched, and she responded enthusiastically when Janie deepened the kiss.

They spent a few minutes reconnecting, before Janie reluctantly pulled away. "I'll come by and see you after work tomorrow, I promise." She exhaled heavily in an attempt to calm her racing heart and took in the exhaustion that was evident on Sam's face. "You look like the drive over wore you out. I'm glad you're lying down."

"Yes, mom." Sam turned a serious expression on Janie and then asked, "Do me a favor?"

"Sure."

Sam held out her good hand until Janie took it. "Don't go out after dark. I know you like walking to and from work sometimes, but play it safe, please?"

"All right. You've got my cell number if you need anything?"

"Yeah." Sam squeezed Janie's fingers. "Don't worry. I'm sure Betsy will keep me in line."

The more she thought about it, the less Janie liked leaving Sam. She knew Betsy was more than capable of tending to Sam's needs. But now that she'd taken that first step, Janie was anxious to see where their relationship could lead. She thought about what had happened earlier, in her living room. Maybe a little space *was* a good idea. She kissed Sam's forehead. "Get some rest."

"All right." Sam closed her eyes, and was asleep before Janie closed the door.

Janie stood in front of the door for a moment. She took a deep breath and headed for the kitchen.

BETSY HANDED HER a mug of coffee after she joined her at the table. "Had a rough go of it, huh?"

"You could say that." Janie sipped her coffee. She shifted in her chair as the silence grew. "Is something wrong?"

"No, not wrong." Betsy paused to get her thoughts in order. "You look like something's on your mind."

Janie stared at the cup in her hands, evidently deliberating something, while Betsy silently observed her.

"You keep your own counsel, don't you Janie?"

"I've never been one to speak freely with anyone except my grandmother." A smile touched Janie's lips as she spoke about her grandmother. "I have an idea that the two of you would be great friends, even considering your age difference." She raised her head. "Can I ask you a question?"

"Sure."

"Sam told me that you practically pulled her in off the street. Why would you do that? I mean, you had to have known she wasn't from around here."

The older woman nodded. "That's true. She definitely stood out amongst the ugly old rednecks I'd seen." She became serious. "I saw something in her eyes. She reminded me of someone I once knew. And my heart went out to her."

They both sat quietly, each absorbed in her own thoughts for a few moments until Janie quietly said, "It's hard for me to believe that anyone in Piperton could be so trusting. I was raised to fear anyone different."

"Why do you think that is?" Betsy asked.

Janie decided she could trust Betsy with the truth. "My mother ran away with a traveling evangelist. After that, my dad, Harvey..." She shrugged her shoulders. "Old news. You said Sam reminded you of someone. Who?"

Betsy sighed. "You know, Sam asked me the same thing. I lied and told her she reminded me of myself, because I didn't want her to be afraid. Now, after what's happened to her, I wish I'd told the truth." She paused, the ticking of the kitchen clock seemed amplified in the small room. "My Jack had an older sister, Kathleen. She'd ended up right here in Piperton, teaching high school history."

"Really? I had Mr. Graham for history. I don't recall—"

"No, you wouldn't. She passed away in seventy-one. Her death was the reason Jack and I came here." Betsy poured more coffee into her cup, even though it was over half-full.

Janie placed her hand on Betsy's forearm. "I'm sorry. Was she ill?"

Shaking her head, Betsy blinked away a tear. "No." She took a deep cleansing breath and sat up straighter. "She and Jack spoke frequently. She'd told him about falling in love with a fellow teacher. The problem was her lover was another woman. And married."

"Here? In Piperton?"

"Yes. They'd made plans to run away together, from what Kathleen told Jack. We were living in New Mexico at the time, and offered to put them up. But before they could leave, Kathleen was killed in a hit and run accident." Betsy wrapped her hands around the coffee mug, as if trying to draw strength from its warmth. "After the funeral, Jack spoke to the police. They were ready to chock it up to a drunk driver, but he never believed that. We went back to Santa Fe, packed up our stuff, and moved here. He was bound and determined to find out what really happened to her, but we never did."

"What about the other woman?"

Betsy shook her head. "I don't know. She never came forward." She shrugged. "We hadn't expected her to, anyway. Poor thing was probably terrified."

"I suppose. But still." Janie thought about Betsy's story. "Do you think Sam's attack could be related to what happened to Kathleen?"

"No. Heavens, that happened over thirty years ago. The only reason I mentioned it was because it shows how intolerant this place is. I should have warned Sam to be more careful."

Janie gripped Betsy's hand and squeezed. "You know, a wise woman once told me that Sam was the type of person to draw attention to herself all on her own."

Betsy laughed. "Throwing my own words back at me, eh? Guess I deserve it." She sobered quickly. "Seriously, though. As much as Sam stands out, you don't. Please be extra special careful. This whole mess scares the living daylights out of me."

"Me, too. And don't worry. I'll watch my back."

But even as Janie spoke, Betsy wondered how far Janie and Sam would have to go to protect themselves.

Chapter
Fourteen

JANIE WATCHED THE minute hand of the clock edge closer to twelve. It was only Thursday, much to her disappointment. When the moment arrived, she took her purse from the bottom desk drawer and stood. Five o'clock couldn't have come soon enough. She pushed her chair under the desk and was out the front door before anyone noticed.

Within five minutes, Janie parked her car two spaces away from the gym's front entrance and hurried inside. She stood in the doorway and looked around. Seeing Betsy at her usual place behind the front counter, Janie waved. "Hi."

"Hello there, yourself." Betsy gestured for Janie to join her. "Are you here for class?"

"No, I didn't think—"

Betsy laughed at the befuddled look on Janie's face. "I'm only messing with you. You're right, that class isn't tonight. Run upstairs. Maybe you can get gloomy Gus out of her mood."

"Is she all right?"

"She's a grumpy pain in the butt, that's what she is. But I think you're just what the doctor ordered." Betsy made a shooing motion with her hands. "Go on."

Janie looked around carefully before heading for the back door. The three women on the exercise equipment were too engrossed in their work outs to notice her. "Thanks." In no time she scaled the stairs and stepped into Betsy's living room, where she saw a disgruntled Sam slouched on the couch. "Hi."

Sam's face instantly brightened. "Hey." She started to get up but was stopped when Janie crossed the room and dropped beside her. "Is it after five already?"

"Yes, finally." Janie kissed her lightly on the cheek. "How are you doing?"

"A lot better in the last minute," Sam admitted, placing her arm around Janie's shoulders and bringing her closer. "I've been bored out of my mind today. But things are definitely looking up." She closed her eyes when Janie's hand cupped the back of her head and their lips met.

They spent the next few minutes kissing and touching, until Janie slowly pulled away and rested her forehead against Sam's. "I needed that."

"Me too." Sam raised her head slightly and kissed the tip of Janie's nose. "Need more?"

Janie laughed. "Always." She snuggled against Sam's chest and enjoyed the warmth. "I never thought I'd feel like this."

"Like how?" Sam used her good hand to stroke Janie's arm.

"That if I don't see you, or touch you, I'll cease to exist."

Sam's eyes widened at Janie's heartfelt words. "You know, when I found out my car was history, I almost booked the next bus ticket out of town."

"What changed your mind?"

"You." Sam's fingertips traced up Janie's arm and cupped her cheek. "Even with all the misunderstandings we had there was something about you that I couldn't get out of my mind." She pulled Janie to her, their lips meeting. Unable to get enough, Sam's lips traveled down Janie's throat, causing the other woman to moan. Janie's hands tangled into Sam's hair. Sam pulled away slightly, breathing heavily. "Baby, we need to slow down."

"I know." Janie lowered her hands. She counted to ten in hopes of catching her breath. "It was nice, though." She played with the frayed edge of Sam's cutoff shorts, then her fingers moved lower to stroke the smooth thigh. Her fingers were grasped. "What?"

"You're killing me," Sam ground out, her jaw clenched.

"I'm sorry, did I hurt you?"

Sam closed her eyes and swallowed. "Not like you think. It's just—"

"Oh." Janie blushed. "Sorry."

"It's okay." Sam threaded their fingers together and held Janie's hand in her lap.

Janie turned and brushed her free hand across Sam's jaw. "I can't seem to stop touching you."

"I'm never going to complain about that." Sam turned her head and kissed the inside of Janie's wrist.

"Oh, god." With her heart pounding, Janie scooted closer and hooked her leg over Sam's. She leaned forward and reached beneath Sam's tee shirt and kissed her hungrily.

"Whoa, excuse me!" Betsy's voice caused them to break apart. She stood in the doorway, blushing almost as deeply as the two women on the sofa. "Maybe I should go back downstairs."

Janie climbed off Sam, but didn't move far. She straightened her top and gave Betsy a friendly smile. "Don't be silly. We were just, uh, visiting."

"Looks more like you were visiting her tonsils," Betsy quipped.

"Ah, geez." Sam rubbed her face with one hand. "You're evil."

Betsy laughed. "I'm going to go figure out something for dinner. Janie, you're staying, aren't you?"

"No, that's all right. You don't have to—"

"I know I don't. But it's as easy to cook for three as it is two." Betsy headed for the kitchen. "You two keep *visiting*."

Once they were alone again, Janie fell back against Sam. "We've got to be more careful."

Sam wrapped an arm around Janie's waist and buried her nose in her hair. "I think what we really need to do is find someplace more private."

"How about my place?"

"No."

Janie turned to face her. "Why not?"

"It's not safe. What if he sees me there? I still hear his voice in my sleep every night. I can't risk you. It's bad enough that you come here."

"Are you saying you don't want me to come here anymore?" Janie's earlier elation began to weigh heavily in her stomach. "That we can't be together?" Her eyes started to burn.

"No, nothing like that." Sam hugged Janie to her and kissed her neck. "I'm just terrified that something's going to happen to you."

Janie tilted her head so Sam could have better access. "It won't. But I see what you mean." She sighed heavily as Sam nipped at her earlobe. "I'll only come over here on days I'm going to work out."

"Okay. And, to keep myself from going crazy missing you, I'm planning on going back to work at Danny's tomorrow. I'm hoping Ray has something for me to do." Sam sucked the earlobe between her teeth and nibbled gently, causing Janie to squirm.

"Ah, Sam, I—" Janie brought Sam's good hand to her breast. "I need—"

Betsy's voice called from the kitchen. "You two better cool it in there. Dinner will be ready soon."

"Damn." Sam rested her forehead on Janie's shoulder. "This is worse than living with my grandmother."

"She's a good chaperone, that's for sure." Janie exhaled and leaned her head against Sam's. "There's a park not far from the square, and it's usually deserted after dark."

"Oh? What are you suggesting, Ms. Clarke? A secret rendezvous?"

Janie nodded. "There are picnic tables scattered among the trees on the south side of the lake. Well, actually, it's more like a pond. But we could meet there." She turned so they were looking eye to eye. "It's safe, I promise." She ran a finger down Sam's face. "And very private."

"H-how private?"

"Maybe not *that* private, but at least we can spend some time together without being interrupted." Janie kissed her slowly before pulling away. "Call me tomorrow after you talk to Ray, and we'll figure out when we can meet, all right?"

"Sure. Now, come here." They kissed again, until Betsy hollered vague threats about ice water and lots of it. Buckets of it. And fire hoses. Breaking apart, they laughed and got up from the sofa.

THE NEXT MORNING, Sam was dressed and ready to go. She enjoyed Betsy's company but was tired of doing nothing. After breakfast, Sam struggled into her jeans and work shirt from the bar. She moved slowly down the stairs until she was at the reception counter of the gym.

Betsy looked up from the magazine she had been reading and frowned. "What do you think you're doing?"

"I'm going crazy up there. I thought I'd run by the bar and see if Ray needed any help." Sam adjusted the sling her broken hand rested in. She hated wearing it, but it was the only way to keep the swelling down.

"And just what do you think you're going to do?" Betsy stood from the stool she'd been perched on and straightened the strap that went behind her neck. "Silly kid."

Sam slapped her hand away. "Stop that. I can clean tables and take drink orders."

"And how are you planning on getting there?"

"I'll walk. It's not that far." Although it would be even faster to cut through the alleys, Sam had no intention of doing so.

Betsy grabbed her keys from beneath the counter. "Oh, no you don't. If you're that determined to do this, I'll take you."

"Come on, Betsy. I'll be fine. And you can't leave the gym in the middle of the day."

"Watch me." Betsy scribbled a few words on a piece of paper and taped it to the counter. "I used to do it all the time before you came along." She took the small metal box where she kept the money and locked it in her bottom desk drawer. After locking her office, she limped toward the back of the gym. "Well? Are you coming or not?"

Sam sighed and followed. "Yes ma'am."

RAY HAD HIS back to the door when it opened. "Sorry, we're still closed," he called over his shoulder. Heavy steps coming closer caused him to turn around. "Are you deaf? I said, we're—" his words cut off when he saw Sam's face. "Holy hell, Sam. You look like shit."

"Thanks a lot, Ray." Sam was embarrassed by the scrutiny. Betsy had stopped by the doctor's office on the way over so that she could have her stitches removed, and Sam hated how the red scars stood out on her face. "I thought I'd come in and see if there was anything I could do around here. I can't play for a while, but I was getting bored at home."

He filled a couple of glasses with ice water and motioned for her to sit at the bar. "Don't worry about it. I can always use some help. You mind clearing tables?"

"No, not a bit." She raised her cast away from her body. "As soon as I can get rid of this damned sling, I can take care of the floors and stuff, too."

"Ever worked behind a bar? It's not hard, at least around here. All you have to do is pour a few shots, open beer bottles and fill mugs with draft."

She twisted her glass around, making patterns with the pool of condensation. "Can't say that I have. What's your plan?"

"If you could come in, set things up and work until about four or five during the week, I'd be forever in your debt."

"What about Fred?"

Ray shook his head. "Asshole walked out a couple of days ago and never came back. I've been working opening to close ever since, except on the weekends. Tracy opens then. She's not available during the week because of her college schedule."

"Damn, Ray. I'm sorry. You should have called me." Sam shifted on the barstool, trying to find a more comfortable position.

"Nah, it's not that big of a deal, especially since we're closing earlier now. But it would be nice to sleep in for a change," he hinted.

Sam's laughter echoed in the quiet bar. "Subtle, buddy. But yeah, I can handle the early stuff. What all do I need to do?"

He walked around the bar. "Come on. I'll show you. It's easy."

Within an hour, Sam learned enough to handle the day shift at the bar. Since they didn't open for business until two, she didn't see any reason why Ray needed to stay. "Why don't you go home and take a nap? I think I can take care of things here."

Ray headed for the door. "You don't have to tell me twice. See you about five-thirty, if that's okay."

"Sure." Once the door closed, Sam leaned against the bar and looked around the room. She was filled with a sense of accomplishment, proud to have the responsibility she had run from for so long.

AS MUCH AS she wanted to call Danny's and see if Sam was working, Janie decided to use her lunch break to have a quick visit with her grandmother. She'd talked to Lucille several times on the phone, but hadn't seen her since before Sam had gotten hurt. She walked down the familiar hallway and exchanged greetings with several staff members before tapping on her grandmother's open door.

Lucille spun her electric wheelchair around and grinned. "Hello there, stranger. Come give me a hug."

After they embraced, Janie sat on the edge of Lucille's bed. "Are you getting enough sleep? You look a little tired."

"Please. That's all they want us to do in this place. I get more than my share. How's your friend? Is she doing better?"

Janie blushed when she thought about the kisses she and Sam shared the previous evening. She was definitely feeling better. "Uh, yes. As a matter of fact, Sam has gone back to work at the bar."

"I'm glad she's doing so well. Didn't you tell me she was a singer?"

"Yes, among other things. Although I doubt she'll be able to sing for a while, since she can't play the piano until the cast comes off her hand." Thinking about the sexy timbre in Sam's voice, Janie felt a warmth spread through her.

"That's a shame. You look a little flushed, dear. Are you feeling okay?"

Janie's eyes widened and her face turned a deeper shade of red. "Um, well, I—"

Lucille wheeled closer and covered Janie's hands with her own. "You know, the last time I saw you this flustered was when you were in junior high. I believe his name was Larry or something like that."

"Gary Lane," Janie murmured, looking at their joined hands. "He'd asked me to the Halloween dance."

"That's right. So I'm figuring it must be a young fellow that has you so riled, and giving you this beautiful glow. Are you back with Doug?"

Janie couldn't believe she was having this conversation with her grandmother. "God, no."

"Then who?"

"Oh, damn." Janie tore her hands away from Lucille's and covered her face. "It's not like that, Nana."

The older woman inhaled slowly, as if to gather her strength for the revelation she knew was coming. "It's all right, child."

Janie raised her head. "I'm scared."

"Of what?"

"Everything." Tears fell from Janie's eyes and she lowered her gaze again. "Why now?" Her voice dropped lower. "Why *her*?"

Lucille's tone was forcibly light. "So, when do I get to meet this woman who's stolen your heart? That's what this is all about, isn't it?"

Janie covered her face again as she began to cry softly. Her greatest fear was of losing Lucille, who'd been the only person she could count on throughout her life. But she couldn't deny what was in her heart.

"Janie?" Lucille squeezed Janie's knee. "Honey," her voice softened, as if trying to calm a frightened child. "The only thing that matters to me is that you're happy. Please don't cry." Her gentle words had the opposite effect, as Janie sobbed harder. She turned her chair sideways until she was against the bed and tugged her granddaughter to her shoulder. "Sssh. Everything's going to be fine, I promise."

RAUCOUS LAUGHTER FROM the three tables shoved together caused Sam to wince. It seemed the entire lawn mowing workforce had turned up at Danny's. She checked the clock behind the bar. The men had showed up at four, and it was now only ten minutes after five. She lost count of how many pitchers of beer she'd filled for the rowdy men. She reached for another as Doug came to the bar.

"Hey, we need another refill." He placed the empty pitcher on the counter. He'd lost the coin toss and it was his first time to pay for a round. "Shit! What happened to you?"

Sam wanted to spit out a nasty retort, but held her tongue. "Someone didn't like me being here, I guess." She traded his empty pitcher for a full one, and scooped the ten-dollar bill off the bar. She watched his face as he digested her remark, wondering if he had anything to do with whoever beat her.

Doug took the change she gave him and stuffed a dollar into the tip jar. "Well, I guess that sucked for you." He returned to his co-workers, not giving Sam another glance.

Several more men came in and joined the group. Sam automatically filled two more of the plastic containers with draft beer and carried both with one hand to the tables. "Here you go fellas." She accepted the wad of cash from a dirty hand and thanked them for the extra. "Let me know if you need anything else." As she was leaving, a cold chill went down her back as she heard the voice from her nightmares. She quickly turned, but with the heavy smoke and boisterous chatter she was unable to tell who had spoken.

Sam returned to her position behind the bar. She kept staring at the group of men, hoping to figure out who her assailant could be. The slam of the back door caused her to jump and she reached beneath the bar and grasped the wooden baseball bat that was kept for security. She released it when Ray came out of the back room.

"Wow, looks like a busy afternoon," he remarked, joining her. "You okay?"

"Yeah." She turned so that she wasn't facing the large group of men. "What do you know about those guys?"

Ray shrugged. "Not a whole lot. They all work together, but I guess you figured that out by their matching shirts. Why?"

"No particular reason. Just curious." She watched as Doug and an older man got into a lively discussion. She couldn't hear them over the din the others made, but Doug didn't seem very happy.

Doug stood and scooted his chair away from the table. "Fine, I'll go! Whatever it takes to get you off my ass." He followed the older man from the bar, cursing the entire way.

Several more of the men pushed away from the tables and started to leave. It was as if once their leader was gone they no longer had a reason to stay.

Sam waited until they cleared the door before gathering a wet towel and a tray. Ray's hand on her arm stopped her. "What?"

"I'll take care of that. Why don't you go on home, and I'll let you open tomorrow?"

She placed the tray on the bar. "You sure?"

"Yeah. Tracy's coming in around seven. She'll help me take care of the tables." Ray took the towel out of her hand and lightly shoved her. "Go on. I'm sure you've got better things to do than hang around here."

"Great. Hey, is it okay if I use the phone in the office before I go?" At Ray's nod, Sam weaved through the tables and headed for the back room. She stepped into the office and closed the door behind her, taking a seat beside the old wooden desk. She dialed a number from memory, anxiously twirling the cord around her finger as she waited for an answer.

"Hello?"

"Hey, Janie. This is Sam. What's up?" Sam rolled her eyes at her own nervous attempt to sound cool.

"Hi. I was just changing out of my work clothes. How was your first day back?"

The implications of Janie's words hit Sam hard. "You're getting undressed?" The thought of a scantily clad Janie caused her breath to quicken. "What are you wearing?" She whacked her forehead with the handset of the phone. *Idiot! Quit sounding like an obscene phone call.* "I, uh, well," she stammered.

"Actually, I was standing here in front of my closet, trying to figure out what to put on." Janie laughed when her comment was met with silence. "What was that sound? Did you drop the phone?"

Sam rubbed her head where she had thumped herself with the handset. "No, must be the connection." She took a deep breath and released it slowly. "Work was okay. I'm taking the day shift behind the bar for the time being."

"That's great." A rustling of cloth, and Janie continued. "There. I've got my jeans on. Hold on while I slip on a blouse."

Closing her eyes, Sam imagined Janie in only jeans and her bra. The vision certainly wasn't helping to calm her down. "Maybe I should call back."

"No, I'm done."

"Ah. Okay." Sam turned in the chair to check the thermostat by the door, wondering if Ray had turned the heater on. "Are you going to go visit your grandmother this evening?"

"No, I went at lunch today." Janie quieted. "We talked about us."

"Us? As in you and me?" Sam wished she could see Janie's face. "What brought that up?" When she didn't get an answer, she started to panic. "Janie? Baby? Are you okay?"

Janie sniffled. "I'll be okay. Nana was great, actually."

"Really? Then why are you crying?"

"I'm not," Janie lied. "Hold on."

Sam could faintly hear Janie blow her nose. She tapped her fingers nervously on the battered desk.

"Sorry." Janie cleared her throat. "What are you doing tonight? I'd love to see you."

"I think that can be arranged. Want to try the park tonight? As soon as it's dark?"

"That would be wonderful. Directly behind the old dock there's a picnic area. Around eight?"

"Sure."

"All right. See you then." Janie was the first to hang up.

Sam stared at the wall as a wave of anticipation flowed through her. She placed the handset on the phone and leaned back in the beat up leather office chair. Now if she could just figure out what to do with herself for the next couple of hours.

THE SMALL FRAME house where he grew up felt more confining than usual to Doug. He sat silently in the same chair where he'd taken his meals for the last thirty-four years, while his parents bickered back and forth. They'd been at each other's throats for as long as he could remember. More than once Doug wondered why they ever married to begin with. He wiped a piece of bread across his plate before stuffing it in his mouth. The quicker he finished, the sooner he'd be able to find something better to do. He almost choked when his father slammed a hand on the table, causing the dishes to rattle.

"Goddamn it, Sue. Do you have to harp at me non-stop?"

Sue brushed her gray hair away from her face. The neat bun she'd put it in at the beginning of the day had come loose, adding to her frazzled appearance. "All I asked was if you'd paid the water bill today. You told me you would drop it off on your way to work. And if you weren't such a nasty drunk, you'd be able to have a normal conversation." She gave her son an apologetic smile. "Honey, when are you going to bring Janie over again? It's been ages since I've seen her."

"I'm not, Ma. We're not seeing each other any more." Doug took another helping of scalloped potatoes. He'd try to stay longer, for his mother's sake.

"When did this happen?" Sue turned to her husband. "Did you know about this? Why didn't you say anything?"

Reggie drained the first of the three beers he had near his plate. "Wasn't any of your damned business, woman. Besides, it's only temporary."

"You're wrong Pop. We're not getting back together." Doug shoved a forkful of potatoes into his mouth. "Jus' drop it."

"Bullshit! You don't have the balls to do what needs to be done. Swallow your damned pride and beg the girl to take you back," Reggie demanded, popping the top on his next beer.

Doug dropped his fork. "Back off old man. I ain't interested in Janie no more. She's changed."

"Well, *unchange* her! Be a man, for once." Reggie pointed a grease-stained finger at his wife. "This is all your fault! If you hadn't coddled him when he was a boy his girlfriend would have never turned queer."

Almost spitting his tea out, Doug forced himself to swallow. "What do you mean? Janie ain't no dyke. We've fu —" he glanced at his mother.

"Sorry, Ma. I mean, had relations."

"That's all right, hon." Sue glared at her husband. "Leave him alone, Reggie. And quit spreading rumors about Janie."

"Ain't a rumor. I've seen...uh, why else would she leave Doug?" Reggie belched. He picked up an empty can and waved it at Sue. "And don't tell me what to do, you damned ol' cow."

Doug stretched across the table and took the empty can from his father. "Cool it." He crumbled the can and tossed it in the trash. It was time to change the subject. "How'd school go today, Ma?"

"About the same, I suppose. It's getting harder and harder to get today's students motivated. Principal Weston told me he heard the school board is considering dropping my art classes altogether if things don't pick up."

"But you've been at the high school for over thirty years. How could they do that to you?" Doug took the napkin he had tucked under his chin and wiped his face. "What would you do?"

Sue shook her head. "I'm not sure, son. But maybe it's time for me to retire."

Reggie snorted. "Well, that's fucking great. Then you'd be around here all the time. But I guess it's just as well. That damned place has always been a breeding ground for freaks." He drained his beer. "You just want to sit around the house all day and watch TV."

"You may be surprised at what I'll do when I stop teaching," Sue snapped. She began to remove the dishes from the table. "And I sure as hell don't want to spend my golden years cooped up in this dump with you."

"Well, fuck you!" Reggie snarled. He got up from the table, beer in hand. "I need some air." Without another word, Reggie tromped through the house and out the front door.

Sue set the dishes down and patted Doug on the shoulder. "That was one of our better dinners, wasn't it?"

THE PARK WAS deserted when Janie arrived. She hurried past the old dock. Very few ever ventured to the far side of the small lake anymore. It was well-removed from the new picnic area, which boasted wooden tables and free-standing barbeque grills. The chipped concrete picnic table beneath the trees had lost one of the accompanying benches and it was nearly invisible from the road.

She pulled up short when she saw the table. There was a folded blanket padding the bench and a checkered paper tablecloth covered the surface of the table. A small battery-powered lantern in the center cast a warm glow and an oversized basket rested on one corner. "Oh, my."

Sam stood next to the table looking slightly embarrassed. She held out her good arm out and shrugged. "I thought it would be nice to have dinner together without worrying about who saw us."

"You're so sweet." Janie stepped into her arms and tucked her face against Sam's neck. The clean scent of soap mixed with Sam's own natural scent was intoxicating. "Thank you."

"My pleasure." Sam trembled when Janie's lips touched her neck below her ear. "You look great."

Janie held the dark green skirt out slightly and ducked her head. The foam-colored sleeveless top hugged her body, and it was brighter than most of the clothes in her closet. She'd decided to change from her jeans, hoping for this reaction from Sam. "Really? I...I bought it for you."

"Then I'm a very lucky person." Sam led Janie to the bench. "I'm afraid this was the best I could do." She waited until Janie was seated before taking her place next to her, straddling the bench. "You deserve a nice restaurant, not a picnic in the middle of nowhere."

"This is perfect. Show me what's in the basket." Before her eyes, a marvelous meal appeared. She watched as Sam removed plastic containers and situated them on the table. Inside was spaghetti, breadsticks and a tossed salad. "Wow."

It was Sam's turn to blush. "I'm not much of a cook, but I figured I wouldn't poison you with something this easy."

"I'm sure it's wonderful."

They spent the meal in silence, although they both peeked at each other when they thought the other wasn't looking. Once they'd finished, Janie sighed in contentment. "This was the best spaghetti I'd ever eaten. Did you do something special to it?"

Sam packed away the dirty dishes. "Thanks. Yeah, I added a touch of brown sugar to the sauce, like my grandmother used to do. I'm glad you liked it." She sat again and smiled when Janie edged closer.

"Thank you." Janie leaned over and gave Sam a kiss to show her gratitude. She surprised herself with her own boldness. Janie well knew that even though it was dark, there was still an element of danger involved. But the sensations she felt became all that mattered. She deepened the kiss, exploring Sam's mouth in earnest. Her fingers threaded through Sam's hair, lost in the silky texture.

Sam pulled Janie even closer, until Janie also straddled the bench. Sam's good hand began to slide up and down along the outside of Janie's thighs as they continued to kiss.

Janie gasped and tilted her head back while Sam explored her throat. The touch along her skin felt like fire. "God, Sam. That feels so good."

Sam moved her hand upward to cup Janie's rear. In response, Janie's legs went around Sam's waist.

"Oh, Sam. That feels so good. But, we shouldn't, we can't—"

Her words brought Sam to where they were. "Damn. I know this isn't the right place—" She was surprised when Janie kissed her again, this time even more urgently. All thought left her and she squeezed

Janie's rear again.

Janie moaned. "Don't."

Sam removed her hands. "I'm sorry." The breath was knocked from her when Janie hugged her tightly.

"No, don't you dare *stop*." She kissed her harder. "I swear, if you don't touch me soon, I'll explode."

"But—"

"It's late and there's no one else here. I need you, Sam."

"Janie," Sam moaned, "I want you so bad, it hurts." She moved one hand to the inside of Janie's thighs.

"Yessss," Janie hissed. "Touch me." The sound of rustling leaves caused her to almost slide off the bench. "What was that?"

Sam scooted away and got to her feet. "Let me go check it out."

The rustling got closer. Janie stood behind Sam. "No, please. Stay." When a dark blur broke through the brush, she screamed.

The gray rabbit raced around the pair, never slowing down.

Janie dropped her head onto Sam's back and exhaled heavily. "Well, that killed the mood."

Sam turned and put her arms around Janie. "Yeah. And it makes it very clear we need to find someplace safer to be together. That could have just as easily been a person." She left a light kiss on Janie's lips. "I'm sorry, baby."

"That's all right." With her arms around Sam's neck, Janie returned the kiss with fervor. Her pulse quickened as she felt a strong hand caress her backside. "Come home with me."

"What?"

"Let's go back to my place." Spinning away from Sam, she started folding the tablecloth.

Within ten minutes, everything was put away in the trunk of Janie's car. Sam climbed into the passenger seat. "Are you sure about this?"

"Definitely." Janie started the car and backed out of the parking space. She held out her right hand and Sam grasped it. "I hope you don't have any plans for the weekend."

Sam flushed. "I guess I do now."

They were almost to Janie's apartment when her phone rang. "Damn it." She released Sam's hand and dug the device from her purse. "Hello?"

"Janie? I've been knocking on your door for five minutes. Is everything okay?" Sandra's voice cracked.

"Sandra? What's going on?" Janie wheeled the car to the side of the street and parked. "What are you doing at my apartment?"

Sam sighed and pointed at her door. They weren't far from the gym. "Should I leave?" she mouthed.

Janie shook her head. "What was that, Sandra? I'm sorry, I couldn't hear you."

"I came home tonight and they had a notice on my apartment door.

Something about fumigating for termites. Can I stay with you until Sunday?"

"Uh, well," Janie glanced at Sam. She ached to touch the younger woman. "The place is a mess. What about your boyfriend?"

"Terry?" The name came from Sandra in a half-sob. "I don't think his *wife* would approve."

"He's married? Oh, honey, I'm so sorry." Janie realized her weekend plans had just changed drastically, and not in a good way. "Look, I'll be home in about ten minutes, okay? Just hang in there." She exchanged goodbyes with her friend and tossed the cell into her purse. With a heavy heart, she clasped Sam's hand again. "I'm sorry. But she needs me."

Sam gave her an understanding smile. "I heard. Rotten timing, huh?"

"The worst." Janie unbuckled her seatbelt and slid closer to Sam, ignoring the discomfort of the bucket seats. She caressed Sam's face and leaned close to gently kiss her. When they pulled apart, she reluctantly returned to the driver's seat. "Let me take you home."

"Nah." Sam climbed out of the car. "I think I could use a little cooling down." Closing the door, she ducked into the open window. "I'll be working days at the bar, so maybe we can get together some evening."

"I hope so. Please be careful."

Sam winked. "You too." She walked down the sidewalk, not looking back.

Janie leaned her head against the shoulder strap and sighed. "I hope she's as bad off as I am."

Chapter
Fifteen

BY TUESDAY, JANIE had had all she could take of Sandra. Her friend's overnight stay turned into an unwanted slumber party, the end nowhere in sight. She had come home after work and found Sandra stretched out on the sofa, dirty dishes covering the coffee and end tables. "Didn't you go to work today?"

"Yeah, but it was slow, so they sent me home. Hey, do you want to go out tonight? I've been bored silly around here today."

Janie moved a pair of jeans from a chair to the floor and sat. "You could have always gone home and cleaned. Didn't you tell me it was safe to go back to your apartment yesterday?"

"Well, yes. But I'm trying to get the landlord to pay for a cleaning service. You should see the place. There's a layer of film over everything!" Sandra pulled a cigarette from the case. "I wish you'd let me smoke in here. It's such a pain in the ass to go downstairs and outside."

"No way. I'd never get the smell out of the furniture." Janie had grown up living with a smoker, and vowed to herself to never allow it in her own home. "And I already have plans for tonight. I've got an aerobics class at seven."

Sandra got off the couch and straightened her blouse. "Since when? You've never been interested in things like that. Come on, go change into something more casual and we'll hit Danny's. Maybe that singer will be there."

Not thinking about what she was saying, Janie stood as well. "No, she's working the day shift for a while. And she can't play because of her hand."

"What? Since when were you the expert on the comings and goings of the bar? And it sounds like you've become pretty friendly with that woman."

Sandra's superior attitude angered Janie. "Am I not allowed to have other friends?" She started gathering the dirty dishes. When her arms were full, she headed toward the kitchen, with Sandra on her heels.

"Friends? I thought you said you only shared a table at Fern's with that woman. Now you're telling me she's your friend?"

Janie spun away from the sink and rested her hands on her hips. "Sam's a very sweet person, and a good friend to have. She's done nothing to anyone around here, yet all she gets is grief. So I wish you'd just lay off her."

"Whoa, calm down." Sandra backed up a step. "I didn't mean anything by it. It just seemed kinda strange, you talking about her like that."

Before Janie could answer, her cell phone rang. She rushed to the living room and took it out of her purse. "Hello?"

"What the hell do you think you're doing?" Harvey ranted. "I thought I told you to make up with Doug."

Janie dropped into the nearest chair and closed her eyes. The last person she wanted to talk to was her father. "We've been over this before, Harvey. I have no interest in Doug, so just drop it."

"Like hell I will. You'll do as I say, girl. Or I'll—"

"Or you'll what? Don't you dare threaten me." Years of being bullied had festered until Janie felt a burning hatred for the man who'd done nothing but belittle her throughout her entire life. "Until you're ready to talk to me in a civilized manner, don't bother calling. Goodbye, Harvey." Janie disconnected the call and tossed the phone onto the coffee table. "Asshole."

Sandra's eyes were wide from where she stood in the doorway of the kitchen. "Wow. If I hadn't seen it with my own eyes, I'd have never believed it. You've changed."

"What? No, I haven't." Janie stood and returned to the kitchen. At the sink, she started running water.

Sandra sidled up beside her. "Yes you have. Don't get me wrong, it's not a bad thing. Well overdue, if you want to know the truth. First your hair and clothes, and now this kick-ass attitude." She bumped hips with Janie. "I like it. Now scoot over tough stuff, and let me take care of these dishes. Don't want you going off on me next."

THE GYM WAS full of women, yet the only one Sam saw was Janie. Standing next to Betsy at the reception counter, Sam released a heavy sigh.

"If you keep staring at her like that, she's going to burst into flames," Betsy teased, speaking low so as not to be overheard by anyone else. She took the towel that Sam was using to wipe the counter. "Give me that. You're wearing a hole in the wood."

Sam's face turned a deep red. "Sorry." Her fingers tapped out a nervous beat while she forced herself to look away from the aerobics class. "Maybe I should go put a load of towels in to wash."

"You did that five minutes ago."

"Damn." The upbeat music which drove the aerobics class was giving Sam a headache. At least that's what she told herself. It had nothing to do with the fact that Sandra had accompanied Janie to the gym. Sam sent some decidedly unfriendly thoughts toward the blonde. She hadn't been alone with Janie since Friday evening and her mood continued to deteriorate. "I think I'll go upstairs," she announced to Betsy. "That is, if you don't need me for anything."

"I guess I'll survive down here without you moping around."

"I wasn't moping." Sam spared a final glance at the class before she left. She bumped into the doorframe when the class bent at the waist, giving her a great view of Janie's rear. Ignoring Betsy's laughter, she closed the door and stomped up the stairs.

TEN MINUTES LATER, the class broke up. Janie hung back from the women who trekked to the locker room, instead stopping at the counter where Betsy was perched on a stool. Wiping her face and neck with a towel, Janie leaned against the counter. "Pamela runs a tough class," she shared, as the last of her group left the room. She exhaled heavily. "Where's Sam?"

"Upstairs." Betsy's smile widened at the look that crossed Janie's face. "Why don't you run up and see her?"

Janie's face fell. "I wish I could. But Sandra's with me. That might be a little hard to explain."

Betsy tapped the counter with a pen while she considered Janie's dilemma. "Okay. How about this? You go get changed, and then both you and your friend come up for dinner. We'll order pizza or something."

"That sounds wonderful. Thank you!" Janie patted Betsy's hand and jogged to the locker room.

"Guess I'd better let Sam know about our dinner guests." Betsy hurried to the office, where the intercom was located. She dropped into her leather chair and used the intercom button to buzz upstairs.

It took Sam less than thirty seconds to answer. "Betsy? Is everything okay down there?"

"Fine, kiddo. Listen, I've invited a couple of ladies to dinner tonight. Would you like to call in a couple of pizzas from Aces? You know what I like."

"Um, sure. But who —" Sam's voice stopped in mid sentence. "You didn't."

Betsy laughed before pressing the button again. "I sure did. Now get busy. We'll be up in a few." She ignored the cursing that came out of the small box. It was always fun to keep Sam off balance. Betsy considered it a great hobby. "Beats collecting stamps." She continued to laugh as she returned to the front counter.

DINNER WAS AN uncomfortable affair, at least as far as Sam was concerned. She struggled to keep from staring at Janie, whose damp hair from her shower curled attractively around her face. She tried to tune out Sandra, who was chattering non-stop about her last boyfriend.

"Imagine my surprise when I called his house and his *wife* answered the phone!" Sandra exclaimed. "I was so humiliated!"

"I'm sure his wife wasn't too thrilled, either," Sam mumbled. "Ouch!" She reached beneath the table and rubbed her leg where Janie's foot had connected with her shin. "What?"

Janie's glare spoke volumes. "Be nice," she mouthed silently. She viciously stabbed her salad with a fork before bringing it to her mouth.

Sandra kept cutting her eyes at Sam and then back to her plate. "Um, Sam? Can I ask you a question?"

"Yeah, I guess." Sam saw Janie's frown and moved her leg before she was kicked again. She grinned and resisted the urge to stick out her tongue.

"What made you the way you are?" Sandra waved her hand. "You know, gay? Did you have a bad experience with a man?"

Sam bristled, but was quickly calmed by the loving look bestowed upon her by Janie. "No. I've never had a 'bad' experience with a man. I've always been a lesbian. I can't remember ever *not* being the way I am."

"Really?" Sandra propped her elbow on the table and rested her chin in her open hand. "What does your family think about it? Is that why you travel around?"

Janie quickly interrupted. "I don't think that's any of our business." She knew family was a sensitive subject for Sam.

"No, it's all right." Sam dropped the pizza crust she'd nibbled on. "I don't have any family, Sandra. But when my grandmother was alive, she didn't have a problem with my sexuality."

"I'm sorry," Sandra offered. Without thinking, she put her hand on top of Sam's. "Really, I am."

Sam managed a smile for the other woman. "Thanks." As much as she had enjoyed spending time with Janie, Sam was ready for the evening to come to an end. She stood and took her paper plate to the trash can. "Does anyone want any dessert? I think we have some ice cream in the freezer."

Janie followed suit and was soon standing beside Sam, peeking into the freezer with her. The half-gallon of chocolate fudge didn't appear to have been opened. "Um, ice cream sounds good. But I'm more of a vanilla person, myself. Want to run to the store with me?" She turned to Betsy and Sandra, who were still eating. "Do you mind?"

Betsy's grin belied her innocent comment. "You know, I think I'd like some strawberry. Are you sure you two don't mind fetching some?"

"Not a bit." Sam slammed the freezer shut. "Sandra, any requests?"

The blonde shook her head as she chewed a mouthful of pizza. She quickly swallowed. "Nope. I'm easy." She pointed her finger at Janie, who stifled a giggle. "No comments from you, smarty pants."

Janie grabbed her purse. "I wouldn't dream of it. Come on, Sam. I'll drive." She grabbed Sam's good arm and dragged her from the room.

They were halfway down the stairs when Sam stopped. "Hold on." She waited until Janie turned then put her unbroken hand behind Janie's neck. "I've wanted to do this all night." Her lips pressed against Janie's, and she almost tumbled back when her belt loops were grabbed and the kiss deepened.

With her libido on overdrive, Janie gently pressed Sam to a seated position on the stairs, straddling her hips. When they finally broke apart to breathe, she rested her forehead against Sam's. "This isn't getting us ice cream very fast, is it?"

"No, not really." Sam brushed her lips along Janie's throat. "But it's infinitely more satisfying."

"Oh, god." Janie tilted her head back to allow Sam easier access. Her eyes closed as the warm mouth moved closer to her pulse point. "We shouldn't —"

"Sssh." Sam sucked tenderly on Janie's neck. "Just a few more minutes," she pleaded. Her hand slid beneath Janie's tee shirt and cupped her breast. "You feel so good."

Janie gasped at the sensation before slowly moving back. "You're not making this any easier."

"Good." But Sam removed her hand from Janie's top. She brushed the hair away from Janie's eyes and kissed her quickly on the nose. "We'd better get that ice cream, huh?"

"I suppose." Janie got to her feet and helped Sam up. "Sandra's moving home tomorrow, whether she likes it or not. I've got plans for you."

Sam almost stumbled down the stairs at the hunger in Janie's tone. "I can't wait."

UNFORTUNATELY, SANDRA DIDN'T move home immediately. She was determined to have her apartment manager pay for the cleaning of her home. Janie and Sam couldn't find the privacy they wanted, making Janie short-tempered at work. On Thursday morning, things quickly got out of control.

Andrea tossed another stack of files onto Janie's desk. "Hey, Janice. Looks like you're getting behind again." She settled her abundant ass on the edge of the desk. "I don't know what your problem is, but you need to get busy."

"Janie," Janie corrected quietly.

"What?"

"My name is Janie. I've been telling you for years, but you only seem to get it right when you want something from me. Now please move."

The redhead picked up a small picture frame and glanced at it. "Wow. Your mom sure was old-looking in this."

Janie snatched the photograph out of Andrea's hand. "That's my grandmother," she grumbled. When Andrea made no effort to move, Janie saw red. "I said, get-off-my-desk!" Each word was louder, until her voice echoed in the room. She shoved Andrea, who wasn't able to catch herself in time and ended up on the floor.

"What the hell is your major malfunction?" Andrea stood and dusted off her tight blue dress. "You'll regret this, Janet."

"Janie!" With a growl, Janie picked up her stapler and was about to throw it at Andrea.

Dr. Richmond poked his head into the room. "What is going on in here?" He stared at Janie, whose face was bright red. "Is there a problem?"

Andrea pointed at Janie. "Ask her! All I did was bring in some files and she practically attacked me." She fluffed her hair and brushed by the doctor. "I'm going to lunch." Over her shoulder she added, "I want those files entered before you go home today, *Janie*." She gave the other woman a wicked grin before leaving the room.

"Argh!" Janie slammed the stapler onto the desk.

Ted Richmond sat in the visitor's chair. "Rough morning?"

"No, I'm sorry." Janie exhaled heavily and brushed the hair away from her eyes. "I shouldn't let her get to me like that." Unable to look him in the eye, she took great care in straightening the papers on her desk. "Is there something I can do for you?"

"I feel like I should be asking that of you." Ted propped his right ankle on his left knee. "How's Sam? Tammy said she'd come in last Friday to have her stitches removed, although I didn't get a chance to see her."

Janie finally smiled. "She's great. I haven't seen her much lately." Her face slowly changed into a frown. "I'm sorry about that scene with Andrea. She seems to push the wrong buttons with me."

Ted got to his feet. "Don't worry about it. If she wasn't Dr. Pelletier's niece, I doubt she'd even work here." He paused at the door. "If you ever need anyone to talk to, my door is always open."

"Thanks, Ted. I appreciate it." Janie opened up the program on her computer and started typing in the data in the first file. The office was slowly transferring all the files to a database, and she feared it was only a matter of time before she'd be out of a job. The only comforting thought was that if there weren't as many office workers, they wouldn't need a manager either. She hoped she'd get a chance to see Andrea in the unemployment line. She picked up the phone, needing to hear a friendly voice.

"Danny's, Sam speaking."

"Hi." Janie lowered her voice and kept her eyes on the door, afraid of being caught.

"Hey, beautiful. What's up?"

"Nothing, really. I was just thinking about you." The sexy growl on the other end of the phone caused Janie to blush. "Stop that."

Sam laughed. "Sorry. So, what are you doing for lunch? We don't open until two, so it's kinda lonely in here, if you get my drift."

"Oh, really? Well, I suppose I could bring you something to eat. I can be there a little after eleven, if that's okay."

"That would be perfect. But you don't have to bring me lunch, I can just nibble on you."

Janie flushed. "Would you behave? I still have to work, you know." But she couldn't keep the smile off her face. "I'll see you in a little while." They flirted for another minute, and then she hung up the phone, looking forward to lunch.

JANIE OPENED THE door to Danny's to see Sam whistling a tune as she wiped down tables. She was no longer wearing the sling, but Janie could tell that the cast that went halfway to Sam's elbow still kept her from doing as much as she wanted.

Sam looked up at the sound of the door opening and closing. She dropped the towel on a nearby table and rushed to meet Janie. "Hey."

Janie stopped inside the door to allow her eyes to adjust to the room. She laughed as Sam scooped her up and swung her around. "You nut, stop! You're going to hurt yourself."

"Nah, you don't weigh anything." But Sam lowered her to the ground to kiss her. "I've missed you." She took the bag of food from Janie's hand and held it by her side.

Her heart pounding from the unexpected ride, Janie returned the kiss with fervor. She linked her arms around Sam's neck as her body melded against the younger woman's. When Sam broke the embrace, she gave her a questioning look.

"Let me lock the door, so we won't be disturbed." Sam relocked the door and led Janie to a nearby table, where she placed the bag of food. She pulled out a chair for Janie, then brought another one close for herself.

It wasn't long before Janie moved from her chair to Sam's lap. "Is this okay?"

"Perfect." Sam put her arms around Janie to keep her from falling.

Janie looked into her eyes and saw the love shining back at her. "I can't believe this."

"What?"

"This." Janie ran her finger across Sam's cheek. "No one's ever looked at me the way you do, Sam."

Sam smiled shyly. "I know it's probably too soon to say this, but I lo—" Sam's lips were covered with Janie's finger.

"Shh." Janie shook her head. "I don't think I'm ready to hear that." There were too many unresolved issues to worry about, without hearing Sam bare her heart. Janie replaced her finger with her mouth and kissed Sam deeply.

They finally got around to eating the sandwiches Janie had brought, and were feeding each other potato chips when Janie noticed the time. "Damn! I've got to get back." She gathered her trash.

"I'll take care of all this." Sam followed her to the door and unlocked it. "I think you need to lobby for a longer lunch hour."

"That kind of defeats the whole 'lunch *hour*' part of the thing, doesn't it?" Janie sidled closer. She placed a soft kiss on Sam's lips. "What do you have planned for tonight?"

Sam cupped the side of Janie's face and kissed her slowly. "You tell me."

"I'm so tempted to call out sick for the rest of the day."

"I could always tie you up and hold you hostage in the back room," Sam offered.

Janie laughed and hugged her. "Don't tempt me."

"I guess I'll let you go, if I can see you tonight." Sam nipped her on the nose.

"One way or another, we'll see each other," Janie promised. She gave Sam one more quick kiss and backed out into the sunlight. "I wonder if Sandra's at work today. Because if she isn't, she'd better be cleaning her damned apartment." She took her cell phone out of her purse and hit the speed dial, growling when Sandra's phone went directly to voice mail. "Sandra, this is Janie. Call me as soon as you get this message, okay? Bye." She hustled back to work, hoping she wouldn't have another showdown with Andrea.

Chapter
Sixteen

AFTER RAY RELIEVED her, Sam hurried home to get cleaned up. She wasn't sure what Janie had in mind for the evening, but she was determined to be ready for whatever came up. She waved to Betsy as she headed for the stairs.

"Hold on there, speedy. Where's the fire?" Betsy asked.

"I was just going up to get a shower." Sam tapped her foot while she stood in place. "Anything else I can do for you?"

Betsy laughed. "Actually, I do need to talk to you about something, when you have the time."

Sam stopped tapping and leaned against the counter. "Are you okay? What's wrong?"

"Good god, kid. Why does everything have to be life and death around you? I said I wanted to talk, not write my will." Betsy walked around the counter and led Sam to the office. "Let's go someplace where it's quiet."

At Betsy's insistence, Sam closed the door behind them and sat on the sofa next to her. "Okay. I'm here, you're here. Now what is it that you want to talk about?" Sam's hand shook where it rested on her leg, until Betsy took it in her own.

"I swear, you worry more than an old woman."

"And I'll turn into one before you get to the point," Sam countered.

Betsy slapped her leg. "All right, fine. I got a phone call from a friend of mine and I was wondering if you'd mind watching the gym while I took a couple of weeks off to see her."

"That's all?" Sam fell back against the sofa and exhaled. "I was worried that something was wrong with you. I'll call Ray and see what I can work out with him."

"No, that won't be necessary. Pamela already said she'd be glad to handle things while you're at the bar. I just need you to keep an eye on things overall. Like making the bank deposits and keeping everything in order. Pretty much what you're doing all ready."

Sam laughed. "I see. How long will you be gone?"

"Oh, I don't know. A couple weeks. I haven't had a vacation in over twenty years. Think you can handle it?"

"Sure. You've done so much for me, Betsy. I'd love to be able to do something for you." Sam leaned into the older woman and gave her a one-armed hug. "Take as long as you need. The gym will still be here when you get back."

"Of that I have no doubt. Now, you want to tell me what's going on with you and Janie?"

"What do you mean?"

"Don't try to bullshit a bullshitter, Sam. The heat you two put off while you're in the same room is unbelievable. How're things going?"

Sam's face turned red. "Better than I could have hoped, although I think I almost blew it today."

"Why? What did you do?"

Sam's answer was unintelligible.

"Excuse me? What was that?"

"IalmosttoldherIlovedher," Sam rushed out.

Betsy had to think about it for a moment to realize what Sam said. "Do you?"

"What?"

The older woman slapped Sam on the leg. "Love her, you big goof."

Lowering her eyes, Sam nodded. "Yeah. I mean, I know it's too soon, but she makes me feel things I've never felt before." She turned her head and looked Betsy in the eye. "I do love her, Betsy. Is that wrong?"

"Hell no, kid. That's the rightest thing I've heard in a long time. How do you think she feels about you?"

"I'm not positive, but I think she feels the same. I mean, she hasn't come out and said it or anything. But I can see it in her eyes."

Betsy patted Sam on the shoulder. "Good. That's the way it should be." She backed away slightly. "You smell like smoke. I think you'd better get upstairs and take a shower."

Sam laughed. "No kidding." She stood and bent to kiss Betsy on the head. "Thanks for listening, Betsy. I love you."

"I love you too, you crazy kid." Betsy swatted her on the rear. "Now go on upstairs and get cleaned up. I figure you've probably got a hot date tonight." She laughed at Sam's wink, before the younger woman left the office. "Brat."

NOT READY TO face her friend if she was at her apartment, Janie went to the gym from work. On her way she stopped at The Wicked Wok and picked up enough food for Sam, Betsy and herself. She'd called Betsy before she left work and offered to bring dinner, which was met with excitement from the older woman. Janie parked behind the gym and headed up the stairs, balancing the take-out bags and her purse.

As Janie rounded the corner into the apartment, she saw Sam stretched out on the sofa, half-asleep. Sam yawned and checked her watch. "Too early for Betsy," she muttered, sitting up.

"You're right about that." Janie stepped into the living room and lifted the bags full of food. "Hungry?"

"Depends on if you're part of the menu." Sam rose from the sofa and took the take-out from Janie. She gave her a quick kiss on the lips. "It's great to see you."

Janie followed her into the kitchen and set her purse next to her usual chair at the table. She'd started spending more time here than she did at home. "I missed you, too." She watched as Sam removed the food from the sacks and placed the containers on the table. "Want me to grab some plates?"

"That would be great." Sam almost dropped a carton of rice when Janie ran her hand across her rear on her way to the pantry. "Whoa!"

"Problem?" Janie inquired playfully.

Sam exhaled quickly. "Uh, nope. Everything's fine. I guess I should buzz Betsy downstairs and tell her dinner's ready."

"No need." Janie melded her body against Sam's back and put the paper plates on the table. "I called her before I left work, and she said we should start without her."

"Really?" Sam turned and put her arms around Janie. "And what exactly should we be starting?" She grinned before nibbling on Janie's neck.

Janie moaned at the sensation and tilted her head back. "Mmm. Whatever you want."

"That's what I was hoping you'd say." Sam's mouth burned a path down Janie's throat. "God, I love how soft your skin is."

Feeling her knees go weak, Janie leaned against the table, causing it to scoot noisily. Her hands threaded through Sam's hair, silently urging her on. Several buttons on her blouse mysteriously opened, but before she could feel a draft, Sam's lips heated her breast. "Yes."

The buzzing of the intercom almost caused Sam to knock Janie over. "Dammit!" She backed away and blinked several times to get her brain to function. "I'm going to kill Betsy," she growled. She watched as Janie shakily buttoned her blouse. "Hold that thought."

Janie couldn't help but laugh at the look on Sam's face. She was certain hers wasn't much better. "It's probably for the best anyway."

Sam poked the outgoing button on the intercom. "What's up?"

"Looks like I'm going to be stuck down here for a while. Would you mind bringing me a plate of food? I can smell it all the way down here."

"Likely story," Sam teased, while Janie loaded a plate for Betsy. "Delivery will cost you extra."

"Put it on my tab," Betsy quipped. "And hurry up! You two can mess around after I'm fed."

Sam blushed and laughed. "I don't know how she does it," she told Janie, before pressing the button. "All right, old woman. I'll be right down."

"Good! Oh, and Sam?"

"Yes?"

"Don't forget to bring me a coke."

Sam watched Janie as she removed a cola from the refrigerator. "Have I ever?"

"Yes." Betsy laughed before she released the intercom.

Before Sam could take the plate, Janie held out her hand. "There's no sense in you having to juggle everything. Let me take it."

"Are you sure?" At Janie's nod, Sam turned over the soda. "I think she's just being ornery while she can, since she plans on leaving Saturday."

"I wouldn't be surprised." Janie kissed Sam's cheek. "Be right back."

Janie peeked over her shoulder and laughed when she saw Sam obviously watching the sway of her hips as she left the kitchen. Halfway down the stairs, Janie heard the sound of running water in the kitchen sink. "I bet she's splashing cold water on her face."

SAM AND JANIE ended up helping Betsy close and clean the gym for the night. Once they finished, the three of them sat at the kitchen table and played cards.

Betsy slapped a card onto a pile and cheered. "I'm out!" She stared gleefully at the handful of cards Sam still held. "Looks like I caught you good this time."

"Again." Sam silently counted the points she held. "I thought you said you were rusty at playing Canasta."

"Guess I limbered up." Betsy exchanged grins with Janie. "Didn't seem to hurt you as much."

Janie shook her head. "The way you've been playing, I didn't trust you. And it looks like I was right." She quickly totaled her cards and gave the number to Sam, who was the scorekeeper.

Sam wrote down her total and added up the columns. "You stomped us Betsy. Good thing we weren't playing for money." She gathered the cards and placed them in the box they came from, before yawning deeply.

"Teach you to beg for a rematch." Betsy glanced at the kitchen clock. "Good lord, it's almost two in the morning. Janie hon, maybe you should bunk down here for the night. I'd hate for you to be out on the streets this late."

"I don't live that far away. I should just go home."

The look on Betsy's face brooked no argument. "Humor an old woman. Please stay."

"That's a good idea. But not on that lumpy couch. You can sleep with me," Sam offered, before realizing how it sounded. Her face grew deep red. "Just sleep, I swear!"

Betsy laughed at her discomfort. "Don't worry Janie. Your virtue is safe with Miss Prude over there. I've never seen anyone so skitterish about sex before."

"Betsy!" Sam covered her face. "Do we have to discuss this now?"

Sam's embarrassment only caused the other two women to laugh louder. She got up from the table. "Yuck it up you two. I'm going to bed." She stopped in the doorway and winked at Janie. "Coming?"

WHEN SAM LEFT the room, Janie turned to Betsy. "Are you sure it's all right?"

"Please! We're all adults here. And I know damned good and well Sam won't do anything, especially as long as I'm around." Betsy stood and leaned closer to Janie. "Of course, I'll be leaving Saturday afternoon, if you catch my drift."

Janie's face turned beet red. "Oh god. I can't believe you said that."

Betsy patted her on the back. "Calm down. I only thought you'd enjoy the chance to spend some quality time together, without anyone else interfering."

"I do. But are you sure you want to leave so soon?"

"I'd have left tonight, if I could have gotten everything ready. I'm long overdue for a vacation, and I haven't seen my friends in years." Betsy gave her a hug. "But you two take care of each other while I'm gone, you hear? And be careful."

Janie returned the embrace eagerly. "We will. And you be careful too. It's a long drive."

"Only about eight hours, which I'll most likely split up into two days. Do a little sight-seeing while I'm at it. Now go on to bed and I'll see you both bright and early tomorrow."

Janie took her time heading for Sam's bedroom. She studied the photographs that adorned the hallway, picking a younger Betsy out of many of them. The one that brought an ache to her heart had to be the last picture taken of Betsy and her husband, Jack. He appeared to be several years older, but it was easy to see the happiness on both their faces. She took a deep breath and continued toward the bedroom. She stood in the door and watched as Sam searched through a dresser drawer. "Hi."

Sam turned, holding a pair of shorts and a tee shirt in her hand. "Hey." She waved the clothing. "Thought I'd dig up something for you to wear to bed."

"That's sweet of you, thanks." Janie held out her hand for the clothes, her face warming when she realized it was a pair of Sam's boxers. "I guess I'll get changed." She quickly escaped to the bathroom.

While she waited, Sam put clean sheets on the bed and changed into her own sleepwear. The threadbare black tee shirt had faded to a charcoal gray and the cartoon boxers had been a gift from Betsy. She played with the hem of the shorts while she sat on the edge of the bed.

Janie came out of the bathroom, her face still damp from scrubbing. She stepped into the bedroom and smiled shyly at Sam. "All yours, if you want it."

"Thanks." Sam gestured toward the bed. "Won't take me but a second. Pick either side, I'm flexible." She slipped by Janie and exchanged words with Betsy in the hall, before going into the bathroom and closing the door.

Betsy peeked in the bedroom and saw Janie staring at the queen-sized bed. "You know, it's more comfortable if you sleep *on* the bed," she teased.

Janie spun around, startled. "You scared me."

"Sorry, that wasn't my intention."

"That's okay. But I have no idea what I'm doing here." Janie sat on the edge of the bed, grateful when Betsy joined her.

"Well, I bet between the two of you, you'll figure it out soon enough." Betsy put her arm around Janie's shoulders. "I may have been teasing before, but it's true. Sam will most likely take her cue from you. She doesn't have it in her to be very aggressive. You have nothing to worry about."

Janie leaned into her. "I'm not worried about *that*," she whispered. "But what does worry me is if I'll be what she needs. I don't want to hurt Sam."

"If you're worried about hurting her, she's in safe hands." She stood and touched Janie's cheek. "I think you both are. Now get some sleep."

The bathroom door opened, and Sam came into the bedroom. The hug she received from Betsy wasn't unwelcome, but she did appear confused after the older woman left. She looked at Janie. "What was that all about?"

"Nothing." Janie scooted to the opposite side of the bed and crawled under the covers.

Sam turned out the light and joined her. Within seconds, she felt Janie snuggle close. "Um, Janie?"

"Shh." Janie put her head on Sam's shoulder and her arm across her stomach. She kissed her on the cheek. "Goodnight, Sam."

"Goodnight." Sam smiled into the darkness and put her good arm around Janie's shoulders. Sleep came quickly for them both.

Chapter
Seventeen

IT WAS CLOSE to one o'clock on Saturday afternoon when Betsy said her final goodbyes and hit the road. Both Sam and Janie stood by the back door of the gym and watched as Betsy drove away, struggling with their emotions. The older woman had been so kind to them in the short amount of time they'd known each other.

"I feel as if a part of my family is leaving." In order to keep the tears at bay, Sam cleared her throat. "I'm going to go see if there are enough towels in the locker room."

"All right." Janie followed Sam into the gym and watched as she headed toward the dressing area. She thought about how she felt when she woke shortly after dawn. Snuggled against Sam, she'd slept better than she expected. Even though she worried about being discovered, Janie knew without a doubt she cared deeply for Sam and was anxious about where their relationship was headed. She was so intent on watching Sam that she bumped into Pamela. "Oh! Excuse me."

"No harm done." Pamela Long set her bag on the floor by her feet. "Is everything okay? You seem a little out of it."

Janie nodded. "Nothing serious. Betsy left on her trip a few minutes ago."

"I'm glad she got off okay." Pamela leaned against the counter. "I meant to say something to her beforehand. I've got enough ladies signed up to start another class."

"What kind of class are you going to do? Will it be another aerobics, or something else?"

Pamela turned to watch several women making the circuit of machines in one corner of the gym. "This one will be the same. But I've also thought of something similar to aerobics, but with boxing moves sprinkled in. After what happened to Sam, I want the women to have a better chance to protect themselves."

"That's a really good idea," Janie agreed.

"I thought so. I've taken boxing, karate, and tae-kwon-do. But that was in Austin, before I moved here. There isn't anyplace close by to study self-defense. Do you think Betsy would mind if I put up a flyer?"

Sam stepped out of the locker area and joined them. "Hi, Pamela. What's up?"

"Not much, Sam. How are you feeling?"

"Better every day, thanks. You're early for your three o'clock class," Sam observed.

Pamela glanced at her watch. "True, but I was going to try and catch Betsy before she left, but Janie informed me that I was too late. Do you think I could talk to you for a moment?"

"Is everything all right?"

"Follow me to the office and you'll see." Pamela linked arms with Sam and led her away. She winked at Janie over her shoulder. "I hope you don't plan on exercising in that dress, Janie. I'm feeling particularly energetic today."

Janie laughed at the look on Sam's face. The teasing tone in Pamela's voice would worry anyone. But she had a point. Janie was wearing the same dress she had worn to work the previous day. "I think I'll run home and change. See you two in a little while."

Ten minutes later, Janie climbed the stairs to her apartment. As she unlocked the door she listened carefully, but all was quiet. Relief flowed through her, even as she maneuvered around Sandra's scattered mess in the living room. It looked as if a fraternity had moved in, but Janie didn't touch anything. She was in too much of a hurry to get back to the gym. The unpleasant odor of unwashed clothes assailed her senses, but she disregarded it and stepped over a pair of jeans and high-heeled boots on the way to her bedroom.

Within minutes, Janie changed into the clothes she'd bought to work out in: Black sweatpants, gray tank top and new white sneakers. She also decided to pack a bag so she could spend some quality alone time with Sam. Her closet floor was a mess and she rooted around until she found her overnight case. The floral-patterned tote had been a gift from her grandmother when she was in high school but had rarely been used. Janie packed it with a blue silk nightgown, her robe, jeans, a casual top and undergarments. She'd return home sometime Sunday afternoon, so she didn't bother to take work clothes. After hurriedly gathering toiletries from her bathroom, she checked her look in the mirror and closed the bag.

On the way to the gym, Janie realized she hadn't left a note in case Sandra returned to the apartment. She decided it wasn't too important, since her friend more than likely had gone home on Friday. As she turned onto the street where the gym was located, she noticed there wasn't any parking. Not concerned, Janie used Betsy's space. She parked next to Sam's "party barge," as Sam jokingly referred to the Oldsmobile. Although the car was unreasonably large, Janie considered it an upgrade from the rusty old Chevy Sam had driven into town. She shouldered her bag and went through the back door, smiling at what the weekend might bring.

AFTER THEY CLOSED the gym for the day, Janie helped Sam straighten and mop the locker room, so as a reward Janie was given first shot at the bathroom to clean up.

The kitchen was filled with tantalizing scents as Sam prepared dinner. She peeked beneath the lid of the pot on top of the stove and took a deep breath. "Perfect." The rolls in the oven were a nice compliment to the pot roast that she'd put in the crock pot that morning. She took note of the time, and knew that Janie would probably be a while in the shower.

Content the meal was well on its way to being done, Sam hurried to her room and gathered her own clean clothes to change into. She took a small trash bag from the box on her dresser so her cast wouldn't get wet. Not wanting to wait, she went downstairs to use the gym's showers.

JANIE STEPPED FROM the bathroom and tightened the robe around her body. It was almost eight o'clock in the evening so she'd decided to forego regular clothes. She could smell the roast, and followed her nose to the kitchen. "Sam, that smells—" her voice trailed off when she realized she was alone. "Now where has she run off to?"

"Right behind you," Sam answered, laughing when Janie whirled around and gave a short scream. "Scare you?"

"Brat!" Janie swatted her on the shoulder, noticing the shirt was stuck to Sam's skin and her hair was damp. "You're wet. How'd you manage that?"

Sam's smirk caused her to get hit again. "Ow. Why'd you hit me again?"

"For whatever you're thinking." The pout on Sam's face charmed Janie and she kissed her on the cheek. "Is that better?"

"A little." Sam laughed and dodged the hand that aimed for her rear. "Ha! You've got to be quicker than that to catch me." She pulled a chair away from the table. "Have a seat and I'll bring you some dinner. It should be ready."

The timer on the oven buzzed. Janie ignored the offered chair and grabbed an oven mitt from the counter. "Nope. I'll help."

They took their time eating, sharing small stories of their past while the food disappeared from their plates. Janie noticed how Sam's hair had grown out since she'd arrived in town. "Looks like you're due for a haircut. Have you always worn your hair that way?"

"No, this was a first." Sam wiped her mouth with her napkin. "I usually get it cut fairly short at the beginning of the summer so I don't have to worry about it for a while. But I had a cold the last time, and while the lady used the clippers on the back of my neck, I sneezed." Sam laughed remembering the woman's look of horror. "She ran it right up the back of my head several extra inches. We both figured it would look better shaved all around the sides, instead of just a stripe. At least I got the haircut for free."

Janie almost spewed her water across the table. She swallowed hastily. "I bet that was something!" She raised her hand and brushed it against the side of Sam's head. "I think it's rather sexy."

"Really? Just about everyone I've met has given me grief over it."

"It suits you." Janie leaned closer and kissed Sam lightly on the lips.

Sam scooted her chair closer and took Janie into her arms. What was left of their meal was soon forgotten as they melted into each other. When Janie's hand snaked beneath her tee shirt, Sam almost tipped backward in her chair.

"Let's go to bed," Janie ordered. She stood and helped Sam to her feet.

Unable to form any words, Sam stumbled after her.

In Sam's room, Janie stopped by the bed and turned to face her. She untied the belt on her robe and slid the garment from her shoulders, allowing it to pool around her feet. A little nervous about her appearance, she watched Sam as she took in the blue satin nightgown. Her fears were erased by the look of love emanating from the younger woman's eyes. Feeling much braver, Janie took Sam's left hand and placed it on her breast. Her eyes closed as she was gently squeezed. "Oh, god, that feels good." She lay back on the bed and pulled Sam down on top of her. "Come here."

Sam pressed against Janie, but kept the majority of her weight on her good arm as she stretched out. She used the fingertips on her broken hand to brush the hair away from her lover's eyes. "I love you, Janie. I know you said you weren't ready to hear it, but—"

"No." Janie smiled. "I'm ready." She traced the smile on Sam's face. "I love you too." She almost cried at the startled look of joy her words caused. Her lips were quickly covered by Sam's and she used her hands to pull the younger woman closer.

HER BLADDER WOKE Janie around three in the morning. She rolled off of a sleeping Sam and made her way quietly to the bathroom. While she washed her hands, she studied herself in the mirror. She wondered what Sam saw in her. As far as she was concerned, she had boring brown eyes and plain features. She adjusted her wire-framed glasses and considered buying contacts. For the first time in her life, she *wanted* to look more attractive. While in school, she'd considered her appearance a blessing, because she didn't want to be bothered by boys. And as she got older, she didn't care much for men, either. Thinking back to the previous evening, she finally understood why. She dried her hands and returned to bed.

Janie rolled onto her side and watched Sam as she slept. Her fingers itched to touch her. Although she was concerned about how they were going to hide their relationship from those that would do them harm, there was no remorse or guilt after their evening together. She'd never felt more right about anything in her life, and Janie felt a fierce determination to protect Sam, no matter what.

With a sigh, Sam turned and faced Janie. Her eyes opened slowly and a smile graced her features. "Hey." She tucked her arm beneath her pillow. "Are you okay?"

"Very." Janie pressed her lips to Sam's. "I was just thinking."

"About earlier?"

Janie smiled. "Among other things." She used her hand to pull Sam closer. "I love you."

Sam's eyes sparkled. "I never thought I'd hear someone tell me that."

"Really?"

"Yeah." Sam kissed her slowly and thoroughly. She smiled against Janie's lips, before moving down her throat. "I love you, Janie." She licked and nipped her way toward Janie's chest, enjoying the harsh breathing and moans her actions caused.

Janie wondered for a moment how long Sam could prolong this sweet torture. With her insistent hands on Sam's shoulders, pressing her lower, Janie realized it wouldn't be long at all.

BY EARLY SUNDAY afternoon, Janie knew without a doubt where her heart belonged. She stood next to Sam in the kitchen, helping prepare lunch. The revelation brought her a sense of peace. She watched as Sam, clad only in her boxers, scrambled eggs on the stove. The tantalizing view was more than she could take and Janie slowly ran her finger down Sam's nude back.

"Stop that," Sam grumbled good naturedly. She waved the spatula. "You're gonna make me burn them."

"You shouldn't tempt me, running around all National Geographic like that."

"You're the one who stole my shirt and wouldn't let me get another one. So don't blame me for how I'm dressed." The grin on Sam's face told Janie that Sam wasn't very upset with the clothing arrangement. She knew Sam liked how the "borrowed" tee shirt barely reached the top of Janie's thighs. It was a wonder they ever made it out of the bedroom. "Would you like to get the plates? I think these are about done."

Janie put the dishes next to the stove before cutting up the cantaloupe she'd found in the refrigerator. She turned in time to see the muscles twitch in Sam's back as she dished out the eggs. Desire shot through Janie and she closed her eyes momentarily. She'd never felt so...wanton, before. This all-encompassing hunger to be with Sam was beyond anything she'd ever experienced. She swallowed and seriously considered sticking her head in the freezer to cool off. When Sam moved the pan off the burner and turned around, the need grew stronger and her hands began to tremble.

"Janie? Are you all right?"

Before Sam could pick up the plates, Janie shoved her against the counter. "God, you make me so damned hot!" she growled, right before she slid Sam's shorts to the floor. Their bodies soon followed and lunch was quickly forgotten.

MONDAY MORNING ARRIVED too soon and Janie was seriously tempted to call in sick to work. In order to not miss a single moment of their time together, she'd shared a shower with Sam. Now she stood in the bedroom with her packed bag and struggled to keep her tears at bay. "I don't want to leave," she admitted sadly.

Sam, also fully dressed, pulled Janie into her arms. "And I don't want you to go, either. But we both have responsibilities today."

"I know, but I'm afraid." Janie snuggled closer and tucked her head against Sam's chest.

"Of what, baby?" Sam ran her fingers through Janie's hair.

Janie sniffled. "Of losing this."

"That's the last thing you should worry about." Sam kissed her head. "Nothing or no one can change the way I feel about you." She used her fingers to gently force Janie to look at her. "We're both going to work, get through the day, and spend tonight together. That is, if you want."

"I definitely want." Janie kissed Sam's chin before moving toward her mouth. The contact was gentle but affirming. "Can I bring you lunch today?"

The plaintive tone was almost Sam's undoing. "I'd like that a lot. I'll leave the front door unlocked for you."

"Please don't. I'd worry about you all morning. I'll knock."

"Okay, if it'll make you feel better." As much as she didn't want to, Sam released her hold on Janie. "You'd better scoot if you're going to stop by your place before work."

Janie took in her appearance. The tee shirt she'd borrowed from Sam was slightly baggy on her smaller frame, and her jeans were wrinkled from being in her overnight bag. She'd definitely need to change into more appropriate work clothes. "I know. But it's hard." She took a deep breath, released it and stepped away. "All right. I'll see you a little after twelve, okay?"

"I'll be waiting." Sam tucked her hand into her pocket to keep from grabbing Janie and dragging her back into the room. "I love you."

"Love you, too." Janie blew Sam a kiss before she disappeared into the hallway. She hurried down the stairs, afraid to look back. If she stopped, she knew she'd end up back in Sam's arms, and neither one of them would get to work.

She barely remembered the drive home. So engrossed in her

thoughts, Janie unlocked her apartment and was halfway to the bedroom before she found out she wasn't alone.

Sandra sat up on the couch and rubbed her eyes. She glanced at her watch. "Janie? Are you just now getting home? Where the hell have you been all weekend?"

Angry at the tone in Sandra's voice, Janie continued to her bedroom. "Not that it's any of your business, but I stayed with a friend. Why aren't you at your own apartment?"

"Well, excuse me for caring!" Sandra followed and stood at the bedroom door. "When I didn't see or hear from you on Saturday, I decided to hang out here in case something was wrong."

"You could have called my cell, if you were so concerned." Janie turned her back and started to strip. She didn't have time to placate her friend. She turned to search her closet for something to wear.

Sandra was about to snap off a caustic retort when she noticed several small bruises on Janie's lower neck and chest. "My god, what happened to you?" She hurried over to get a closer look. "Did Doug do that to you?"

Janie looked down and blushed. "No, I haven't seen Doug in a while." She grabbed the first blouse she saw and rushed to button it closed.

"Wait a minute. Those look like—" Sandra narrowed her eyes. "Hickeys? Just who the hell did you spend the weekend with?" She saw her friend blush and turn away. "I didn't know you were seeing someone else. Who's the lucky guy?"

Tears filled Janie's eyes. She didn't want to have this conversation so soon with Sandra. "It's not a guy."

Comprehension flooded through Sandra and she shook her head. "Oh, hell no. You can't be serious. Not with *her*!" She took several steps back. "You can't be like *that*! My god, we've slept in the same bed!" Her lower lip began to tremble and she held up her hands as if to ward off the thoughts. "We went to *Bible school* together when we were kids."

"Sandra, wait. It has nothing to do with you and me." Janie moved slowly toward her friend. "Haven't you always said you wanted me to be happy?"

"Yes, but—"

"*Sam* makes me happy. I don't know how it happened, but I feel things for her I've never felt before. I love her."

Sandra kept shaking her head as she gathered her clothes from around the living room. "No, that's not possible. She's tricked you or something, that's what it is. You can't be," her voice lowered, "queer." She tossed everything into the satchel that she'd thrown by the sofa.

"Wait, please," Janie begged, grasping Sandra's arm. "Let's talk about this."

"Get your hands off me!" Sandra screamed, flinging Janie's hand away. "I can't be around you, Janie." She opened the front door before digging her key ring out of her purse. With shaky hands, she removed the key that Janie had given her years ago and threw it at her ex-friend. "You make me sick. I hope you both rot in hell."

Janie flinched as the door slammed behind Sandra. She looked at the key lying a few feet away and broke into tears. Wrapping her arms around her body, Janie dropped to her knees and sobbed.

THE OFFICE WAS quiet when Janie slipped in shortly before nine. She placed her purse in her desk drawer and powered up her computer. Before she could log in, Andrea poked her head into the room.

"I see you decided to grace us with your presence today," the redhead quipped. She tossed a thick stack of folders on Janie's desk. "I haven't gotten around to doing these insurance forms. Be a dear and have them done by lunch today, would you?"

Janie opened the top folder and glanced at the date. "These are over a month old, Andrea."

"I know. And we can't bill the patient until the insurance has been filed. Dr. Richmond was asking about them earlier, which you'd have known if you'd bothered to come in on time." Andrea noticed Janie's red and puffy eyes. "Have you been crying?"

"No, it's allergies." Janie wasn't about to get into a personal discussion with her. She stood, gathered the files and pushed them into Andrea's chest. "Do your own work. I'm tired of cleaning up after you."

Andrea's eyes grew wider as she juggled the folders. "Excuse me? Since when do you talk to me that way?" She dropped them on the desk, causing several to fall to the floor. "Now look what you've made me do!" She tried to bend to pick them up, but her tight skirt restricted her movement.

Janie opened the lower desk drawer, removed her purse and stepped around the desk. "I've decided to take the day off, Andrea. I'll tell Dr. Richmond on my way out."

"What? No, you can't! This stuff has to get done today!" Andrea started to cry.

HALFWAY DOWN THE hall, Janie saw Ted about to enter his office. "Dr. Richmond, may I talk to you for a moment?"

He held the door open for her. "Of course. Please come in." Once she was seated he took his place behind the desk. "Now, what seems to be the problem?"

"I have some vacation time left, don't I?" She brushed her hair away from her face and tucked it behind one ear. "I know this is short notice, but something's come up and I would like to take some time off, if at all possible."

"Take all the time you need. You've probably got a month's worth of vacation since you rarely take any." Ted could see that she was struggling to keep from crying. "What is it? Has something else happened to Sam?"

She shook her head. "She's fine. It's just—" Unable to control herself any longer, Janie covered her eyes as a sob tore from her throat. "I'm sorry."

Ted hurried around the desk and sat in the visitor's chair next to her. "Forgive me for saying so, but you look as if you've lost your best friend."

"I think I have." She bent at the waist and continued to cry. It took several minutes for her to get her emotions under control. With a wavering breath Janie accepted the tissue that Ted offered and wiped her eyes. "Thanks."

"You're welcome." He gave her a little more time to compose herself. "If you need someone to talk to, I hope you know you can always come to me. If not me, then consider talking to Sharon."

"I appreciate your concern, but this is something I'm going to have to handle on my own." Janie blew her nose and went to the door. "Thank you for your help, though. I should be back tomorrow."

He sighed. "That's fine, Janie. Just give us a call if you need anything." Ted watched as she straightened her shoulders and left the office. He went to his desk and picked up the phone. "Andrea, please get the backlog of insurance filed before you leave today. No, I want *you* to handle it. Yes, *you*. I don't want to hear it, Andrea. Goodbye."

A SOFT ROCK tune on the jukebox kept Sam company as she wiped down all the tables in the bar. She barely heard the knock on the front door over the music. Sam tossed the damp towel onto her shoulder and unlocked the heavy door. Her surprise at seeing Janie so early left her speechless.

Janie stood in front of Sam, unsure of the reception. "Sam? Is this a bad time?"

"Uh, no. Of course not. Come on in." Sam stepped back to allow Janie to enter. "I thought—" her words cut off when Janie launched herself at her. She automatically wrapped her arms around her lover.

Unable to stop herself, Janie began to cry. She was only slightly aware of being led to the nearest chair and being pulled into Sam's lap. Her head rested on Sam's shoulder and her tears stained the navy blue tee shirt. The light caress on her head only fueled her sobs.

"Shh. Baby, it's okay." Sam rocked and held her close.

It took Janie quite a while to calm down but she was finally able to raise her head. "I'm sorry."

"Hey, don't ever be sorry for coming to me when you're upset." Sam kissed Janie's forehead. Her fingers wiped the damp tracks from Janie's cheeks. "Did something happen at work?"

"No, not at work. Sandra was at my place when I got home this morning." The vicious words kept racing through her head. "She knows about us."

Sam tried to stay calm. "I'm sorry. What happened?" When Janie started to cry again, it took everything Sam had not to hunt down Sandra and tear her apart. "Did she hurt you?"

"Not physically. But she said some pretty hurtful things. She thought I'd found a new boyfriend, and I couldn't lie to her." Janie wiped her nose with the tissue she'd held since leaving the office. "I can't really blame her for getting so upset. It had to be a pretty huge shock. We've been friends since we were little kids."

"Some friend," Sam grumbled.

For some reason, Sam's protective streak calmed Janie. She kissed her softly on the lips. "Thanks." One kiss became two, the second deeper and hungry. She struggled to remove Sam's shirt from her jeans when they heard a heavy pounding on the back door. Shaking, she slid from Sam's lap and backed away. "What's that?"

Sam glanced at the clock over the bar. "A dead man." She stood and tried to straighten her shirt. "Just a beer delivery. I'll be right back."

"Wait." Janie helped Sam with her shirt. "I'm going to run home and get some housework done since Dr. Richmond gave me the day off. Sandra nested in the living room and left a huge mess, and I have to run to the laundromat. I've been neglecting my dirty clothes for too long."

Sam grinned at the flushed look on her lover's face. "All right." The pounding continued. "Will you be over tonight?"

"I'll bring dinner," Janie promised. "No, on second thought, I'll cook dinner. How about fried chicken?"

"Sounds great. Why don't you bring over your laundry? Betsy's got a full-sized washer and dryer."

"All right." Janie gave Sam another quick kiss. "Better go answer the door before he knocks it down." She went out the front door at the same time Sam let the deliveryman inside.

Chapter
Eighteen

THE AFTERNOON CROWD was loud, mostly thanks to the group from Doug's Lawn Care. They had several tables pushed together and were starting to get on Sam's nerves. She couldn't be certain, but she thought she'd heard the voice of her attacker again within the crowd. But with all of them laughing and carrying on, she couldn't assign the individual voices to faces. She exchanged the full pitcher of beer with an empty and returned to the bar.

Reggie lit another cigarette and glared at the retreating woman. "Stupid bitch didn't seem to learn her lesson," he muttered.

"What was that, Pop?" Doug asked while he poured himself another mug of beer.

"Nothin'." Reggie inhaled deeply of the Camel cigarette he'd recently lit. He exhaled, causing Doug to cough. "Damned wimp."

Doug wiped his watering eyes. "Not everyone wants to die of lung cancer, old man. What's gotten into you, anyway?"

Reggie blew more smoke at his son, getting a perverse pleasure over seeing him gag. "You made up with your girlfriend yet?"

"We're friends, if that's what you're asking. But I'm not dating Janie anymore."

"That's a shame. Your Ma really liked her."

Although he liked to make his mother happy, Doug refused to get back with a woman who didn't want him. He took several swallows of his beer and belched. "Too bad."

Reggie scribbled a note on a napkin. "Think I'll run to the john. Have another round brought out, will ya?"

"Sure." Doug waved to Sam, who acknowledged him with a nod.

Reggie took his time, waiting until Sam brought over the drinks. While she spoke to Doug, Reggie took the opportunity to duck into the office and leave the napkin on the desk, where it couldn't be missed.

SAM PLACED SEVERAL empty pitchers on a tray and carefully carried it to the back. She left them next to the sink and was on her way back to the main room when she heard the back door open. "Hey, Ray. You're in early."

"Yeah, it was either come in to work or listen to my brother complain about his wife. I wish they'd make up so he could go home. He's cramping my style." Ray started running water in the sink. "You didn't have to bring these back. I could have gotten them."

"Nah, that's okay. I was afraid we were going to run out."

He joined her in the doorway and peered into the main room. "Yard guys going strong?"

"Definitely. I don't understand how they can take off at three or four every day. They sure keep me busy, though." She watched as several of the men stood and headed for the front door. "Guess I'd better get those tables taken care of."

Ray touched her arm. "I'll do it, if you don't mind taking yesterday's deposit to the bank. It's locked up in my bottom desk drawer."

"All right." Sam accepted his keys. "You really should think about getting a safe."

"Are you kidding? The owner would never go for that kind of unnecessary expense." He gave her a light push. "Go on. Tracy will be in later to take care of the dishes."

She nodded. "I'll bring your keys to you on the way out."

"Don't bother. Just leave them on the desk." Ray waved to Doug, who was standing at the bar. "Be right there."

Grateful she didn't have to serve any more beer to Doug and his cronies, Sam went into the office and sat at the desk. She unlocked the bottom drawer and removed the deposit bag, double-checking to make sure everything was inside. More than once she'd taken it to the bank, only to have to backtrack. Ray was a nice guy, but tended to be forgetful.

She set the keys down and saw the paper napkin with handwriting on it. Curious, she picked it up and read aloud. "Why are you still here – ready for round two?" Her heart started to pound and Sam dropped the napkin as if it were on fire. Flashbacks to the beatings she'd endured during high school caused sweat to break out along her brow. Since she always got the register drawer off the desk every morning, she knew the note hadn't been there earlier.

Sam didn't know what she should do. She understood now that she should have gone to the police after the attack, but was afraid of what could have happened to Janie. Since the written threat wasn't explicit enough, she decided to wait and see what happened. She folded the napkin and tucked it in her front pocket then picked up the deposit bag. She'd be extra careful from now on.

ANOTHER FACE FULL of water was Sam's penalty for turning the bolt holding the showerhead the wrong direction. She wiped her face and cursed, feeling her tee shirt stick to her skin. She twisted the wrench the opposite direction until the dripping stopped. To make certain it was properly repaired she stepped out of the way and turned on the cold water. It sprayed downward and splashed her bare feet. "Finally."

Sam came out of the showers and tried to ignore Pamela's giggles. She knew she looked ridiculous. Her work shirt from Danny's was drenched and the athletic shorts she wore were dripping as well. She was glad she thought to change out of her jeans before tackling the leaky shower. "Yuck it up, Pamela."

"You should have taken some soap in there with you," Pamela teased.

"Thanks for the advice. Next time I'll let you handle it." Sam wiped her wet hair out of her eyes.

Pamela wriggled her manicured nails. "No thank you. That's what I have a husband for." When Sam moved closer and shook her head like a dog, Pamela squealed. "Yuck! Go upstairs and change. I'll stick around until you get back."

"Nah, that's okay. It's only fifteen minutes 'til close. I'll dry." Sam took a towel from beneath the counter and ruffled her hair. "Go on home to your husband. I appreciate you staying as long as you have."

"Okay, if you're sure." Pamela hefted her workout bag and looped the strap over her shoulder. "If you hear from Betsy have her give me a call. I've got a few more ideas I'd like to run by her."

Sam draped the towel around her shoulders. "Sure thing. Have a good night." She heard the ceiling creak and her smile grew.

UPSTAIRS, JANIE SET the grocery bags on the kitchen counter. She put everything away before returning to her car for her laundry.

On her way back in, she left her basket of dirty clothes beside the washer, which was located beneath the stairs. While she sorted the clothes, she came to the realization that she didn't have enough for full loads. Instead of doing three small batches, she went upstairs to see if Sam had any clothes she could add.

After gathering what few of Sam's she could find, she returned downstairs and added them to hers. When she tossed a pair of jeans into a stack, Janie heard the rattling of change. She checked the front left pocket and came up with a handful of coins as well as a neatly folded paper napkin. Uncertain if she should save it or throw it away, she opened it. The handwritten message made her skin crawl. Janie was debating what to do when the door from the gym opened and Sam walked in.

"I thought I heard you upstairs a little while ago." Sam went to Janie but stopped short. "What's the matter?"

Janie held out the napkin. "I brought your stuff down to put in with mine, and I found this in your pocket."

Sam grimaced at the obvious fear in her lover's face. "I was going to tell you about it tonight." She took the note from Janie and wadded it up. "Are you okay?"

"Me? What about you?"

"Yeah, I'm okay." Sam leaned against the dryer and tried to appear unaffected by the conversation.

"What are you going to do about it?"

Sam shrugged. "Not much I can do. Other than keep my eyes open."

Janie clenched her hands into fists and slowly counted silently to five. "That's it?" She moved closer to Sam and grasped her arms. "Aren't you scared?"

"Hell yeah, I'm scared. But I don't know what else you want me to do." Sam broke Janie's grip and backed away. "Whoever this bastard is, he obviously won't be satisfied until I'm gone."

The words frightened Janie more than any unseen attacker. She asked softly, "Is that what you want?"

"Not now, no. I'm not letting some redneck run me out of town. I'll leave when I'm damned good and ready."

Janie felt a sharp pain in her chest. "You're planning on leaving?"

"No!" Sam snapped, then repeated more gently, "No." Her defensive posture relaxed and she took Janie into her arms. "You can't get rid of me that easily," she murmured, kissing the side of Janie's head. "I love you."

AFTER DINNER, THEY sat on the living room sofa and folded the clean laundry. Janie held up a scruffy blue tee shirt and laughed.

"What's so funny?"

"I can almost see through this thing, Sam. Don't you think it's about time to retire it?"

Sam snatched the item from Janie's hands and held it close to her body. Originally navy, the shirt was now a much lighter blue. Whatever lettering had been on the front had peeled away, leaving tiny splotches of darker material. "No way. I've had it since high school."

"And it shows, honey. It has holes under the arms so big you could put your fist through them."

"So?" Sam reverently folded the top and set it beside her, as far away from Janie as possible. "It's just well-ventilated."

Janie gave up. "If you say so." She started sorting through Sam's various styles of socks when the phone rang. "Do you want me to get that?"

"Nah." Sam stood, and with a teasing grin, grabbed the folded tee shirt and waved it as she went to the kitchen. She picked up the phone on the third ring. "Hello? Haley residence."

"Sam, I thought I told you to quit answering the phone like that. You sound like the hired help," Betsy admonished. "It's your home, too."

"Hi, Betsy. How's your vacation?" Sam stretched the phone cord to the kitchen table and sat, placing her shirt close at hand.

"I'm having a wonderful time, and don't think I didn't notice you changing the subject. Is everything okay there?"

"Of course. Well, there *was* that flood in the gym earlier today, but—"

"What?" Betsy yelped. "Flood?"

Sam laughed as she propped her feet on another chair. "Gotcha. Actually, one of the shower heads in the locker room needed a new washer. It was only a slight drip, and didn't take me any time at all to fix it."

"Thank god. I swear, you're just trying to turn my hair completely white, aren't you? No, forget I asked." Betsy was silent for a moment. "Seriously though, are you all right? Any more problems?"

The question caused Sam to pause. She didn't see any reason to tell Betsy about the note she'd just received. "Nope. All nice and quiet."

"How about my neighbors? Any complaints about the noise?"

"Noise? I don't think the aerobics classes are that loud. At least no one's said—"

Betsy's rich laughter echoed through the phone. "I was talking about the *upstairs* aerobics. You can't tell me that you two haven't done anything yet. I haven't seen that many sparks since the last electrical storm," Betsy chortled.

"Betsy!" Although she was alone, Sam still covered her eyes in mortification.

Janie came into the kitchen. She raised Sam's legs and took the chair, allowing Sam's feet to rest in her lap. She took the handset away from her embarrassed lover. "Betsy? Is everything all right?"

The older woman continued to laugh. "Never better, hon. I was just tweaking Sam. She's so easy."

"Uh-huh. How's Santa Fe?"

"Marvelous. You should really think about taking a vacation out here. It's the most amazing place."

Sam left the kitchen, only to return moments later with the cordless phone from Betsy's room. She winked to Janie before joining the conversation. "I take it you're enjoying yourself?" she asked Betsy as she returned to her chair and put her feet up again. "Been chasing any good looking men while you're there?"

It was Betsy's turn to be embarrassed, but it didn't take her long to bounce back. "Let's just say I'm having a good time and leave it at that. But, that's also why I called. Since there aren't any problems, I'd like to stay here longer and visit. I ran into a very dear friend just the other day. His name is Al, and he was my Jack's best friend for years."

"That's wonderful, Betsy." Janie grabbed Sam's sock-covered toes and wiggled them. "Sam's doing a great job taking care of the place."

Sam rolled her eyes. "Pamela's really doing most of the work. I just close up. So, Betsy, tell us about this guy? Is he married?"

"Widowed, actually. His wife Norma passed a couple of years ago.

The four of us used to have all sorts of fun before Jack and I moved to Piperton. He has a couple of restaurants here, and one of them is somewhat of a hangout for people our age. It's been nice to catch up with him."

"I'll bet." Sam yelped when Janie pinched her big toe. "What was that for?" she whispered, covering the mouthpiece.

Betsy went on, ignoring Sam. "Anyway, as I was saying, I'd like to stay another few weeks if you can handle the place. Will that be a problem?"

Sam had her foot in her lap, trying to protect it from Janie. "No problem at all, Betsy."

"Thank you, dear. But don't hesitate to call if you need anything." They chatted a few more minutes before hanging up, Betsy promising to keep them updated.

FOR THE NEXT week things were quiet for Sam. Whoever had left her the threatening note either didn't come into the bar, or had decided to leave her alone. Not one to look a gift horse in the mouth, Sam settled down to enjoy her work. With Janie spending the evenings with her, she also had the nights to look forward to.

She looked up when Doug knocked on the bar. "Need another round?"

"Yeah." He sat on a barstool to wait for her to fill a pitcher. "You're friends with Janie, aren't you?"

Sam nodded as she concentrated on not spilling the brew. "Yes."

"And you've seen her?" He kept his voice low. "Lately?"

"I have. Why?" Sam placed the beer in front of him.

Doug tossed a few bills on the bar. "I was just wondering. She's not been too lonely or nothing, has she?"

"Uh, no. She seems pretty happy to me."

"Good." He waved off her attempt to make change and took the pitcher to his group.

Sam placed the two dollar tip in the tall jar on the counter. If the conversation hadn't been so nerve-wracking, she might have laughed. She was glad Doug seemed to be over Janie. With a quick glance at the clock, Sam silently counted the hours until her relief would arrive.

The Thursday afternoon crowd was quieter than usual. Sam decided to put a dollar in the jukebox to liven things up. Her fingers had almost snagged a bill from the neck of the tip jar when the phone rang. "Danny's, Sam speaking. How can I—"

"Thank god. I was hoping to catch you." Pamela sounded out of breath.

"What's going on? Are you okay?"

"Look, something's come up, and I won't be able to handle mornings at the gym for a while. I know you've got others things to take care of, but this can't be helped. I'm really sorry."

"That's okay, Pamela. You take care of what you need to, and I'll handle the gym."

"Thank you Sam."

After thinking it over, Sam called Ray and asked him to come in early for her. She explained her situation, and he promised to be there as soon as possible. She tried to get everything stocked and cleaned, but hadn't gotten far when he came in the front door.

"Sorry it took so long, Sam." Ray tied an apron around his waist as he stepped behind the bar. "Things look good."

"Yeah, it's been a little slow today. Thanks for coming in early." She loaded the last of the bottled beer in the fridge beneath the counter. "I may have to change my hours. If Pamela can't open the gym, I'll have to spend the day there."

He shrugged. "Not a problem. Would it bother you if I hired another bartender? I had a guy come in yesterday who looked pretty good."

"Actually, that would be great. I don't know how long Betsy will be gone, but two full-time jobs are starting to kick my ass. I can handle some evenings if you need me to, though."

"Nah, that's okay. Take some time off. Maybe come back and play when you get your cast removed?" He dumped the tip jar and handed the money to Sam. "This is yours."

Sam knew better than to turn it down. She'd tried once before, and found out how stubborn Ray could be. "Thanks." She pocketed the cash. "If you need a break some evening, give me a call." She felt the heavy burden on her shoulders lighten as she stepped out of the bar and turned toward home.

Chapter
Nineteen

THE FOLLOWING WEEK moved along without incident. Sam returned to Dr. Richmond's office for a check up, which turned into something more. They were alone in the examination room and she studied her right hand and wrist. It smelled horrible, looked scaly, but Sam couldn't have been happier. She slowly clenched her hand into a fist, pleased that she could do so.

"How's that feel?" the doctor asked.

"Not too bad." Sam sat patiently while he turned her hand over. She flinched as he touched her fingertips with a pin. At his request, she moved each finger independently.

Dr. Richmond moved away and washed his hands at the sink. "You appear to have fully recovered, Sam. Although I don't remember making the cast that short."

"Uh, well," she stammered, embarrassed at being caught. By the time she came to have it removed, the plaster was only a couple of inches below her wrist. "It got in my way." Afraid she sounded ungrateful, she added, "It didn't hurt, though. And I really appreciate you letting me make payments. I don't know what I would have done otherwise."

"That's quite all right. But, as I've told you before, our office has allowances for those who don't have insurance. You didn't have to pay us anything."

Sam picked at the dead skin on her hand. "I know. And I am grateful. But I want to pay. I'm not a charity case."

Ted sighed. "Yes, I understand." He sat on the rolling stool and moved toward her. "Okay, how about this? I could use some help moving the old files that have been entered into the computer to a storage facility. They have to be alphabetically boxed, the boxes labeled, and then transported to the other side of town. It'll probably take a full day to complete the work. Do you think you can do it?"

"That's it?"

"Believe me, it's more than enough. We'll figure out how much money per box, and if it runs over what you owe, I'll pay you the difference in cash."

"Okay." Sam slid off the exam table and held out her hand. "But don't try to overpay on the boxes."

He shook his head. "You are the most stubborn woman I've ever met."

"That's what Janie tells me," she joked. "Will I be able to do the work at night, or maybe on Sunday? I've got the gym to worry about during the day."

"Sure. We can meet here Sunday morning. I've got a lot of paperwork of my own to catch up." He opened the door for her. "Does Janie know you're here?"

"Nope. I figured I'd see her tonight at the gym, when she came for her class. Why?"

Ted tucked his hands into the pockets of his lab coat. "No real reason, I suppose. Just curious." He made a point of looking at his watch. "Hey, it's almost noon. Why don't you stop by her office and see if she'll go to lunch?"

"What are you up to, Doc?"

"Nothing." He followed Sam down the hall, keeping his voice low. "Your friendship has done wonders for her, Sam. I don't think I've ever seen her as happy as she's been these past months."

Sam struggled to keep a neutral look on her face. The last thing she wanted was for him to find out their true relationship. As nice as Dr. Richmond was, she was afraid that if he knew, Janie would lose her job. "She's been a good friend to me."

"I'm glad." Ted stopped outside Janie's door. "I'll see you Sunday morning, around eight?"

"Sure thing." Sam watched him disappear into his office before she tapped on Janie's door. She stuck her head into the room. "Hey."

Janie looked up from her computer, her frown of concentration brightening immediately. "Hi! What are you doing here?"

Sam waved her right hand. "Ta-dah!"

"Oh, Sam, that's wonderful!" Janie hurried around her desk and wrapped her arms around Sam. Before she realized what she was doing, she kissed the younger woman on the cheek. "I'm so happy for you."

The clicking of heels on the tile floor in the hall caused them to quickly separate. Sam leaned against a file cabinet and crossed her arms over her chest, just as Andrea came in.

"Joanie, I have more files for you." She dropped the foot-high pile in the middle of Janie's desk.

Sam pushed away from the cabinet and got into Andrea's face. "Her name's *Janie*. As I'm sure you know."

Andrea's face turned red and she backed away from Sam. "I-I-I, of course. Sorry." She hurried out of the room as quickly as she arrived.

"That was mean," Janie fussed, moving closer to Sam. "But I enjoyed it." She linked her hand with Sam's. "Take me to lunch, my bodyguard."

"You got it, pretty lady." Sam stole a quick kiss before leading Janie from the office.

"THIS WAS A great idea," Sam admitted, as she swiped a fry from Janie's plate. They were in the gym's office with the door closed, sitting close on the old sofa with paper plates in their laps.

Janie swatted at her hand. "Stop that." She nibbled on a fry herself. "I'm glad you agreed. I wanted some time alone with you." She took a bite of her hamburger and moaned in appreciation. "You have totally corrupted me. I bet I've gained ten pounds since we met."

"I think you look great."

"Thank you. But let's see what you think when I'm old and fat." Their age difference was never far from Janie's thoughts, but she was determined to enjoy their relationship for however long they were together. Although Sam often professed her love, Janie believed it was only a matter of time before she'd get tired of Piperton and leave.

Sam set her burger down and put her arm around her lover. "What's wrong?"

"Nothing."

As Janie laid her head on her shoulder, Sam kissed her hair and pulled her closer. "I don't believe you. Something's on your mind."

Janie sighed. She didn't want to upset Sam, but she knew she wouldn't leave her alone until she got the truth. "You know I love you, right?"

"Uh-huh. And I love you."

"I know. But I also understand that Piperton probably isn't where you want to spend the rest of your life." Janie raked her fingernails lightly across Sam's stomach. "Not that I blame you," she muttered.

"Well, that's kind of true, I guess." The silence between them stretched until Sam finally spoke up. "Um, have you ever thought about leaving?"

"What?" Janie raised her head so she could look into Sam's eyes. "Leave Piperton?"

"Yeah. I know you've lived her all your life, and your family is here, and —"

Janie stopped Sam's babbling by placing her hand over her mouth. "I used to think about it a lot. I never really felt as if I fit in here. But I didn't understand why until I met you."

Sam smiled and Janie moved her hand. "Really?"

"Mmm-hmm." Janie nodded and kissed her. "What concerned me most was that I thought I was being too presumptuous, thinking about tagging along with you when and if you left."

"And here I was worried about finding the right words to ask you to come."

They both laughed at their mutual insecurities. Janie snuggled into Sam and closed her eyes. "You know, the only thing I'll miss from this rotten town is my Nana. She's been the only good thing in my life, until I met you."

Sam exhaled heavily. "I'm sorry. Maybe we could —"

"No, don't apologize. Neither one of us can live here safely." Janie snapped her fingers. "I've got a great idea. Why don't we take a quick run to the nursing home? I'd really love for you two to meet."

THE CITY STREETS were fairly deserted as they traveled toward Spring Gardens Nursing Home. Janie glanced at Sam, who kept tapping a beat against the car's armrest. "Maybe this wasn't such a good idea, after all."

Sam's fingers stilled. "No, it's okay. I'm just trying to figure out what to say when we get there." She took Janie's hand in hers and squeezed. "I've never had to meet someone's family before."

"Don't worry. Nana doesn't bite."

"Maybe not, but what if she doesn't like me?" Sam's right leg started jiggling.

Janie stopped at a red light and was able to look Sam in the eye. "No matter what, I love you. Nothing anyone says, including my Nana, will change the way I feel. I'd just like her to meet the woman I've started talking her ear off about."

The heavy feeling in Sam's stomach grew. "You've talked about me with her? What did you say?"

"Oh, you know. How sweet you are, what a great voice you have." Janie's grin widened. "How good you are in bed." The light turned green and they passed through the intersection.

"What?" Sam's voice rose until it cracked. "Y...you don't actually —"

Janie laughed. "Honey, calm down. I was only kidding." She parked close to the front door and turned off the engine. "Come on. Nana's waiting."

The sterile smell turned Sam's already nervous stomach as she followed Janie into the nursing home. She fumbled with her shirt, tucking it into her jeans for the third time.

Janie tugged on Sam's sleeve. "Relax. You look great. You're not seeing the President. Just my Nana."

"Yeah, but she's more important."

"What do you mean?"

Sam longed to hold Janie's hand, but didn't want to draw any undo attention. "Because she means a lot to you. And I want to make a good impression."

"You will." Janie took Sam's hand and squeezed. She paused in front of an open door and took a deep breath. "Here we go." Using her free hand, she knocked on the threshold.

LUCILLE LOOKED UP from the book she had been reading. She closed the book and placed it on her dresser. "Come in, come in." She adjusted the afghan across her lap and gave her guests a smile. "I see you brought a friend this time."

"Nana, this is Sam." Janie gave Sam's hand another squeeze before releasing it. "Sam, I'd like you to meet my grandmother, Lucille Clarke."

Sam stepped forward and held out her hand. "It's a pleasure to meet you, Mrs. Clarke. Janie's told me a lot about you."

"I'll just bet she has, Sam. And please, call me Lucille." Lucille patted Sam's hand before letting go. "You two girls have a seat. Would you like something to drink? I think I have a couple of sodas in my fridge." She gestured toward a small dorm-sized refrigerator beside the dresser.

Janie kissed her grandmother's cheek and joined Sam on the edge of the bed. She sat close enough so that their thighs touched. "We're fine, Nana. Thanks."

Her granddaughter's proximity to Sam didn't go unnoticed by Lucille. She could see a difference in Janie. Gone was the mousy woman who tried to hide behind her thick-rimmed glasses and plain, oversized clothes. Janie exuded a confidence that she'd never seen before. She couldn't remember the last time she'd seen her wearing jeans and a casual top. It made her look years younger. Lucille mentally girded herself for the upcoming conversation. She'd heard a lot from Janie about this woman, but was ready to hear directly from the source. "So, tell me about yourself Sam."

"I'm afraid there isn't much to tell, Mrs., I mean, Lucille. I've traveled most of my life, and was lucky enough to have my car break down in Piperton." She shared a smile with Janie, when their fingers twined together.

"I see." Lucille moved her chair closer. "So you're just passing through?"

"Well, that was the original plan," Sam admitted. "But for now, this seems like a pretty good place to be."

Lucille touched Sam's knee, forcing the younger woman to look at her. "Those fresh scars tell another story, dear."

Sam's free hand went to her cheek, lightly touching the healed mark. "Yeah, but overall, people have been pretty good. I can't blame an entire town for the actions of an individual."

"That's a good attitude to have." Lucille wheeled back a few feet. "Although there aren't many jobs available in a town this size. What is it that you do?"

"Work is pretty easy to come by if you're not picky. Right now, I'm managing Haley's Gym."

"She does more than that, Nana," Janie added. "She sings, too."

Lucille tried to keep the smile off her face at Janie's defense. It was obvious her granddaughter was totally smitten with the younger woman. And if she were honest with herself, she was beginning to like Sam, too. "Is that how you've supported yourself, Sam? By singing?"

"Among other things."

"What made you start to travel?" Lucille asked. "You're not wanted by the law anywhere, are you?"

Sam laughed and shook her head. "No ma'am. I was raised in a small town in Oklahoma by my grandmother. When she passed away, there wasn't anything left for me there. I've been on the road ever since."

It wasn't hard for Lucille to see the sadness in Sam's eyes. "I'm sorry, dear."

"It's all right." Sam straightened. "She would have liked you, though."

Lucille nodded. She had another question for Sam, but wanted to ask it privately. "Janie, would you be a dear and run to the cafeteria? There should be some leftover brownies, and I'm dying for one."

"Uh, okay. Sure." Janie stood and looked at Sam. "Would you like one, too?"

Sam shook her head. "I'm fine." She faced Lucille after Janie left the room.

"I know it wasn't very subtle, was it?" Lucille moved in front of Sam. "My granddaughter cares for you, I can see that. But what about you?"

"I love her."

Pursing her lips, Lucille stared at her for a long moment. "And what are your plans?"

"Plans?"

"Yes. You know, plans. Intentions, if you will."

"We haven't really discussed it."

Lucille finally smiled. "And would you? Discuss it, I mean? You're not planning on sneaking out of town in the middle of the night, are you? That would break Janie's heart."

"No, ma'am. Like I told Janie, she's stuck with me until she says otherwise."

At that moment, Janie returned, bearing a paper plate with several brownies. She gave her grandmother a glare before placing the treats on the nearby dresser. "You could have just asked me to leave, Nana. Not sent me on an errand like a child."

"I know sweetie, but I really did want a brownie." Lucille pinched off a corner of the dessert and popped it into her mouth. She picked up the plate and waved it toward Sam. "Don't make me be a pig alone."

Chapter
Twenty

SATURDAY MORNING STRETCHED into afternoon, both occupants of the bed not bothering to move. Janie woke to find herself snuggled against Sam. She raised her head to peer at the alarm clock on the nightstand. "Sam, are you awake?"

"Yeah," Sam yawned, tightening her grip on Janie. "What's up?"

"I'm hungry."

Sam turned her head and noticed the time. "Now that you mention it, so am I. It's almost one in the afternoon. Whatcha hungry for?"

"Well," Janie started walking her fingers along Sam's bare chest. "It's not very nutritious, but thanks to you, I can't seem to get enough."

"Janie," Sam warned. They'd never get out of bed at this rate. Not that she minded much.

Janie's mouth moved close to Sam's ear. "I'd love," she nibbled on an earlobe.

Sam moaned.

"One of your gooey cheese omelets," Janie whispered. She squealed when Sam rolled over and started tickling her. "No fair! Stop!" She tried to fight back, but Sam apparently wasn't ticklish. "I'm going to wet the bed if you don't stop!" she warned, which finally gained her a reprieve.

Sam laughed as her lover hurried out of bed and raced to the bathroom. "Go ahead and shower and I'll get lunch started," she yelled, getting up as well. She slipped on her boxer shorts, and, as an afterthought, grabbed a white ribbed tank top as she headed toward the kitchen. The last time she'd cooked topless, she'd gotten a few small burns from popping grease. It wasn't something she wanted to repeat.

A SHORT TIME later, Sam had a large omelet going in a pan. She stood over the stove singing softly. She heard a noise behind her. "I thought you were going to spend all day in the shower," she teased, turning her head. "Holy shit!" She dropped the spatula on the floor.

Betsy and a man she'd never seen before stood in the doorway. "That's a new way to say hello, Sam."

"Sorry." Sam laughed and met Betsy halfway, embracing the older woman. "I've missed you."

"Me too, kid." Betsy cleared her throat and pulled away. She took Sam's hands in hers. "You're looking better than when I left. I see you got the cast off."

"Yeah." Sam peered over Betsy's shoulder to the man still standing quietly by the door. "Hi."

Betsy rubbed her on the arm. "Forgive my lapse in manners. Sam, I'd like for you to meet a very dear friend, Al Martin." She held out her hand, which Al quickly took. "Al, this is Sam."

Al Martin was a slender man of average height, his salt-and-pepper slicked back away from his face. His smile and twinkling blue eyes were genuine as he released Betsy's hand and shook Sam's. "I've heard a lot about you, Sam. It's a pleasure to finally meet you."

"Same here, sir. Would you care for some lunch? I was just whipping up an omelet."

"No, we've already eaten."

Betsy pushed Sam toward the door. "Why don't you get a few more clothes on before you catch cold? I'll keep an eye on your food."

"Thanks." Sam realized how thin her shirt was and crossed her arms over her chest. "I'll be right back." She rushed into the bedroom, almost knocking Janie down. "Betsy's here," she warned. "With her friend, Al."

"Really?" Janie watched as her lover changed clothes. "Good thing I decided to come in here after my shower then." She was already dressed in a pair of Sam's sweatpants and work shirt from Danny's. "Maybe I should put on something else."

Sam buttoned the fly on her jeans. "You look great. I doubt they'll care what we're wearing." Finally dressed, she gave Janie a kiss. "Ready for some teasing? I'm sure Betsy will have a field day with us."

"She'd better behave," Janie warned, following Sam from the room. "Especially since I'm betting she and Al are closer than she's let on."

"Oooh, good point." Sam yelped as Janie pinched her on the rear. "Watch it, woman. Paybacks are a bitch."

AFTER SAM AND Janie had finished their lunch, the foursome moved to the living room to share a pot of coffee. All pretense gone, Janie sat as close to Sam as possible on the loveseat, leaning into the younger woman and sighing in relief when Sam's arm snaked around her shoulders. She gave Betsy a defiant look, daring the other woman to say anything.

Betsy grinned at the couple. She and Al were on the sofa, he on the end and she on the next cushion. "I see you two have been busy while I've been gone."

"Yeah, the gym's holding its own," Sam answered, purposely obtuse. "Although we have changed the hours a little, since Pamela had to scale back her time."

Betsy nodded. "She told me about that when I talked to her the other day on the phone. Such a shame, too, having to move in with her mother-in-law. I hear they have to look for a new house, since the one they were renting had been foreclosed. But that's not exactly what I was talking about."

"I know." Sam appeared pleased with herself. "But since you seem to be wearing some new jewelry, I was going to give you a break."

Betsy blushed. The grip Al had on her hand grounded her, and she glanced down to see the handmade turquoise and silver ring he had bought her from a local Navajo artisan. "That's a big reason why we're here." She found it hard to speak as her emotions got out of control.

Al stepped in. "Betsy has done me the greatest honor and agreed to become my wife," he shared. "We've known each other most of our lives, and have been friends forever." His eyes softened as he looked at his intended. "And when she came back into my life, the most amazing thing happened — one look and I was lost."

"Oh, Al," Betsy sniffled, burying her face in his shirt. She spent a moment in his embrace before sitting up. "How could I refuse? The man's a poet." Blowing her nose on the handkerchief Al handed her, Betsy composed herself. "I don't have much worth moving, just some clothes and pictures. It shouldn't take long to pack up."

"You're leaving again?" Sam asked. "But what about the gym?"

"Probably within a week, if possible. And I was hoping you'd stay on here and look after things." Betsy sat up and moved to the edge of her seat. "Maybe even buy me out someday."

Sam shook her head. "You're kidding, right?" As much as she loved Janie, Sam couldn't see herself living in Piperton for good. "I'm sorry, Betsy. I'll help you as much as I can, but I hadn't planned on staying here permanently." As soon as the words left her mouth, she knew they were a mistake, especially when Janie jumped up and left the room. "Damn." Sam heard footsteps race down the stairs and the back door slam. "I'll be right back." She hurried after her lover.

Janie paced along the alley, wiping the tears from her cheeks. She heard the door open and purposely turned her back, not wanting to see Sam. "Go away."

"I can't do that." Sam stepped behind Janie. "What I said, up there—" She tried to put her hands on Janie's shoulders, but Janie moved away.

"Don't."

"Baby, please. Let me explain," Sam begged, her own voice cracking.

Janie turned around. "You told me you weren't going to leave," she accused, tears still falling from her eyes. "Was that a lie?"

"No, I meant what I said."

"Then, why?"

Sam exhaled and reached for Janie again. "I love you. And I'd do anything in the world for you, including staying here."

"But?"

Lowering her hands, Sam looked at the ground. "No buts. I

promised I'd be here for as long as you'll have me. The thought of owning a business here in Piperton isn't that appealing. Once word got out the gym was mine, clients would run away in droves. It would never work. I didn't mean those other things I said." She raised her head as Janie moved toward her.

"I'm sorry, Sam. Forgive me for being so insecure?" Janie's tears stopped as Sam's arms went around her body.

"There's nothing to forgive." Sam nuzzled Janie's hair with her cheek. "We're both pretty new at this stuff." When Janie's face rose to hers, Sam kissed her. "Come on. Let's go back inside and pick on Betsy."

JANIE CHECKED HER watch. It was shortly past one in the afternoon, and she hoped her grandmother was in her room. Sundays were a big social day at the center, and Lucille tended to be in the thick of things. She knocked on Lucille's door, not surprised to find the room empty. With a roll of her eyes, she headed for the activity room.

As she approached, Janie heard music and laughter. She stood in the doorway and watched as several of the seniors danced in the center of the room. Hearing her grandmother's distinctive laughter, she turned toward the sound.

Lucille had her wheelchair parked next to the piano, while a silver-haired man played a lively tune. She was as close as the chair would allow, and her head was bent close to his. He said something to her, and she threw her head back and laughed again.

Shaking her head, Janie slipped through the revelers until she was a few feet away from the piano. Once the tune was finished, she placed her hand on Lucille's shoulder. "Hi, Nana."

Lucille turned and gave Janie a smile. "Hello, sweetie. This is a nice surprise." She held out her arms and enjoyed the embrace she received.

"I'm sorry to interrupt your party. Maybe I should just come back another time." Janie turned to leave, but stopped at Lucille's request.

"No sense in that, dear. This is just a normal Sunday, you know." Lucille waved her hand at the piano player. "You remember Jeremy Michaels, don't you dear? Jeremy?"

He stood and bowed slightly toward Janie. "It's a pleasure to see you again."

Janie shook his hand and almost curtsied in response to his courtly manners. "Thank you, Mr. Michaels." She blushed as he kissed her knuckles before releasing her hand.

"Well, I see you two ladies have things to talk about." Jeremy leaned down and kissed Lucille on the cheek. "Until later, my dear."

"I'll catch up with you in a while," Lucille promised. She took Janie's hand. "Let's go back to my room where it's quieter."

Allowing Lucille to take the lead, Janie followed her down the hallway. "I'm sorry to take you away from your friends, Nana."

"Don't worry about it, sweetie. They'll party for hours, or at least until dinnertime." Lucille waited until Janie was in the room with her. "Don't get me wrong, but I figured you'd be with Sam today."

"She's doing some work for Dr. Richmond. But I'll see her later, when we help Betsy finish packing to move to Santa Fe."

Lucille nodded as Janie sat on the bed. "Betsy's your friend that owns the gym, isn't she?"

"Yes."

"How's Sam taking the news?"

Janie brushed her hands across her denim-clad legs. "What do you mean?"

"If Betsy's leaving, I'm assuming she's closing her business, right?"

"She's not sure yet. She may sell to someone else."

"Well, it could be for the best." Lucille adjusted the afghan on her lap and moved closer to the bed. She placed one hand on Janie's knee. "I know you've told me how fond of her Sam is, so perhaps this would be a good time for her to move on as well."

"What?" Janie scooted off the bed. "I thought you liked Sam."

"I do, dear. But even you will have to admit, it's not very safe for her here." Lucille held out her hand and pulled Janie to her. "Nor for you, sweetie."

"But—"

Lucille shook her head. "I can't pretend to understand the relationship between you two, but even an old woman like me can see how happy you are."

"Thanks, Nana. That means a lot to me." Janie gave the older woman a hug. "I've never felt like this for anyone before."

"I'm glad." Lucille looked at their joined hands as Janie sat close by. "What are your plans, Janie?"

"I don't understand the question. What do you mean?"

Lucille gave her granddaughter's hand a squeeze. "Well, I'm assuming you're spending a lot of time with Sam, correct?"

"Yes."

"And you're both happy with the arrangements you have?"

Janie frowned. "Arrangements?"

"The physical side of your relationship," Lucille hinted, causing Janie to blush. "I don't mean to be a busy-body, but I know sex is an important part of a young couple's life." She lowered her voice. "Are your needs being met, dear?"

"Oh, my god. We can't be having this conversation." Janie pulled her hand back and covered her face. "Nana, please."

Lucille snickered. "I'll take that as a yes. Good." She patted Janie's knee. "Have you two discussed the future?"

"I don't—"

"Because I worry about you both, you know. I'd hate for anything else to happen to Sam. Or, God forbid, to you."

Janie adjusted her glasses and cleared her throat. "I appreciate that, Nana. We're being very careful, I promise."

"I'm glad, dear." Lucille wheeled across the room and opened her lowest dresser drawer. She searched for a moment before coming up with a small notebook. She returned to Janie's side and handed her the book. "Here."

"What's this?"

Lucille waved her hand. "Open it."

The black leather was creased with age, but opened easily. Janie blinked when she realized it was an old-style bank book. "But—"

"I've had quite a bit squirreled away for when you got married, Janie. But, considering the circumstances, perhaps it would do more good as traveling funds." She glanced at the pages, using her hand to flip to the back of the book. "As you can see, it's not a fortune. Although I'm sure you can make good use of it."

Janie shook her head and blinked the tears away. "There's close to nine thousand dollars here, Nana. I can't accept this."

"Of course you can." Lucille laughed. "Your father doesn't know anything about it. I started saving when you were born. Your name is on the account as well." She sobered, raising her hand to touch Janie's cheek. "Take it and see the world, dearest. Or at least find someplace where you and Sam can be happy."

A sob tore from Janie as her tears fell in earnest. "But what about you?"

"My life is here. I wouldn't be as happy anywhere else." Lucille pulled Janie into her arms and held her. "They have these new-fangled things called phones, you know," she teased, kissing her granddaughter's head. "And just because you leave Piperton, doesn't mean you can't come back for visits. I'll be fine."

SAM PUSHED THE old mower into the shed and locked the door. She waved to the diminutive older woman on the porch, trudging across the freshly mowed yard to join her. She gratefully accepted the sweating glass of lemonade handed to her. "Thanks, Mrs. Parker."

"I should thank you, Samantha. My yard hasn't looked this nice in years."

After drinking half the glass, Sam licked the residue from her upper lip. "I'm glad I could do it for you. Although I think the grass has pretty much gone dormant for the winter. I'm sorry I was so late getting over here, but I had another job before this one."

Estelle Parker patted the younger woman on the arm. "Don't you fret about it." She tugged on Sam's shirt. "Come inside for a moment."

Sam looked down at her jeans and boots. "I shouldn't. I'm covered with grass."

"Nonsense. Come along, now." Estelle walked slowly into her dining room, where she opened a drawer on the antique buffet. She found what she was looking for and handed a piece of paper to Sam. "Here you go. I signed it just the other day."

"What's this?" Sam turned the paper toward the light. "Mrs. Parker, this is the title to your car."

The older woman nodded. "As agreed. I think you've done more than your share to pay for it. Goodness knows I had no use for the thing. I haven't been behind the wheel in years. Reverend Dinkler was coming over after church every Sunday and driving it around the block for me. He's as happy as I am to have it gone." She looked up at Sam. "Between the yard work, the things you've fixed around here, and the money you keep leaving behind, you've paid much more than that old clunker was worth. So no more arguing with me."

"Yes ma'am." Sam folded the paper neatly and tucked it into her wallet. "Thank you, Mrs. Parker." She tugged off her gloves and held out her hand. "If there's anything else I can ever do, just let me know."

Not caring that Sam was covered with grass and sweat, the older woman pulled her into an embrace. "You're a good person, Samantha." She took the glass from Sam and swatted her. "Go on home and get cleaned up. I'm sure a nice young woman like yourself has better things to do than spend time with an old lady like me."

Sam shook her head. "Not necessarily better, Mrs. Parker. But I do need to run back to the gym and help Betsy get packed up."

"That's fine. You tell her to take care, and give me a call sometime. I'd love to hear about her new fellow." The elderly woman shooed Sam out of her house.

Chapter
Twenty-one

THE LIVING ROOM was cluttered with boxes. Those labeled "donate" were neatly lined against one wall, while several of the "keep" boxes were haphazardly strewn around the room, still open. Betsy brought in an armful of linens and dropped them on the sofa, landing with a thud beside them. "I can't believe I have so much junk," she lamented to Janie, who brought a tray filled with glasses of ice tea from the kitchen.

"You've lived here for years. Of course you'd have accumulated a lot of things."

Betsy took a glass. "Thank you." She drained half of the contents in one gulp. "Damn, that's good. Have I thanked you for being here? You've been a great help."

"You're welcome. But I haven't really done that much."

"I have to disagree with you," Al interrupted. He stood in the doorway with another filled box. "Your organizational skills have kept us from going crazy." He stacked the box neatly with the others before joining his fiancée on the couch. "If you ever decide to leave Piperton, give me a call. I could use a good office manager for my restaurants."

Now that she was tucked against her fiancé, Betsy relaxed. "That's a great idea. Janie, maybe you and Sam could come to New Mexico."

Janie moved a pile of newspapers from the loveseat. "What on earth would we do there?"

"Lots of things." Betsy warmed to the idea. "You're both young, bright, and not afraid of hard work. I'm sure it wouldn't be hard at all for you two to find jobs." She looked up into Al's face. "Right?"

"Definitely." He nodded. "I meant what I said, Janie. I think you'd be great at managing my restaurants. Look at how quickly you've helped Betsy get things done around here. And Betsy tells me that Sam is very versatile, too."

"Well, I'm not sure what we've got planned right now. But thank you." The prospect excited her, but Janie sipped her tea and thought about how to bring up the subject to Sam. "What's it like?"

Al brought Betsy closer with his arm around her shoulders. "Santa Fe?"

Janie nodded.

"Wonderful," Betsy replied. "I'd forgotten how beautiful it was, Janie. In fact, I can't wait to get back. The people are friendlier, the food tastier, and the company can't be beat," she finished, closing her eyes blissfully as Al kissed her head.

"You two ought to get a room," Sam teased, as she came into the room. She stopped by Janie and leaned down to give her a light kiss on the cheek. "Hi."

Betsy tossed a throw pillow at Sam. "Look who's talking, Stinky. What on earth have you been up to?"

"Working." Sam saw the full tea glass next to Janie. "Mind if I steal some of that?" At Janie's nod, she scooped up the glass and finished it off quickly. "Thanks."

"Are you going to clean up, or just shed grass and dirt all over my perfectly clean living room?" Betsy asked, gesturing to the piles of boxes. She shifted out of Al's grip and stood. "Come on, Al. Let's go finish packing my bedroom."

Janie stood as well, careful to keep her distance from Sam's filthy body. "Why don't you grab some clean clothes and meet me downstairs?"

"Downstairs?"

"Mmm-hmm," Janie ran a finger down Sam's face, lingering on her lips. "Since the gym's closed, I'd be more than happy to scrub your back in the showers."

Sam's eyes grew larger as she considered her options. She bit down lightly on Janie's finger, sucking the tip into her mouth, grinning at her lover's gasp. "Race ya."

TWO DAYS LATER, Betsy, Al and Sam surveyed the empty apartment. The older woman put her arm around Sam's waist. "One last chance, Sam. Are you sure?"

Sam returned the embrace. "I'm very sure, Betsy. Janie already said I could stay with her. I think selling to Pamela and her husband is a perfect solution. She's been in and out of here half a dozen times since yesterday, waving paint and carpet samples."

"I know. I think she's happiest about moving out of her mother-in-law's old house. She told me the woman makes them keep their bedroom door open, so the cats can have the run of the place."

Footsteps on the stairs caused the trio to turn. Janie smiled as she came into the room. "Thank goodness. I was afraid I'd miss you."

"Aren't you supposed to be at work?" Sam stepped away from Betsy and gave Janie a brief kiss.

"I was, but Dr. Richmond said I could take an early lunch." Janie rubbed Sam's hip before backing away and giving both Al and Betsy hugs. "I knew you wanted to get as early a start as possible."

Betsy blinked away an errant tear. "We did, but we would have gladly waited to see you before we headed out." She put her arms around Janie and whispered in her ear, "Remember what else we talked about. I'd like to see you and Sam in Santa Fe before the end of the year." She kissed Janie's cheek and pulled away. "You girls take care of each other, you hear?"

"We will, I promise." Janie wiped at her own face. "Let us walk you two downstairs." She held out her hand to Sam, who immediately took it.

The foursome was silent as they trekked down the stairwell for the last time. Sam had already moved her meager belongings to Janie's apartment. The building wouldn't be empty for long, as Pamela and her husband were set to take over the following week. The last person out, Sam locked the door behind them and pocketed the key. She'd pass it along to the new owners later.

Betsy stopped and stared at the back of the old building. The white paint had long-ago been faded by the sun, and the steel metal door had rust in several places. Some of the best times of her life happened upstairs, as well as her greatest heartache. Jack had collapsed on the kitchen floor, never to wake. She sniffled once and shook her head. "Well, I guess this is it." Al's comforting arm around her waist helped her get past the ghosts and she looked up into his knowing eyes. "Ready to go home, handsome?"

"As long as you are, my dear."

More hugs were shared before the couple climbed into the rental truck. Betsy got behind the wheel, much to Al's chagrin. "Don't worry, hon. You know I don't see well at night, so I thought I'd take the first shift." Her window was down and she hung her head outside. "Be good, kids," she yelled, before putting the truck in gear.

THE VEHICLE LUMBERED down the alley as Sam and Janie watched. They continued to wave until it turned out of sight. Sam brushed her cheek with her hand. "I'm really going to miss them."

"I know, honey. So will I." Janie put her arm around Sam and rested her head on her shoulder. "What are your plans for the rest of the day?"

Sam shrugged. "I guess I'll pick up a paper and find myself another job. Singing at the bar won't get me very far."

"I suppose that's a good idea." Janie kissed Sam's neck below her ear. "I'm not expected back at work for a couple of hours," she hinted.

"Yeah?" Sam turned her head and met Janie's lips with her own. Her hands followed the contours of her lover's ribs until the sound of a car backfiring caused them to jump apart anxiously. "Meet you at home in five?"

Janie nodded. Without another word, she got into her car and sped out of the alley, while Sam took the opposite direction. She knew Sam would park a block or two away from her apartment and walk the rest of the way, which gave her a few extra minutes to prepare.

Not far away, Sam found a good parking place behind the

abandoned dry cleaners on the square. She locked her car and glanced around before jogging down the alley. It was less than two blocks from Janie's apartment and she was anxious to get there. She started across the street, jumping back when a black truck honked.

"Watch it, dyke!" the driver yelled, his gravelly voice punctuated by a watery cough. His tinted windows were only partially lowered, keeping him hidden from view. "Stupid bitch!" He honked again and spun away, curse words floating on the wind.

The voice was one she'd never forget. Sam tried to get the license plate number, but the back tag had been dented and scraped too many times by a trailer to be legible. She backed away from the street, waiting to make certain it was gone before heading toward Janie's.

INSIDE HER APARTMENT, Janie lit another candle in the bedroom. She placed the book of matches on her nightstand before heading into the bathroom to change. After she pulled the shimmering nightgown over her head she looked at herself in the mirror. The waif-like body was gone, replaced by womanly curves and a more confident posture. Janie smiled at her image, sliding her hands across the cool satin and imagining Sam's expression when she saw the new clothing. She heard the front door open and close, and she quickly dabbed several strategic points on her body with perfume.

Sam stepped into the bedroom and looked around, still breathing heavily from her run. The fragrant candles flickered around the room and their spiciness tickled her nose. When Janie came out of the bathroom, Sam stopped breathing altogether at the vision in front of her. "You're...beautiful," she finally gasped.

"Thank you." Janie noticed how winded and sweaty Sam was, and she didn't think it was due to her outfit. "Are you all right?"

Sam nodded, her eyes glued to the vision before her.

Janie moved closer. Her hands went to Sam's belt, while their eyes stayed locked on one another. "How far did you run?"

"Old...cleaners."

Janie slipped Sam's belt out of the loops and she started to smile as she heard it hit the floor. Sam's shirt and bra were removed next, then her nimble fingers popped open each button on Sam's jeans. Once they were pushed around her ankles, Janie gently shoved Sam onto the bed, as she made quick work of relieving her of her boots.

Once Janie had Sam completely stripped, she held up a finger and backed out of the bedroom. "Don't move," she ordered. "I need to get something," she called from the kitchen.

Sam had raised herself up on her elbows to say something, but when Janie returned to the bedroom holding a can of whipped cream and began decorating her skin Sam fell back onto the bed and gave herself over to her lover's creativeness.

SEVERAL HOURS LATER, Sam woke with a very sticky Janie stretched across her. She glanced at the clock and panicked. She shook her lover's shoulder. "Janie?"

Janie moaned but didn't open her eyes. "Later, Sam. I don't think I can move."

"Baby, it's four o'clock."

"Ugh." Janie raised her head and pried open her eyes. "So?"

"What about your work?"

Janie stretched, her body peeling from Sam's uncomfortably. The whipped cream had been fun, if messy. "I called on my way home and took the rest of the day off." She moved slowly toward the bathroom. "Come on. I think we could both use a hot shower."

Not having to be asked twice, Sam quickly followed. She heard Janie's curse and started to laugh. "Don't like the hairdo?"

"It's not funny," Janie grumbled, staring at herself in the mirror. Between the activity and the sticky treat they played with, her hair was standing up in every direction. "I look deranged."

Sam patted her on the rear before she turned on the water in the shower. "Well, you *were* a bit out of control," she teased. When the water was the right temperature, she climbed in, but didn't see Janie's hand slip in and turn the knob toward the right. She shrieked as the cold water hit her.

"Out of control, huh?" Janie readjusted the water and stepped in beside Sam. She gave her lover a sweet smile. "Problem, hon?"

"Nope." Sam ran her fingers down Janie's sides, causing her to squeal. "You?"

Their giggles and laughter lasted longer than the hot water.

Much later, when they were snuggled together in the clean sheets, Sam decided it was time to tell Janie about her earlier troubles. She explained how the driver of the black truck acted, and was surprised when Janie stiffened in her arms. "What's the matter? Nothing happened. I don't think he was trying to run me down."

"No, it's not that. Could you describe the truck again? And could you tell me exactly what the guy said?" Janie listened carefully to Sam's narrative, becoming more concerned by the moment. "Oh, no."

"What? Does he sound familiar?"

Janie nodded. "I'm afraid so. Doug's father, Reggie, has a black truck. And since he's a chain smoker, he's had a nasty cough for as long as I've known him."

"But, why? What did I do to him?"

"I think he might have seen me talking to you, back behind the bar one time. He was walking home after a few too many. Doug told me once he and Harvey were determined to see he and I married. I don't know why."

Sam tried to remember if she'd ever seen anyone besides Janie in the alley. "There was an old guy, once. Tall, thin? Not much hair?"

"That's him. He's always given me the creeps." Janie tightened her hold on Sam. "We should go to the police."

"We don't have any proof, just some vague memories. There's nothing they could do." Sam wrapped her arms more securely around Janie and yawned. "Besides, I doubt if he'll try anything again. It would be too hard to get away with it a second time, and I'm being a lot more careful now."

Janie kissed Sam's chest before closing her eyes. "All right."

THE FOLLOWING AFTERNOON, Janie used her lunch break to drive to Doug's shop. Knowing her ex for so long, she knew all about how his place operated. Reggie worked as a mechanic for his son, and the crews were usually gone until late afternoon every day.

The converted service station appeared deserted when she arrived. Janie was about to leave when she heard the clank of tools and loud cursing from one corner of the shop. She gathered her courage around her and walked purposely toward the sound.

Reggie was kneeling beside a riding mower, his arm wedged beneath it and a look of concentration on his face. Something clattered, and he pulled out his arm. "Damned piece of shit," he yelled, slamming the wrench on the concrete floor.

"Reggie?"

The soft voice caused him to look up. "Well, lookie here. The queer's girlfriend." He glared up at Janie. "What the fuck do you want?"

"I know it was you," Janie said, as calmly as she could. She took a step back when he got to his feet and stood over her.

"Me? I don't know what the hell you're talkin' about, girl." Reggie wiped his greasy hands on an equally greasy rag. He gave her a sly grin. "But if'n I was...knowing, that is, what should I care?"

Janie watched as he shook an unfiltered cigarette from the pack he always kept in his shirt pocket. With a flick of his lighter, Reggie inhaled deeply. She attempted to blink the smoke out of her eyes. "Since you're Doug's father, I wanted to talk to you about things first. Leave Sam alone, or I'll go to the police."

He laughed. "Bullshit. You ain't got nothin'." He leaned in closer. "You tell that dyke this; faggots don't have much luck around here. Accidents have been known to happen. Sometimes, they can be downright fatal."

"Is that a threat?" Janie hated how her voice quivered. "Because, if it is—"

"Just statin' a fact of life, Jane. Now get the hell out of here. I've got work to do."

She watched him carefully as she backed away. Reggie had always seemed a little off to her, but up until now, she'd never thought he was dangerous. But she knew, deep in her heart, he was not only involved in Sam's attack, but capable of much worse.

SAM SHOVED THE newspaper away and sighed. One of the few jobs she was even remotely qualified for was as a mower for Doug, and she knew better than to even consider it. She didn't know how she was going to support herself in a town this size by singing in Danny's. Odd jobs would only get her so far, and if she wanted to stay with Janie, she'd have to find something more suitable and permanent. She looked around Janie's apartment. Small as it was, it hadn't taken her long to clean it from top to bottom. The furnishings were old, but well-taken care of.

She left the living room and went to the kitchen. After checking the pantry and freezer, she decided to go shopping for dinner supplies. Janie wouldn't be home from work for another hour so she had more than enough time. Sam was halfway to the front door when it opened, startling her.

Janie came in and closed the door behind her. "Good, you're here." She dropped her purse on the coffee table and went to Sam, who immediately embraced her.

"Yeah, I was just about to run get something for dinner. What's up?" Sam felt Janie shudder and tightened her hold. "Janie?"

"I quit my job."

Sam pulled back so she could look at her lover. "Why? What happened?"

"I'm scared, Sam. I can't live in this town any longer, looking over my shoulder and worrying about something happening to you." Janie allowed Sam to lead her to the sofa, where they sat close together. "I talked to Reggie at lunch today."

"You shouldn't have done that, baby. We don't have any real proof—"

Janie sighed. "That's what he said." She studied Sam's face. The scars still stood out against her skin, which made her decision all that much easier. Her hand lightly touched Sam's cheek and traced over the healed marks. "Let's get out of here." At her lover's questioning look, she continued, "This town ceased being home to me the moment we met." Janie leaned closer and placed a gentle kiss on Sam's lips.

"What about your family? Your grandmother?" Sam felt a thrill at the thought of leaving Piperton behind and taking Janie with her. "I don't have much money saved, and traveling can be expensive."

Janie took her purse from the coffee table and put it in her lap. "Funny you should say that. My grandmother suggested we leave." She dug through the purse until she found Lucille's bank book. "I think we'll have more than enough funds to get us somewhere." She handed it to Sam.

Sam opened the small leather notebook. "Is this for real?"

"Yes. Nana told me she'd been saving it for me since I was born." Janie put her purse aside and took Sam's hands in her own. "Take me away from here, Sam. I want to go someplace where we can sit in public and have lunch together, without worrying what will happen."

"All right." Sam kissed her, excited about their upcoming adventure. "Any idea on where you want to go?"

Janie's smile lit up her face. "I hear Santa Fe's nice this time of year."

SAM WENT TO work early the following day, hoping to catch Ray before he turned over the shift to the evening bartender. Aaron was working the bar and pointedly ignored her as she came in. Even though it was barely three in the afternoon, several patrons were scattered around the room. To her surprise, a couple even greeted Sam as she headed for the office.

"You playing today?" one of the men asked as she passed by his table.

"Probably a little later. Are you going to stick around?"

One of the man's tablemates thumped him on the arm. "Yeah, Randall. You gonna stay and buy a few rounds?"

Randall glared at his compatriot before giving Sam a sheepish grin. "I was going to bring my wife by. She likes your singing."

Sam lightly blushed but smiled all the same. "That's great. I should start around five." She continued on to the office while Randall's friends gave him a hard time. She found Ray at his desk, filling out the deposit from the previous day. "Ray?"

Ray turned at the sound of her voice. "Hey, Sam. I wasn't expecting you here so early. Not much of a crowd for you, yet."

"Yeah, I know. There's something I needed to talk to you about." She came into the office and closed the door behind her.

He studied her for a moment and nodded. "You're leaving."

"How'd you know?"

"You just had the look about you, I guess. Tired of putting up with us rednecks?" Ray joked.

Sam leaned against the tall filing cabinet and tucked her hands into the front pockets of her jeans. "Nah, it's not that. And I wouldn't call you a redneck. It's just time for me to move on. You've been really great to me, Ray, and I appreciate it."

"Hey, I should thank you." Ray stood and held out his hand. "You've brought life back to this old dive. Can you stay for at least a week?"

"Sure." Sam shook his hand. "Why?"

"There's this group of kids who've started their own band, and they wanted a chance to play for the crowd. But they have to wait until their drummer turns twenty-one."

Sam laughed. "Super. I was worried about leaving you in a bind, but I guess you've got everything figured out. That's great."

"Well, they're not you, but they're not bad." He grinned. "And they're a country band."

"Thank god. Once I leave here, I hope I never have to sing another Reba McEntire song for as long as I live."

HEAVY SMOKE HUNG in the air, and only a handful of tired looking men sat scattered around the room. Conversations of the day's events were covered up by the sounds of the piano.

Janie sat at the bar, her attention fully focused on the woman playing the piano and singing in a low voice. She never tired of looking at Sam. From her dark hair to her smoky gray eyes, the singer exuded a quiet intensity that had drawn Janie to her in the first place.

The music stopped, and a tiny smattering of applause broke Janie from her musing. She clapped along with the others. When her eyes met Sam's, she felt her heart pound.

Sam thanked the crowd and stood. She stretched, showing her lanky body off well by the worn jeans and tight long-sleeved tee shirt she wore. Her eyes never left Janie's as she maneuvered through the maze of tables toward the bar. She sat on the stool next to Janie's. "Hey there. I thought you were going to visit with your grandmother today."

"Change of plans. I have to go to Harvey's this afternoon, so I probably won't be home for a while." She picked up her beer bottle and took a sip, then set it close to Sam's hand. The action allowed her to brush her hand against her lover's, which was about as much as they dared. She leaned closer, in order to be heard over the jukebox the bartender had just plugged in, but kept her voice low. "And I didn't want to wait that long to see you." Her voice lowered further. "I have plans for you tonight."

Sam's eyes tracked to her lips. "Not fair." It was definitely getting warmer in the bar. Sam waved to catch the bartender's attention.

He rolled his eyes, but dropped a few cubes of ice into a short glass then filled it with water. He placed it in front of her and walked away without a word.

"I think Aaron's starting to like me," Sam joked.

"How can he not?" Janie touched Sam's hand before taking another swallow of beer. She longed to do more, but knew all too well what could happen if anyone noticed. "I'm sorry to leave so soon, but he wants me there for dinner. It's the least I can do, so I can properly say goodbye."

Sam nodded in understanding. "That's okay. I guess I'll hang around here a bit longer and see if I can earn a few more tips. I'd like to get as much as I can, since this is my last week here."

Janie slid off the stool and placed a five dollar bill on the bar. She glanced around, and, seeing that no one was paying any attention to them, quickly squeezed Sam's arm. "Be careful going home."

"Always." Sam tipped her head toward the back, where the restroom was located. "Maybe you should wash up before you go."

"Sounds like a good idea." Janie adjusted the shoulder strap on her purse and walked away.

Sam picked up her drink and carried it back to the piano. She removed the tips from the jar and placed them in her pocket. Once a couple of minutes passed, she went to the bathroom as well.

The door was barely closed behind her when Sam was pushed against it. Janie was slight, but her hands were strong as she pinned Sam's shoulders. Sam grinned playfully before her lips were captured. When they finally broke apart to breathe, she leaned her forehead into Janie's and sighed. "I love you so much."

"I love you too." Janie used her thumb to brush her lipstick from Sam's lips. "Guess I'd better get going." She hugged her lover and slipped out the door.

"Bye." But the door had already closed before Sam's words left her mouth. She walked to the sink and splashed a handful of water into her face.

THE APARTMENT COMPLEX looked the same as any other. Beige, with dark brown doors and stairs, it was old and run-down. Janie parked in the space beside her father's latest car, a shiny black Buick. She fought the temptation to run her key down the side, marring the perfect finish. She took the stairs to the second level, where his apartment was located.

Harvey opened the door before she had a chance to knock. "I was expecting you sooner," he chastised, turning and leaving her at the threshold. He moved to the kitchen, where he stirred a pot of spaghetti on the stovetop. His beady eyes glared at his daughter. "You said you'd be right over. Where have you been?"

"I had an errand to run." She sat in one of the two chairs beside the kitchen table, placed her purse under her chair and picked up the water glass next to the empty plate. "I told you that when you called today."

"Errands don't usually take an hour and a half. You didn't go to work dressed like that, did you?" He dipped the wooden spoon into the pot and tasted the sauce. The empty jar sat on the counter, so it wasn't as if he made it from scratch. He shook the pepper shaker several times over the pot, before tasting it again. "Better."

Janie frowned, but kept quiet. Still afraid of her father, she hadn't told him she no longer worked at the medical office. The only reason she had come to see him today was to tell him she was leaving town. "Why? What's wrong with the way I'm dressed?"

"You look like a boy, wearing those jeans." He coughed heavily and wiped his mouth with the back of his hand. "Women are supposed to wear dresses."

"I don't want to argue about my clothes, Harvey. What was so important that I had to rush right over?"

He carried the pot to the table and sat it on a folded newspaper. With a groan, Harvey sat on his own chair, which creaked under his weight. "Watch your mouth, girl."

The conversation was quickly going downhill. "Look, maybe this wasn't such a good idea." Janie took the paper towel she'd draped across her lap and set it on the table. "We can't even have a meal together without arguing."

"Eat," Harvey ordered, slurping a strand of spaghetti into his mouth, the red sauce sticking to his chin. He used the back of his hand to wipe at his face and continued to eat.

Janie poked at her food. "I'm not hungry. I don't know why you even asked me to come over here."

Harvey raised his eyes and licked the sauce off his lips. "Maybe I just wanted to see you. Is that so hard to believe?"

"You never call unless you want something, Harvey. What is it this time?"

He shrugged his shoulders. "I've found you a new fella. His name's David, and he works with me at the hospital."

"What? Have you lost your mind?" Janie pushed her plate away. "How many times do I have to tell you that I don't need anyone? This is ridiculous."

"Don't talk like that, Jane. I think you'll like him." He took a drink of water, leaving a tiny bit of spaghetti on the rim of the glass. "You're going to invite him over for dinner."

Janie shoved her chair away from the table and got to her feet. "Like hell I will." She picked up her purse.

Harvey grabbed her arm. "Hold it. You're not leaving." He wiped his mouth on a paper towel and stood as well. "He's going to call you to make arrangements."

Janie jerked her arm away. "You gave him my number?"

"Of course I did. He's looking forward to talking to you."

"That's never going to happen, Harvey. I'm not interested."

He wouldn't be deterred. "Bullshit. You need a man to take care of you, Jane. You've embarrassed me long enough by being single."

"I don't need, or want, a man! I'm perfectly happy with Sam." Janie gasped as she realized what she'd said.

"Who the fuck is—" Harvey's face turned red when he figured out what she said. "No! Not *my* daughter!" He took a firm grasp on her arm and started to shake her. "There's no way in hell you're with that fucking dyke!"

Janie tried to pry his fingers away. "Stop it, Harvey. You're hurting me." She cried out when he threw her against the wall.

"Get the fuck out of my house! I don't have a daughter!" he screamed, spittle flying from his lips.

"Fine with me. You were never much of a father anyway." Janie hurried to the door, holding her aching arm. She'd be damned if she'd let him see her cry. She slammed the door behind her and raced down the steps.

SAM HAD JUST finished a song when Aaron caught her attention by waving the telephone handset at her. "I'm going to take a quick break," she announced. No one in the bar looked up as she went to the phone. "Hello?"

"Sam?"

The rough sound of her lover's voice worried Sam. "What's wrong? Are you okay?"

"Can you come home?" Janie sniffled. "Please?"

"Of course. I'll be there in five minutes." Sam hung up the phone and waved Aaron over. "I've got to go."

He shrugged. "Whatever."

Sam grabbed her tips and hurried out of the bar. Not caring how it looked, she took off toward the apartment at a jog, dodging the few pedestrians she came across.

JANIE WIPED HER eyes, feeling foolish. Every time she thought of the altercation at Harvey's, she started crying all over again. She moved listlessly around the living room, picking up things and putting them back down, in an effort to keep herself busy until Sam got home. She looked up as the front door opened and her lover stepped inside.

"What happened?" Sam was met halfway across the room by Janie, who wrapped her arms around her and buried her face in Sam's chest.

Janie snuggled closer and choked back a sob.

Sam rubbed Janie's back as she led her to the sofa. She sat and brought her lover close to her, never relinquishing her hold. She hummed a favorite song of Janie's in an attempt to comfort her. When Janie finally calmed and raised her head, Sam brushed her tears away with her fingertips. "Better?"

"A little." Janie leaned against the back of the sofa and rubbed her eyes with the heels of her hands. "I'm sorry."

"Hey, there's no reason for you to apologize. I'm glad you wanted me to come home."

"I needed you." She turned away, embarrassed by her admission. She took a deep breath and released it slowly. "Harvey knows about us."

"What happened?" Sam brushed her fingers through Janie's hair.

The gentle touch was soothing, and Janie allowed herself to lean into it. "It kind of slipped out tonight. He was going on and on about this new guy he wanted to set me up with, and I just snapped."

"I'm sorry." Sam kissed Janie's head. "Are you okay?"

Janie closed her eyes and huddled closer. "I will be, I think. As long as I have you."

"Always."

ACROSS TOWN, A recently laid-off educator walked into her house, carrying the small box that held over thirty years of teaching memories. She placed the container on her bed and sat next to it, staring at the dingy walls. For years she had wanted to paint, but was thwarted at every turn by her husband.

She took a worn photo album from the box and flipped through its crumbling pages. Pictures, faded by time, took her back to before Doug was born. Her younger self, arm in arm with another young woman, stared back at her, causing Sue to cry. "Kath," she sobbed, holding the album to her chest.

She wished she had been stronger then. Soon after Kathleen was killed, Sue had tried to move out of the house. No one in town would rent to a married woman. She was told to go back to her husband and take care of her family like she was supposed to. Leaving town wasn't an option without money, which Reggie controlled and drank away.

The shadows of the room lengthened, reminding Sue that Doug and Reggie would soon be home from work. Still holding the photos, she brought out the suitcase that stayed beneath the bed, tossing it on the aged quilt.

Sue left most of her clothes in the closet, only taking the most comfortable things she owned. When the valise was full, the last item she placed on top was the picture album. She looked around the bedroom one last time before gathering the suitcase and leaving.

As she moved through the living room, a framed photograph of her son caught her eye. She paused by the television and picked up Doug's high school graduation picture. "I'm sorry, son. But I can't stand to stay in this town another minute." She kissed the glass and tucked the frame under her arm, not bothering to lock the front door as she walked out.

She had filled up her car on the way home from school, and now all Sue had to do was pick a direction. Her eyes filled with tears as she passed the cemetery, but her heart lightened as she passed under the final flashing yellow light on the way out of town. She saw the open road ahead of her, and for the first time in over thirty years, Sue Howard smiled and looked forward to her future.

TWO WEEKS LATER, Sam loaded the final box into the trailer and closed the door. "Well, that's it." She turned to her lover, who stood nearby. Janie looked years younger in the faded jeans, sleeveless blouse and sneakers that were now a regular part of her wardrobe. She had donated the majority of her old clothes to charity, vowing to never again allow someone to dictate how she dressed. Sam grinned at Janie's confident stance. "You about ready?"

"As ready as I'll ever be." Janie opened the passenger door to the sports utility vehicle and tossed her purse inside. They'd decided to trade-in Sam's Oldsmobile and Janie's Escort, getting a gently-used Explorer. Some of the money Lucille gave them went toward an enclosed utility trailer. Janie climbed up into her seat, grinning at Sam who slipped in behind the wheel. "We're really doing this, aren't we?"

"Yeah, we are." Sam returned her smile. "Any last minute stops you want to make?"

Janie bounced in her seat and laughed. "The only thing I want to see is the city limits sign as we drive past it."

"All right." Sam started the truck and put it in gear. "Goodbye, Piperton."

Janie waited patiently until they were under way. Her fingers twined with Sam's on the console between them. "Hello, life."

Other Carrie Carr titles published by
Yellow Rose Books

LEX AND AMANDA SERIES

Destiny's Bridge - Rancher Lexington (Lex) Walters pulls young Amanda Cauble from a raging creek and the two women quickly develop a strong bond of friendship. Overcoming severe weather, cattle thieves, and their own fears, their friendship deepens into a strong and lasting love.

Faith's Crossing - Lexington Walters and Amanda Cauble withstood raging floods, cattle rustlers and other obstacles to be together...but can they handle Amanda's parents? When Amanda decides to move to Texas for good, she goes back to her parents' home in California to get the rest of her things, taking the rancher with her.

Hope's Path - Someone is determined to ruin Lex. Efforts to destroy her ranch lead to attempts on her life. Lex and Amanda desperately try to find out who hates Lex so much that they are willing to ruin the lives of everyone in their path. Can they survive long enough to find out who's responsible? And will their love survive when they find out who it is?

Love's Journey - Lex and Amanda embark on a new journey as Lexington rediscovers the love her mother's family has for her, and Amanda begins to build her relationship with her father. Meanwhile, attacks on the two young women grow more violent and deadly as someone tries to tear apart the love they share.

Strength of the Heart - Lex and Amanda are caught up in the planning of their upcoming nuptials while trying to get the ranch house rebuilt. But an arrest, a brushfire, and the death of someone close to her forces Lex to try and work through feelings of guilt and anger. Is Amanda's love strong enough to help her, or will Lex's own personal demons tear them apart?

The Way Things Should Be - In this, the sixth novel, Amanda begins to feel her own biological clock ticking while her sister prepares for the birth of her first child. Lex is busy with trying to keep her hands on some newly acquired land, as well trying to get along with a new member of her family. Everything comes to a head, and a tragedy brings pain — and hope — to them all.

To Hold Forever - Three years have passed since Lex and Amanda took over the care of Lorrie, their rambunctious niece. Amanda's sister, Jeannie, has fully recovered from her debilitating stroke and returns with her fiancé, ready to start their own family. Attempts to become pregnant have been unsuccessful for Amanda. Meanwhile, a hostile new relative who resents everything about Lex shows up. Add in Lex's brother Hubert getting paroled and an old adversary returning with more than a simple reunion in mind and Lex begins to have doubts about continuing to run the ranch she's worked so hard to build.

SOMETHING TO BE THANKFUL FOR

Randi Meyers is at a crossroads in her life. She's got no girlfriend, bad knees, and her fill of loneliness. The one thing she does have in her favor is a veterinarian job in Fort Worth, Texas, but even that isn't going as well as she hoped. Her supervisor is cold-hearted and dumps long hours of work on her. Even if she did want a girlfriend, she has little time to look.

When a distant uncle dies, Randi returns to her hometown of Woodbridge, Texas, to attend the funeral. During the graveside services, she wanders away from the crowd and is beseeched by a young boy to follow him into the woods to help his injured sister. After coming upon an unconscious woman, the boy disappears. Randi brings the woman to the hospital and finds out that her name is Kay Newcombe.

Randi is intrigued by Kay. Who is this unusual woman? Where did her little brother disappear to? And why does Randi feel compelled to help her? Despite living in different cities, a tentative friendship forms, but Randi is hesitant. Can she trust her newfound friend? How much of her life and feelings can Randi reveal? And what secrets is Kay keeping from her? Together, Randi and Kay must unravel these questions, trust one another, and find the answers in order to protect themselves from outside threats — and discover what they mean to one another.

ISBN 1-932300-04-X
978-1-323300-04-8

DIVING INTO THE TURN

Diving Into the Turn is set in the fast-paced Texas rodeo world. Riding bulls in the rodeo is the only life Shelby Fisher has ever known. She thinks she's happy drifting from place to place in her tiny trailer, engaging in one night stands, and living from one rodeo paycheck to another – until the day she meets barrel racer Rebecca Starrett. Rebecca comes from a solid, middle-class background and owns her horse. She's had money and support that Shelby has never had. Shelby and Rebecca take an instant dislike to each other, but there's something about Rebecca that draws the silent and angry bull rider to her. Suddenly, Shelby's life feels emptier, and she can't figure out why. Gradually, Rebecca attempts to win Shelby over, and a shaky friendship starts to grow into something more.

Against a backdrop of mysterious accidents that happen at the rodeo grounds, their attraction to one another is tested. When Shelby is implicated as the culprit to what's been happening will Rebecca stand by her side?

ISBN 978- 1-932300-54-3

The Heart's Longing
by Anna Furtado

Trinn Wells is an award-winning chef in one of the finest hotel restaurants in Boston. She should be content, but she's not. She hates her boss, her ex-girlfriend has left her in debt, she finds it impossible to meet her mother's expectations, and she's having strange dreams that disturb her sleep.

Sidney Wycombe is a prestigious London solicitor driven to preserve the memory of a place that no longer exists. When she tries to convince Trinn to help her in her efforts, Trinn hesitates, but finally arrives in London looking forward to an all-expenses paid holiday, a respite from her troubles.

As Sidney reveals the knowledge and lore of Briarcrest, Trinn's dreams become an alternate reality where she meets a man known only as Catty. As Trinn becomes more involved in Catty's world, she discovers that not everything is as it seems at the Briarcrest of old. When she learns that Catty is involved in some very dangerous activities, the two women from the future begin to worry for Trinn's safety.

While the women try to unlock the secrets of the past, they battle their growing feelings for one another—feelings that neither one of them is prepared to deal with, but which, in the end, neither of them can deny. Will Sidney be able let down her guard as noble protector of Briarcrest? Will Trinn let go of living up to other people's expectations and express her true feelings for Sidney?

The women of Briarcrest live! Travel back in time to find what the future holds for those who love the great castle and its inhabitants.

Available March 2010
ISBN 978-1-935053-26-2

Storm Surge
by Melissa Good

It's fall. Dar and Kerry are traveling—Dar overseas to clinch a deal with their new ship owner partners in England, and Kerry on a reluctant visit home for her high school reunion. In the midst of corporate deals and personal conflict, their world goes unexpectedly out of control when an early morning spurt of unusual alarms turns out to be the beginning of the shocking nightmare that was 9/11.

Available March 2010
ISBN 978-1-935053-28-6

OTHER YELLOW ROSE TITLES
You may also enjoy:

The Sea Hawk
by Brenda Adcock

Dr. Julia Blanchard, a marine archaeologist, and her team of divers have spent almost eighteen months excavating the remains of a ship found a few miles off the coast of Georgia. Although they learn quite a bit about the nineteenth century sailing vessel, they have found nothing that would reveal the identity of the ship they have nicknamed "The Georgia Peach."

Consumed by the excavation of the mysterious ship, Julia's relationship with her partner, Amy, has deteriorated. When she forgets Amy's birthday and finds her celebrating in the arms of another woman, Julia returns alone to the Peach site. Caught in a violent storm, she finds herself separated from her boat and adrift on the vast Atlantic Ocean.

Her rescue at sea leads her on an unexpected journey into the true identity of the Peach and the captain and crew who called it their home. Her travels take her to the island of Martinique, the eastern Caribbean islands, the Louisiana German Coast and New Orleans at the close of the War of 1812.

How had the Peach come to rest in the waters off the Georgia coast? What had become of her alluring and enigmatic captain, Simone Moreau? Can love conquer everything, even time? On a voyage that lifts her spirits and eventually breaks her heart, Julia discovers the identity of the ship she had been excavating and the fate of its crew. Along the way she also discovers the true meaning of love which can be as boundless and unpredictable as the ocean itself.

ISBN 978-1-935053-10-1
1-935053-10-8

Twenty-four Days
by Janet Albert

Sometimes life forces us into uncharted territory, as Dr. Miranda Ross discovers when circumstances lead her to seek employment on a cruise line specializing in all lesbian cruises. Although she's single and surrounded by women, she has little time to socialize and even less inclination. She's made promises to herself, promises she intends to keep.

And keep them she does, until she meets the ship's head fitness trainer, Jamie Jeffries. Jamie has the kind of body and good looks most people only dream of and unfortunately, a reputation to match. The buzz on the ship is that she can have anyone she wants and often does.

Miranda fights valiantly to avoid Jamie and the unwanted attraction that seems to have a will of its own. She's strong and determined...but a lot can happen in twenty-four days.

ISBN 978-1-935053-16-3
1-935053-16-7

OTHER YELLOW ROSE PUBLICATIONS

Janet Albert	Twenty-four Days	978-1-935053-16-3
Sandra Barret	Lavender Secrets	978-1-932300-73-4
Georgia Beers	Thy Neighbor's Wife	1-932300-15-5
Georgia Beers	Turning the Page	978-1-932300-71-0
Carrie Carr	Destiny's Bridge	1-932300-11-2
Carrie Carr	Faith's Crossing	1-932300-12-0
Carrie Carr	Hope's Path	1-932300-40-6
Carrie Carr	Love's Journey	978-1-932300-65-9
Carrie Carr	Strength of the Heart	978-1-932300-81-9
Carrie Carr	The Way Things Should Be	978-1-932300-39-0
Carrie Carr	To Hold Forever	978-1-932300-21-5
Carrie Carr	Piperton	978-1-935053-20-0
Carrie Carr	Something to Be Thankful For	1-932300-04-X
Carrie Carr	Diving Into the Turn	978-1-932300-54-3
Anna Furtado	The Heart's Desire	1-932300-32-5
Anna Furtado	The Heart's Strength	978-1-932300-93-2
Melissa Good	Eye of the Storm	1-932300-13-9
Melissa Good	Hurricane Watch	978-1-935053-00-2
Melissa Good	Red Sky At Morning	978-1-932300-80-2
Melissa Good	Thicker Than Water	1-932300-24-4
Melissa Good	Terrors of the High Seas	1-932300-45-7
Melissa Good	Tropical Storm	978-1-932300-60-4
Melissa Good	Tropical Convergence	978-1-935053-18-7
Lori L. Lake	Different Dress	1-932300-08-2
Lori L. Lake	Ricochet In Time	1-932300-17-1
K. E. Lane	And, Playing the Role of Herself	978-1-932300-72-7
Helen Macpherson	Love's Redemption	978-1-935053-04-0
J. Y Morgan	Learning To Trust	978-1-932300-59-8
J. Y. Morgan	Download	978-1-932300-88-8
A. K. Naten	Turning Tides	978-1-932300-47-5
Lynne Norris	One Promise	978-1-932300-92-5
Paula Offutt	Butch Girls Can Fix Anything	978-1-932300-74-1
Surtees and Dunne	True Colours	978-1-932300-52-9
Surtees and Dunne	Many Roads to Travel	978-1-932300-55-0
Vicki Stevenson	Family Affairs	978-1-932300-97-0
Vicki Stevenson	Family Values	978-1-932300-89-5
Vicki Stevenson	Family Ties	978-1-935053-03-3
Vicki Stevenson	Certain Personal Matters	978-1-935053-06-4
Cate Swannell	Heart's Passage	1-932300-09-0
Cate Swannell	No Ocean Deep	1-932300-36-8

About the Author

Carrie Carr is a true Texan, having lived in the state her entire life. She makes her home in the Dallas/Ft. Worth metroplex with her wife, Jan. She's done everything from wrangling longhorn cattle and buffalo, to programming burglar and fire alarm systems. Her time is spent writing, traveling, and trying to keep up with their two dogs - a Chihuahua/Boston Terrier mix named Nugget, and a Rat Terrier named Cher. Carrie's website is www.CarrieLCarr.com She can be reached at cbzeer@yahoo.com

VISIT US ONLINE AT
www.regalcrest.biz

At the Regal Crest Website You'll Find

- The latest news about forthcoming titles and new releases

- Our complete backlist of romance, mystery, thriller and adventure titles

- Information about your favorite authors

- Current bestsellers

Regal Crest titles are available directly from our web store, Allied Crest Editions at www.rcedirect.com, from all progressive booksellers including numerous sources online. Our distributors are Bella Distribution and Ingram.

LaVergne, TN USA
12 November 2009
163743LV00005B/17/P